ETHIC III

BY

ASHLEY ANTOINETTE

Ashley Antoinette Inc.
P.O. Box 181048
Utica, MI 48318

ISBN: 978-1-7328313-3-9

Trade Paperback Printing October 2018
Printed in the United States of America

This is a work of fiction. Any references or similarities to actual events, real people, living, or dead, or to real locales are intended to give the novel a sense of realism. Any similarity in other names, characters, places, and incidents, is entirely coincidental.

Distributed by Ashley Antoinette Inc.
Submit Wholesale Orders to:
owl.aac@gmail.com

APR 2019

ETHIC III PLAYLIST

Unravel Me, Sabrina Claudio
Frozen, Sabrina Claudio
Someone, Musiq Soulchild
Every Kind of Way, H.E.R.
Rather Be, H.E.R.
The Point of it All, Anthony Hamilton
The Line, dvsn
Down, Ella Mai
Found, Ella Mai
Missing You, Mary J. Blige
I Put a Spell on You, Nina Simone
Blackbird, Nina Simone
If You Let Me, Sinead Harnett
Blue, ELHAE
Codeine Dreaming, Kodak Black featuring Lil' Wayne

It is highly recommended that you listen to these songs as you read

LETTER TO THE FANS

Ashley Antoinette novel #14 and I'm just getting started. In book two I broke your hearts. Let's see if I can mend them. Grab your wine.

-xoxo-

Ashley Antoinette

To the Ladies…
never settle for less than an Ezra "Ethic" Okafor.

*To the young ladies . . .
never love a Messiah more than you love yourself.*

To the Fellas...
ask yourself...
what would Ethic do?

LET'S GO!

CHAPTER 1

The sound of Nina Simone filled the room, as Ethic sat in the old, wooden chair. His legs spread wide, hunched over, elbow to knees as his fingers balanced a cigar. He didn't usually prefer to indulge, but on rare occasions when he did, it was always the best…authentic Cuban. The slim leg, tailored suit fit him like a designer's dream. His broad shoulders and lean strength wore it well and the navy rested against his smooth, black skin. He never understood why some men preferred to dress casually. Some business just couldn't be handled in jean or cotton. Some shit you just had to get your grown man on for. Today, he was delivering a eulogy. He couldn't dress down for that.

"I understand how you were easily fooled. I'm not in the streets anymore. I'm not visible. You hear the stories, but then you meet the grown man and I'm raising three kids, fixing cars, going to PTA meetings and shit." Ethic's cheeks puffed, as he held smoke in his mouth. He tasted it, let it dance on his tongue, nodding before blowing it out. "I understand. None of that says I'll kill your mama and fuck your bitch," Ethic stated. "But make no mistake about it, nigga. I killed your mama and fucked your bitch." Ethic drew in another toke of the cigar, because it was a good fucking cigar, and then stood. He walked over to the body that hung from the meat hooks in the empty freezer. The hooks dug into the skin of Cream's back, stretching it as his body weight caused a slight sway. Ethic blew the smoke out in Cream's face. He picked up a severed hand that laid bloody on the table beside him and smacked it across Cream's face, patting him, patronizingly. "I told you what would happen if you touched her again. Didn't I?"

Cream cried, as he hung there, both hands were detached, and he was bleeding out. Ethic was taking his time delivering this death. He was tapping into a part of him that he kept under lock and key. "I don't know why men like you insist on going to war with me. I can never understand it. I've tried to leave this alone because it gets us nowhere as a people. Black men killing black men only strengthens our opponents," Ethic schooled. "But I can't even call you a man. You're vile. You pushed your woman," Ethic paused, as he put the tip of the cigar out on Cream's forehead. He knew the burn it caused, and he gritted his teeth while Cream howled.

"Agh!!!!"

"Excuse me. Slip of the tongue. You pushed *my* woman, my pregnant, beautiful woman over a two-story balcony. That's no man. That's an animal, a desperate, filthy, fucking animal. So, to catch something like you, I have to be an animal, but I'm not just any animal. I'm not like you, hiding and creeping and lurking in the bowels of the city. I'm the king. I'm a lion. You took my son from me. For that, nothing but murder will do. Your mama, the unfortunate woman who lives at 444 Baltimore Street..."

Cream's eyes flickered in recognition, as his second child's mother's residence was revealed, but he was too weak to do anything but groan.

"Your mama's sister, and your granny, nigga. All dead because of you." Ethic turned up the volume on his phone and closed his eyes, sucking in the soulful, painful croons of the incomparable Ms. Nina Simone.

Why you wanna fly Blackbird
You ain't ever gon' fly
Why you wanna fly Blackbird
You ain't ever gon' fly

"Shouldn't be long now," he said. He would sit and watch Cream bleed out. He had already inflicted so much pain. The beating Messiah had put on Cream looked like child's play, compared to the brutality Ethic had rained upon him. Every bone in Cream's back had been broken, as Ethic expelled the pain from his soul. He had to take it out on Cream to avoid taking it out on Alani. He would never harm her, but the feelings of resentment that were shrouding him because of her was blocking the love. His stomach was hollow, and he heard the echoes of her screams as she tried to birth his son into the world. It was on a loop in his head. It tortured him; so Ethic, in turn, tortured Cream - the cause of it all. There were no more passes to be given. Ethic had tried that route. He had extended that olive branch because he knew he was wrong for taking Cream's daughter. Cream hadn't accepted it. Cream had wanted to dance. So, now, here he was waltzing with the devil inside Ethic.

Ethic hated to admit this part of him even existed. He was ashamed of this part. This type of man didn't deserve to be a father or deserve to even get a whiff of a good woman, but he couldn't scrape this part of himself away if he wanted too. He was who he was, and he had the best reason for this savagery today, so fuck it. The king was holding court. Ethic was a patient

3

man and he didn't miss a second of the horror as blood leaked onto the floor. The cold temperatures prolonged the inevitable. It curdled the blood and made it drip slower, made death follow a speed limit that Ethic set. It was an excruciating way to die and Ethic held no remorse. The moment the last breath escaped Cream, Ethic stood to his feet. He sniffed, pinching the bridge of his nose. He gathered his jacket that hung on the back of the chair and slipped into it before stepping out of the meat freezer. Ethic reached into his inner breast pocket and pulled out a white envelope filled with money. Fifty thousand dollars, to be exact.

"Basil," he greeted, as he slapped hands with the man in front of him. "I appreciate the privacy and access to your place."

Basil shook his head and waved off the envelope. "No favors amongst gentlemen, my G. Anytime I'm able, I'm willing," he said.

He embraced Ethic in a gentlemen's handshake.

"He'll make good food for the hogs," Basil said.

Ethic nodded, knowing that Cream's remains would never be found. The African-bred hogs Basil owned would devour everything, bones and all.

"I'll send a crew to clean up the mess," Ethic said.

"It's already on the way," Basil responded. "No half stepping."

Ethic walked to the front of the building and emerged out into the sunlight. He hadn't realized how much time had passed. An entire day and an entire night. It was a long time to be encompassed in death. He needed life. He needed his children, but first he had to lock this rage back in the cage inside him. He drove to the cemetery in a haze. He was directionless, on auto-pilot going, to the only place where he could seek comfort. No one understood him like the dead. He was living on borrowed time and belonged in a plot somewhere, so they were like kin to him…the un-breathing…the forgotten. The dead was his family. Raven Atkins was in the ground and her memory pressed on his soul so greatly that he had wanted to join her for years. She drew him to the graveyard today like a shepherd leading sheep, and before he knew it, his Range was parked there. He put one Ferragamo to the uneven gravel and then let the other fall beside it. Burdened steps carried him to her grave. He could find it with his eyes closed. That's how often he visited. Sometimes, in the middle of the night when his children were asleep, he would sneak away to spend hours with her. He hadn't felt the need to since meeting Alani, but she had lied to him…her lie had put half of him in the grave Raven's death had dug. He was fighting to revive the other half…fighting to live…fighting for purpose but God damn if it didn't hurt. Even Cream's extermination had done nothing to ease that. That was the thing with murder. It didn't heal anything. It only exasperated the hate, it fueled it. Only love could heal, but he was short on that these days. Even Alani's love was tainted now, with her lies, even Bella's with the deceit. He was angry with them and he needed to get a hold on that before he faced them. He sat on the grass in front of Raven's grave and leaned his back against her headstone. Right now, she felt the realest on his team. She was the only one he could break in front of who wouldn't judge him. Ethic shook his head back and forth, trying to keep up the wall, trying to secure his façade, but his eyes prickled. His son. His blue son. So small. So lifeless. Ethic cried. He cried like he never cried before, letting his body slack against Raven's stone as he bared his soul. He was exposed out here under the clouds. He felt every single moment in his life that had contributed to the destruction of his happiness. The memories marched through his brain like a parade, one after another, culminating to this moment. This breakdown. He was weakened. He was just a boy trying to be a man; but how could he do that without a blueprint? Age wasn't a factor in manhood. Influence was. His father had left him long ago, before he even had a chance to be groomed. Everything Ethic knew, he had learned on his own. He was doing the best he could, and the world was rejecting his effort, taking away people he loved because he wasn't enough…enough of a man…enough of a father…enough of a lover to the women he coveted. What the fuck else could he do to evolve into a man he could be proud to face in the mirror? He felt everything and nothing all in this moment. It was so excruciating that it was numbing. How had he gotten to this place?

Get it the fuck together. Nobody cares about your pain. Your hurt don't matter. You just can't let them feel it.

Ethic reigned in his emotions and pinched the bridge of his nose. He stood and then bent to press his lips to her stone. He walked back over to his car feeling depleted. He had caged the madness, now he had to go home to face all the destruction that lay in his wake.

CHAPTER 2

Bella's heart was anxious. She couldn't think straight. Her father hadn't been home, and Lily wouldn't answer any questions. Alani wasn't answering her phone and that only added to Bella's dismay. She could feel her world changing but she wasn't sure exactly how. Something felt wrong...extremely so, and Bella couldn't calm her concerns. She heard the front door open and close. A slight panic settled into her. She smelled him before she saw him; and when Ethic came into view, his eyes pierced her. His eyes were red.

If he's been crying that means she's hurt. Something's wrong with her.

Bella's eyes welled with tears, not only at the possibility of injury but at the disappointment she saw in her father's gaze. He had never looked at her like that. She could feel his discontent. There was no need for conversation.

"Big Man?" Ethic called to Eazy who was sitting on the floor with a handheld video game occupying him.

Eazy looked up. "What's up, Dad?"

"Can you go to your room? I need a moment with your sister," Ethic said.

"Sure, Dad," Eazy replied. "Can we start my science experiment later?"

Ethic's forehead creased, in deep contemplation. His home was like another world. How he could step over this threshold and turn into the type of man that built homemade volcanos with his loving child floored him. He wasn't worthy of this simplicity. It felt like God had made a mistake when he had gifted him with these beautiful souls to govern. How could he make sure Eazy turned out differently? How could he raise a man if he was just guessing? Ethic was stumbling through life without guidance. He made up his own rules because none were ever given, structure was never taught. He didn't want to fuck that up and be responsible for another human like him walking around the Earth, ruining others, destroying lives, hurting women.

"Dad?" Eazy looked to him in confusion, as Ethic stood there stuck, emotion in his eyes.

"Of course, Big Man. We're going to be spending a lot more time together. Every day. I got to make sure I get this right," he said, nodding, speaking more to himself than his son.

"Get what right?" Eazy wore his perplexity on his face.

"Nothing, son. Give me a minute, okay?"

Eazy departed and Bella sat deathly still. Emotion clung to her eyelashes and her lip trembled. "You don't want to spend time with me because I lied, right?"

Ethic rolled eyes down to her. Bella played tough, but her sensitivities were deep rooted. Like a Southern oak tree, historic tragedy hung from her branches. A motherless child. His beautiful baby had told a lie, trying to win over a new one. That was the part that angered him most. Alani's manipulation of his child. Alani's alliance with his own flesh and blood. The two most valuable girls in his world had linked up and drew a moat around themselves, blocking him out. The cost to pay had been a hefty one. Ethic pulled a chair out next to Bella and sat beside her. Not only did he need to address the lying, but he had to break the news to her about the baby, her brother, whom he was sure she had grown an attachment to. Alani had given Bella a privilege she hadn't even extended to him.

Type of shit is that?

Now, she wasn't around to break the news and he had to be the bearer.

"Of course not, Bella. I want to spend all the time in the world with you, baby. You're my flesh and blood. I want to run up as much time with you as I can before I leave this Earth. Nothing will ever change that," Ethic stated, as he stared her in her eyes. He didn't hesitate. She knew it was true. "I'm disappointed in you though, Bella. The secret you kept was a dangerous one. I'm your father. You don't keep anything from me. Ever. I can't do my job as a father if I don't know what's going on."

"Alani asked me not to," Bella whispered. "I couldn't break her trust."

"So, you broke mine?" Ethic asked. "What if he had come back while you were there?"

The thought made him want to revive Cream just to execute him all over again.

Bella lowered her head.

"It's hard for her to accept me without thinking about you, Daddy. I just wanted to keep it separate. You lost her, but I didn't want to lose her too," Bella pleaded. "She's my family."

Ethic swiped both hands down his face. Alani had made an imprint on his child. She had bewitched her with her authenticity, her love, her laugh - he was sure, because it was one of his favorite parts. Bella had fallen in love. How could he be mad at her for that? He knew firsthand how hard it was to do what you knew was right when around Alani. Somehow, deceit seemed like a small price to pay for a piece of her time. He had done the same thing when he had gotten close to her, knowing that he was behind her child's murder.

"Is she okay?" Bella asked, with doe eyes that he couldn't refuse.

"No, B, she's not. She's hurting real bad. The baby didn't make it." He could barely utter the last of it and Bella's face twisted in agony, instantly. Her eyes prickled, and he could see her trying to hold it in, but the tide of emotions rushed her. They flooded his baby girl and a wrenching sob fell from her parted lips. Strain destroyed her pretty face, as her shoulders caved. He was witnessing heartbreak in the purest form...that of a child...of his child...over the murder of his other child...one he didn't even get the chance to know. His anger toward Alani intensified. He pulled Bella into his arms and she cried as she sat on his lap.

"Shhh," he whispered. He needed her to stop because she was going to break him. She was going to weaken him, again, and he had to be strong. He had gotten his tears out in private. He couldn't let her witness his storm. "Where is she? We have to go see her. Can we please go, Daddy?"

Bella was up and heading towards the door, but Ethic

didn't move. He knew the bomb he was about to drop on her would be devastating.

"You're not going anywhere, Bella," he said.

She looked at him, face wet, eyes red.

"You need distance from Alani. I can't trust her with you. She should have never asked you to lie. She should have never put you in that position," Ethic said.

"So, I can't see her anymore? What about the pageant? That's not fair!" Bella screamed. "Daddy, I'm sorry! Please!"

Ethic shook his head. "No, B. I know you don't understand, but I'm the parent. I decide. You don't have to understand my logic. What Alani asked you to do was wrong and we've all paid too big of a price."

"Daddy, no! I'm sorry!" Bella screamed.

Ethic shook his head, as he pinched the space between his eyes, hoping the pressure would levee his tears. His chest was hollow. Aching. "No, B."

"I hate you!" she shouted.

Ethic's lip trembled. "I hate you! You just don't want her to love me because she doesn't love you! Daddy, please!"

His daughter's pleas were devastating, her words were injuring, her hate peeled layers of his soul away and it was agonizing. She was drawing her allegiance in the sand. If she had to choose between a mother and a father, she was choosing Alani. She wanted a mother because she had experienced a father her entire life…she had just gotten used to the thought of a mother and Ethic was taking it away. Burden filled him.

He carried himself up the stairs. He just needed sleep.

He needed respite from this agonizing reality that had become his life. When he was halfway up the stairs, he heard his daughter sobbing and the sound of something breaking. He understood. Her need to break shit. He had broken dozens of bones inside Cream's body to get that aching out, and still it lived in him. Ethic wanted to cave. He wanted to give her Alani, but they were done. He was done. The level of malice Alani possessed. It floored him. It was too calculating to invite into his home. *She hid my kid from me.*

He had given Bella every single thing she had ever asked him for in her lifetime. He had never said no, but he couldn't oblige this. He wouldn't, but the cries broke him down. He lowered his head and ascended the remaining steps before shutting himself off from the woe that had taken over his home.

Alani closed her eyes, as the gentle hand stroked her hair. This was the most tumultuous time of her life; and on one hand, she wanted to question if God was real, but on the other, she knew He was. This woman soothing her was proof of that. Alani didn't know how, but Nannie had come out of her debilitation. She had heard the confrontation with Cream. After months of not walking and barely speaking, Nannie had found the strength to cross her bedroom to reach the panic remote that came with the hospital bed she slept in. It was the only reason the police had come. Alani believed with all her heart that God had restored her aunt. There was no other explanation for it. As she laid in Nannie's lap and let her tears run free, she prayed for God to take this pain away. She needed some of that strength he had bestowed upon Nannie. Life just kept spiraling. Just when she had thought she could see a glimpse of light at the end of the tunnel, Cream had come to cloak her in darkness. She didn't know how she had survived the fall. She had hit the floor so hard. A part of her wished she hadn't. She would have been grateful to not feel any of this…to die right there in her living room, on the floor, and go to Heaven with her babies. Depression had its hold on her and this time it was vice tight. This time, she knew Ethic wasn't an option for revival. The first time she had held the cards in her hand. He had been the offender of her heart, so she made the rules, but this time was different. This time she had lied, and he had walked away. She hadn't heard from him since and Bella had all but disappeared from her life. Alani needed them both, but she would never reach out. She couldn't. It was all too complicated of a puzzle to solve.

"Why does this hurt so bad? I didn't even want the baby. It shouldn't hurt like this," Alani whispered. "He killed Kenzie."

"You've got to stop with that Alani. You hear me, child, and you hear me good. You're not fooling anybody with this hate you're trying to keep up. You think I didn't hear you in your bedroom at night, crying and carrying on over that man. He killed your brother. Murdered him with the intent to take him away from this Earth. Kenzie was a tragic mistake. I was in that boat with you, hating him, cursing him. I was laid in that hospital, couldn't move, couldn't speak, but I could hear just fine. He came into my room every day, bossing the nurses around and good thing too. Little hussies were barely putting soap and water on my ass, but he was there, right on top of them. Then, he would talk, and I would listen. If nothing else is true about that man. He loves you. He's loved you better than any other man in your life, but you're broken. What you can't see is that he's broken too. The things he shared..."

Alani sat up and blinked through blurry eyes. "What things?"

Nannie shook her head. "That's not my history to repeat. It's his, but he can't tell you anything if you block him out. You can't get to know a man that you're shunning. Kenzie's death is weighing on him enough. He doesn't need you to remind him of what he's done. He knows," Nannie said.

"I'm her mother. I'm allowed to hate him," Alani defended. "I'm allowed to judge him!"

"And he's Love's father. He's allowed to judge your ass too!" Nannie snapped back. "You can't have it both ways, Alani. You've always been that type of child. You want to be mad on your terms. You want the attention and be able to turn your nose up at the same time. The way you hold a grudge is unhealthy, baby, and I know you get that from your father leaving you all those years ago. Him hopping in and out your life, you hated him every second he was gone, but he pops in for 20 minutes and you relished in the attention. Your mama did the same thing. In and out. No consistency. When she's here, you're doing everything to impress her, trying to convince her to stay. You're soaking up all of her in a moment because you know it's going to pass and then you're back to hating her when she's gone. Ezra is not your mother and he is not your father. If you allow him to prove it, he will show you he isn't here just to pass through. You can't lay his faults out but not allow him to put a mirror up to yours. God is the judge, Alani, and forgiveness is for the strong. Be strong, baby," Nannie said. "Even if you don't forgive him for the sake of him. Do it for you. Pick yourself up so you can live. You can't heal and hate at the same time."

Alani curled up on Nannie's lap and closed her eyes. If she didn't have so much respect, she would have had more than a few words to say in return. *I don't have to forgive. I don't care about his past. I don't care about his intentions. She was my baby! I will forever hate him.* But what she couldn't understand is how she still loved him too. The attention part was true. When Ethic graced her with his, she felt like she was flying. The paradox was cryptic. It was a connection that would forever haunt her because she hated herself for being so weak for a man who could do such a heinous thing. She could still smell the scent of him. The ghost of him clung to her psyche and she could describe every detail, as if he were standing right in front of her. It was ridiculous, and she was ashamed of the potency of her connection to him. What Alani didn't realize was that love and hate were the same emotion just channeled in different ways. The fact that she now had to bury a child that they shared only made things more complicated.

"Absolutely not," Alani said, as she sat at the table across from James Masters. His face was friendly enough, but he was someone she wouldn't mind never seeing again. Twice in one year was too much for anyone to bear. The funeral home owner sat, perplexed. He pulled at the knot of his tie and pushed his glasses up on his nose with one finger, before blowing out a breath of frustration.

"I'm sorry? Mr. Okafor has a family lot. He's already paid for the plot to be dug, Ms. Hill."

"My son will not be buried there. My son will be buried next to his sister. If that's a problem, I can take my business elsewhere," Alani said.

How dare he!

"If Ezra wanted to make decisions regarding this burial, he would be here. He's not. I'm here. I'm always the one here because of him," she said, her voice shaking, as she pointed a stern finger into the table.

"I understand. Please, just let me make a few calls," Mr. Masters said. He stood, and Alani waited with impatience. She was in the anger stage of grief. She was like a force, blowing through her day, challenging everyone she encountered, sprinkling her negativity all over the place. She couldn't help it. Ethic hadn't called. Not once in days. Not to check on her. Not to console her. Not to scream at her. It was just silence and she desperately just wanted to communicate. She wanted to grieve with the father of her child, but he left her alone and the solitude was killing her. It made her disdain deepen for him, but she knew this was a taste of the medicine she had served him. It hurt to be on the receiving end. She had no support. Nannie's health didn't allow her to come to the funeral home with her, so Alani was alone, again, saying goodbye. The fact that Ethic hadn't shown made her feel like he never really cared at all. To put his card on file and not show up felt cold. The animosity inside her brewed hot and Alani was taking it out on the world.

Mr. Masters walked back into the room. "Mr. Okafor says to do whatever you want. He'll cover all expenses. So, please, let's continue."

Alani put her body on autopilot and made the arrangements. There was something about burying her second child that felt robotic, like she was just going through the motions, but not really feeling it. When she walked out, there was no tragic breakdown, there was just a woman void of emotion. She was a shell of who she used to be. She was tired, and she just wanted it all to be over. Everything. Even this back and forth rancor with Ethic was too much. After the funeral, they could bury everything. They could forget they knew one another and go back to being strangers.

I might take off on you peons and go back to Venus
I'm a star so I put a neutron on my pinkie

Messiah stood posted in the back of the club's VIP, as Morgan did her thing on stage. She was a star. Hands down. When she graced the stage there was an undeniable pull of attention from every other dancer up there. Eyes shot directly to her. Aria held her own, but Morgan was an entire vibe and Messiah ate it up, eyeing her like prey, appreciating the esthetic but his facial expression never changed. The crowd, however, hyped her up. Her arrogance poured through every move she made, and she did this thing with her mouth and tongue that made Messiah's blood run scolding hot in his veins. She was showing the fuck off for him. He knew it because she threw her fingers up in the shape of two M's and rubbed them in a circle over her sex to let him know. M&M. Morgan and Messiah. *Forever*, she signed. That got a rise out of him, pulling a small smirk out of him. She exuded sex on the stage. He both hated and loved it. He hawked her, as he leaned over the railing, eyes low from the blunt he had smoked, locs trapped in a shoulder-length ponytail. Little Morgan wasn't so little anymore. She was finding her way in the world, making a name for herself, and not just on campus. Her social media presence was blowing up. Her story...the dancer who couldn't hear...had made hundreds of thousands of people curious. He had made it a point to stop going on her page because niggas were just out of pocket in the comments. He could only imagine her DM's. The world was taking notice, realizing the potential he had seen in her all along.

Isa, Meek, and even Bleu sat around him, enjoying the show. His entire team came out to support Mo. Isa had intentions of his own, but he didn't blame him. If Messiah was a single man, Aria would be as good of a candidate as any.

"Yo, we eating after this?" Ahmeek asked.

"Oh, a nigga definitely eating after this, but it ain't a group thing," Messiah said. Meek snickered.

"Bro, on some real shit. *You* with *her*, shit's legit. You're my man and I'd never tell you no bogus shit. That other bullshit. It's time to dead that. Let sleeping dogs lie. Some shit ain't worth losing, my G." Ahmeek nodded toward the stage. "That ain't worth losing."

Messiah slapped hands with Meek and turned away from the stage to face the rest of his crew. "We mobbing to the diner after this," he said. Perhaps he would kick it with Mo, in public, vibe with her outside the four walls of a private residence. He had to remember that she was young and probably craved the scene. Better with him then without him.

Bleu shook her head. "No, y'all mobbing. I'm a whole mother out here. It's way past my bedtime."

Isa tossed an arm around Bleu's shoulders. "You act like an old lady. You the oldest 25-year-old I know," Isa cracked.

"Whatever, boy," Bleu said. "Raise a kid by yourself, run a business, and work on a doctorate and then tell me how I shouldn't be tired. As soon as I speak to Morgan, I'm heading home."

Isa kissed the side of her head. "I'm just fucking with you, B. We get it. We're all real proud of you."

Messiah wasn't close to many people, but these three he would die for on any given day. The only other was hopping off the stage and making her way through the crowd toward him. She tucked herself right under him, wrapping her arms around his body and lifting her face to accept his tongue into her mouth.

He pulled back and his lips found her ear.

"I'ma have to stop coming to this shit. I'm jealous than a mu'fucka, shorty," he whispered.

Morgan gripped his face, as he pulled her waist into him.

"You feel that?" he asked. The hardness pressing against her stomach made her breathing shallow. She had danced with the intention of doing this to him, exciting him, frustrating him...she knew the reward that would be waiting for her as soon as the music had begun, and she spotted him in the crowd. She nodded and pulled his lips into her mouth. It was like they were the only ones in the club. The commotion and boisterous celebration around them didn't even matter.

"Okay, Messiah! Let her breathe. The rest of us want to say hi too," Bleu said, infiltrating their bubble.

He snickered, as he rubbed his lips, the red lipstick she wore came off on his fingers. She had marked him, and he didn't even care.

Morgan stepped back from Messiah, slightly irritated that they had been interrupted.

"You're dope. The dance, the hair, the clothes. Everything, girl. Seriously. You killed it," Bleu complimented.

Morgan didn't know much about Bleu, all she knew was that she was Messiah's only female friend. One he claimed to have never slept with. She was possessive, however, and a little weary about Bleu's friendliness. She felt Messiah tap her ass and she knew it came with a hidden message. He wanted her to be nice. He was telling her that Bleu was no threat. Morgan was jealous that the girl meant so much, but if she was close to Messiah, Morgan had to make it a point to find out why. She would be nice until Bleu gave her a reason not to be.

"Thank you," she answered. "Are you coming out with us?"

Bleu shook her head. "Maybe next time. I've got to get the kiddo from his father and head home. I really want to do lunch or something soon, though. Messiah gave me your number. I hope that's cool."

Morgan nodded. "Yeah, that's cool. Lunch sounds like a plan," she answered. "Thank you so much for coming." Bleu waved goodbye.

Morgan watched, as Aria approached Isa, walking directly into his space as he looked down at her with intoxicated eyes. Isa wrapped a dominant hand around her waist and jerked her forward. Morgan snickered and shook her head. *Aggressive-ass niggas. What they run in packs?*

She looked up at Messiah. He had never stopped looking at her. It was like he was studying for a test and the answers were embedded in her skin, he was staring so hard.

"Double date?" she asked.

"You a funny mu'fucka," Messiah said, as he kissed her nose. She knew it would never happen. His time with her was his and his alone. He didn't like to share. "You want to go out? I don't want you to feel like the only place I'm interested is in the bed." His eyebrows dipped in concern, as he pierced her with his stare.

"I don't think that," she whispered. "And tonight, I'm a little more excited about what's going down when we get home. They can have the turn up. I just want you." Her tone was suggestive. She reached behind him and pulled the rubber band from his locs, freeing them, so she could bury her hands in them. They were her leash. She gripped them tightly; and as she pulled him to her face, she bit into his bottom lip so hard she drew blood, leaving it throbbing and then kissing the pain away. Morgan simply couldn't get enough. To love somebody so much had to be wrong and she didn't care. She had never understood how her sister had gone against her father all those years ago for Mizan, but she got it now. If Ethic ever found out she would be placed in the same position, and the way her heart felt, she knew she would choose Messiah. She needed him. Even when everything was going right between them, the mere notion of it ever ending kept a subtle pang of hurt in her heart. She feared the possibility of it. She was so attached...too dependent and she was growing more aggressive by the day. Dealing with him was transforming her. His every quality, good and bad, was becoming hers. She stood on her tip toes and whispered in his ear. "I want to taste you."

"Word? That's how you feel?"

She nodded.

His dick jumped, and she felt it. Her body clenched, and her clit throbbed.

"You coming home with me tonight. Your scent ain't on my sheets no more. That's a problem."

She knew it had been awhile since she had been to his house. A few weeks since Christmas. She was ending the semester and finals were coming up. She hadn't had much time to make the trip back and forth.

"I have an early class," she warned. "I'd have to wake up at like six to make it back on time."

"I'll drive you back," he promised. He looked at Ahmeek and Isa. "Yo, we up."

"Nigga, what happened to going out?" Isa protested. He knew that if Morgan left, Aria would too. Everybody thought they were intimate, but truth was, Aria was making him chase it. The first night after ice skating, she had made him feed her and then insisted that he drive her all the way back to State. He hit her up from time to time, but she was hard to read. He wanted to keep time with her, but he knew if it wasn't a group outing, she was going to decline.

"Plans changed, my G," Messiah replied, snickering because he knew Isa had it bad for Aria.

"I'm going to call it a night too," Aria announced, just as expected. She pulled away from Isa, who was buried in her ear, saying something to spread a smile on her normally-bitchy face. She waved her finger and Morgan knew it was only a matter of time before Isa won whatever game they were playing. She had to give Aria credit, though, the girl had discipline. Women twice their age couldn't resist Isa. It only made him want her more.

Air kisses between the ladies and handshakes for the fellas were the departing ritual before they headed out the club.

"You drove?" Messiah asked.

"I rode with Aria," she answered.

"I'm on my bike," Messiah said. "I can have Meek ride it back and take his car. It's too cold to have you on the back."

"I'm fine," she whispered. The January winds were biting but Morgan wanted to have her hands wrapped around him. She didn't want the distance that a car would force. Even the center console would be too much space between them. Messiah suffocated her with his love, stole her breaths, and killed her softly and Morgan was willing to die, if it was at his hands.

"Why don't we just go back to my place since it's closer?" she asked. "You can sleep in tomorrow while I go to class and then I can come right back to you. I promise I'll send the sheets with you." She smiled and laced her fingers in his. Messiah was the most dangerous man she knew. His rage should have intimidated her, it should terrify her. It was a foreshadowing of darker days to come, but Morgan felt nothing less than adoration for him. Even their fingertips connecting made her heart race. "I love you in ways I can't explain," she said, as she

23

stood in the middle of the parking lot, resting her head against his chest while he shielded her from the wind.

"Ditto, shorty," he answered. "Let me get you home before you get sick. Half-naked-ass."

He climbed on first and handed her a helmet before kicking off the stand and taking off into the night. The speed was a turn-on. Only Messiah would have his bike out in the middle of winter. It was just like him to say fuck the rules and take risks no one else would. It was just like Morgan to follow him there... to reckless land, because fuck it, if he was riding, she was riding too. If he died, she was prepared for that too because there was no living in a world where he didn't exist. She was loyal, and it knew no boundaries. She was too young to set them for herself.

Young women went into love with the purpose of proving how true theirs could be. They measured their commitment by how much they could endure for a man. They would do anything asked and often even what hadn't been asked to attempt to symbolize their allegiance. It wasn't until after a woman knew herself did she establish parameters. It wasn't until she was wiser did she determine that she was the prize and a man either had to love her within her limits or get out the way, so the next man could. Morgan's hands found their way under his leather, Valentino, moto jacket and warmed her hands on his bare skin. His abs tightened at her cold touch. She was freezing, but they weren't too far from her house. She slid her hands down and snuck them into the band of his denim and then down to his dick. Messiah brought wild thoughts out of Morgan...he made her a wild girl and she felt him harden in anticipation. She kept her hands warm there and felt the motorcycle lunge forward as he went faster. He was eager, and the speed reflected it. He pulled into her parking lot, turned off the beautiful machine and then followed her into the building. He was silent, as they stood on opposite sides of the elevator but the energy in their stares was palpable. It was like foreplay. The looking but not touching. The elevator released them, and she put her key into her door, feeling him behind her, his breath on her neck.

They stumbled through the entry way and Morgan wasted no time. She peeled out of her clothes and then walked over to him to start on his. Everything about Messiah was strong, from his manhood to his thighs, to his broad chest and defined back. He was built tough and he had to be to survive the things he had been through. They stood completely naked. Messiah cleared her hair out of her face and wrapped four fingers around the nape of her neck, as he swept a gentle thumb across her cheek. He shook his head.

"What?" she asked. "You put a spell on me." Messiah's voice was low and held a bit of awe, as if he were a young boy trying to figure out the secret behind a magic trick.

"Nina Simone?" she smiled, and boy did it blind him. He didn't know how he had become so lucky to possess the sun.

"What you know about it, shorty?" Messiah asked.

"I know a lot," she defended. She did, in fact. Ethic used to wallow in Nina Simone when she was younger. "Because you put a spell on me too."

CHAPTER 3

Ethic sat on the side of his king-sized bed, leaned over in turmoil. He was doubled over from the unbearable pain that coursed through him. In his hands he held the little hat that had graced his son's head. He hadn't stuck around to help name him, but Alani couldn't have chosen a more suitable fit.

Love Ezra Okafor.

He brought the hat to his nose and breathed in the aura. Whatever DNA had been left behind on that hat he wanted inside him. It was all he had left. He eyed the black suit hanging on his closet door across the room. He had been at a standoff with it for an hour. They were at war and the suit was winning. He couldn't will himself to put it on. Today was Love's memorial and he couldn't even rise from where he sat. He rubbed hands over the top of his weary head. Alani had made all the arrangements and it was his duty to show up, but he was stuck. She had chosen to lay his son down next to her daughter and the juxtapose of that sight he couldn't bear. He knew it was his son's sister, but damn, he just couldn't witness that. His son lying next to the little girl he was responsible for ending. It was fucking with him. A man who had never feared anything, was terrified of the sight of that. He knew it would keep him away from not only the funeral but from Love's grave in general. Alani had made his son's gravesite Ethic repellant and he wasn't sure if it was her intention or not, but it was devastating. Men thought they held the power. Men were arrogant to think that they controlled anything. Men weren't shit compared to women. Alani had made one decision. She had done one subtle thing…moved her piece on the chess board just a little to the left and it had done enough damage to bring him to his knees. Women were a motherfucker when scorned, and her burying his son next to his greatest sin was payback, whether she was aware or not. Even if it wasn't done purposefully, the passive aggression behind the decision floored him. Alani was a queen and she ruled with beautiful passion toward the ones she loved, but the ones she hated felt her wrath. He was learning that the hard way.

He stood to his feet and forced himself to dress. He was glad his children were in school. Bella had begged to attend, but this was something he couldn't do with her at his side. He needed her to be removed from the situation, removed from Alani. He had always lived his life in pain, but it was always dulled, always in the back of his psyche, easy to disguise. The pain that surrounded he and Alani was different. It took center stage in his life and nothing else could distract from it. He couldn't function with that kind of weight on him, and he didn't want his daughter involved. Bella was too young to process that type of anguish. He didn't want it to change her.

He walked over to the closet and pulled his manhood off the shelf - along with the suit. It was time to cover his weaknesses and face the world. It was time to reinforce the stereotype that black men were unfeeling and couldn't cry, that they were hardened. As he slipped into his clothes, he felt obligated to keep up the façade. He built up those bricks around his sensitivity, as he added each layer of clothing on top of his body. His clothes were pristine, sharply pressed thanks to Lily, but the rest of him was ragged. The full beard was a direct contrast of the clean-cut goatee he was accustomed to. It was lined to perfection, however, but still it reflected the grit that had become his life. It was unruly, uncaring, overgrown. He ran his hands over his waves and then moved to his accessories. A simple watch, no ring, because the only one he would ever wear was a wedding band, which he couldn't ever foresee possessing. No chains today. Not on top of a black suit. A black suit was meant to be classic. A classic suit for a classic man. No flash required.

Ethic stood in front of the mirror looking a like a grown man. A strong man. A man's man. But as he slipped that tiny hat into his inner jacket pocket, he felt like a boy, a boy who needed his father; or better yet, his mother to wrap her arms around him and tell him everything would be okay. He had neither. He hadn't had that type of support in a long time. He looked out the window at the black Cadillac Escalade that sat in front of his home. The suited white man was standing outside, waiting patiently. Ethic would need the driver today. His head wasn't clear enough to be behind the wheel of a car, and if he relied on himself to steer his way to the cemetery, he knew he would never make it.

He cleared his throat and headed out the door to face the hardest day of his life...the burial of his child.

Caskets aren't supposed to be this small.

Alani stared at the closed, metal box, her eyes brimming with emotion.

*I just had him. Why is he in a box? How did this happen?
Why is any of this happening to me?*

Alani stood there in front of not one but two graves. She
didn't even know how her legs were still holding her up.
She was so weak. Her womb still bled from the birthing of
a child, but she held no child in her arms. Life had never
seemed so unfair. Her lip trembled through the short prayer
and eulogy. She didn't want to make a spectacle, so the
service was short. She was tired of her pain being a circus...
it was such an elaborate show. Love's funeral wouldn't
be that...she wouldn't allow it. A few members from the
church had come to show support. It was too cold of a day
for Nannie to brave the temperatures in her feeble state, so
Alani stood next to people who felt like strangers. How was
Alicia, the church ho, supposed to be her support?

It was a cold day. Freezing, in fact. The wind caused Alani's
tears to crystalize on her cheeks. Icicles of grief stuck to her.
Alani was so empty she just needed to be filled. She needed
Ethic, today. She would give him back and not ask for him again
for any other thing, but for this, she needed his touch; even if
it was only her hand in his. This was *their* baby. They had gone
half on it. Why wasn't he here to take 50 percent of the grief?

Where is he?

When it was over, Alicia approached her. "I'm so sorry,
Alani," Alicia whispered, as she pulled Alani into a quick
embrace. Alani couldn't even lift her hands to receive the hug.
They seemed to be stuck at her sides. Her body was limp. Her
energy gone, and she had no patience for fake love. She knew
that Alicia was only present to get a glimpse of the father. She
knew it was a question that burned in the minds of many. *Who
is Alani pregnant by so soon after losing her daughter?* She

had heard the whispers at church, seen the judgement on their faces. She hadn't cared. It was nobody's business, but as she stood there alone on this day, she felt abandoned. His presence would have made her feel stronger...strong enough to handle these inquisitive stares. *How could he not show?*

"We will be postponing the pageant to give you time to heal. I can't imagine what you must be feeling?" Alicia said. "If you need anything..."

Alani nodded. She just wanted this woman out of her face. She wanted everyone gone. If he hadn't shown, she didn't want anyone to show.

He doesn't care.

That thought was enough to make Alani stumble. She reached for a headstone, as she walked through the cemetery and wept there. She had no idea that the headstone she found solace at was that of Raven Atkins'. God was peculiar that way, sending angels to hold you up without you knowing it. Alani pulled in the crisp air through her nose and continued on, rushing to her car. She couldn't bear to stick around all this death, all this darkness. Her insides felt like they were leaking out of her, like the bleeding from the birth was getting worse with every cry. Her soul was leaving her. Her children were all she had. She was so distraught that she didn't even see the Black Escalade as she stepped in front of it. She rushed to her car and pulled away, her heart in pieces.

Ethic sat behind the black tint of that Escalade feeling like a coward. The sight of her took his breath away. He could see she was weak, but he was weak too. He didn't want to burden her further without being able to lift some of the weight off her shoulders. It wasn't the place of a man to make life feel worse. If he couldn't make it better, what was his purpose? So, he stayed inside the car.

So beautiful.

Even through the agony etched on her face, she was exquisite. It felt like she was pulling through those ribs she had fractured, trying to tug his heart through the bandages still wrapped around his torso, pulling it on a string, trying to undo the snag that kept it from being in her possession. Letting her leave was the hardest thing he had ever had to do. She was his entire fucking world and he was just watching her drive away. He hoped it was for the best, despite the agony. He hoped the temporary hell he was causing would leave room for a brighter day ahead. He was toxic for her. They were deadly. Two children in the ground proved that much. It was like a moth to a flame, only he didn't know which role he played in that equation. Was he the flame to her moth? Was it the other way around? Did they kill each other? Something that could be so simple was complicated when it came to them; and as much as he craved her, he had to let her go. She deserved a much better man.

"Are you getting out, sir?" the driver asked.

Ethic nodded, and as the driver went to exit, Ethic motioned for him to stop. He opened his own door and put sharp shoes on snowy pavement as he stepped from the truck. The long, Burberry coat kept the cold out well as he trekked across the lawn to where his son's casket sat. The groundskeepers were just about to lower it into the ground when he lifted a hand to halt them as he approached. It was a dismal sight, odd even. The casket was so small. Rarely did you see them this size, and when you did, it just felt wrong. Ethic worked hard to ensure that his children outlived him. He had failed this one. It was a nick in the armor he called fatherhood. He had messed up somewhere. When a child went askew, a father blamed himself.

Ethic carried all the blame for this tragedy on this day. He placed his lips to the cold exterior of the casket and was grateful for the icy temperatures because they froze his welling tears, stopping them from falling.

"I love you, boy," he said.

The groundskeeper went to move, and Ethic shook his head.

"He's my son. I'll bury him."

The man handed over the shovel, reluctantly, and then lowered the casket into the ground. Ethic's tears blurred his vision, as he scooped the pre-dug pile of dirt over his seed. Flesh of his flesh, blood of his blood, was going into the ground. It was a different devastation, unlike anything he had ever felt. It was like being buried alive. When he was done, he tossed the shovel aside in anger and stepped back to look at his work. This was his work. This side by side exhibit of the greatest crimes ever committed. The murder of children. Graves he was responsible for filling, and yes, Love's death was on him too because he hadn't prevented it. Kenzie and Love. Brother and sister. Victims of Ezra Okafor. It was too much to withstand. Ethic came to his knees, landing in the wet snow, as he brought bawled fists of frustrations down to the snow. It was the worst day of his life and one that he wouldn't soon recover from; one he may never recover from at all.

CHAPTER 4

TWO MONTHS LATER

Winter had been brutal, and Spring was trying to break through the last, lingering frost. Ethic hoped that it brought enough warmth with it to break through the gloom in his life. He needed the sun to shine down and brighten his days because nothing was flourishing around him. He needed this season of his life to bloom. Bella had been distant. Her grades had dropped, and she was acting out in class. Ethic had even found a BIC lighter in her backpack and the thought of what she was doing with that was enough to enrage him. She hadn't forgiven him for banning her from seeing Alani and Ethic knew she missed her terribly. Hell, he missed her terribly. Mo was busy with her life and she was flourishing. That gave him some comfort, at least. Eazy was still his man, consistently happy, always hyper, and smart as a whiz. Eazy felt normal, he provided balance in the tension-filled space. It was the morning of the debutante ball and Bella was less than enthused. She had begrudgingly continued to go to practice, oftentimes coming home in tears so bad that he thought of calling Alani himself. The thought was fleeting, however. He hoped she was well and didn't want to interfere in her life any further... for fear of messing it up. He knocked on Bella's door.

"It's open," she called.

Ethic pushed open the door and reveled at her beauty.

Her long, wooly, coiled hair was straightened to pure silk. Her full lips held a nude color, to his disdain, and her brown eyes had a sparkle on the lid. She was growing up and it hurt, but witnessing it was a blessing. She was a treasure to Ethic. His heart ached because he knew that she would one day become vulnerable to the ills of the world. Black women were public enemy number one and he would have to put in extra hours of parenthood to make up for the fact that she was being raised without a mother. It wasn't for a lack of trying. Ethic had put his all into four women during his 30 odd years on Earth. Bella's mother, Melanie, had been the first black woman he'd experienced and lost. Raven had been the second woman to give him a child. Death had taken them both. Grief had darkened too many of his days behind their unfortunate demise. Just when he thought he would never love another, a heartbreaker by the name of YaYa had been the third; and while she didn't die, she was simply not his to keep. Another man had already imprinted onto her soul and he had known their days were numbered from the moment he got lost in her green eyes. Each of these women had inevitably left. Whether it be by choice or circumstance, their love had been fleeting, slipping through his fingertips as if he had tried to hold onto water. Their love had felt that pure, like a natural element, as necessary to man's survival as water and air. One man couldn't possess those things, they were for everybody, God-given, universe-created, needed by everyone, but owned by no one. They were three of the world's greatest wonders and he considered himself lucky to know what it felt like to love them at all, despite the pain that came along with their desertion. All these women had left him to figure out how to raise his princess into a queen. He had witnessed three women, with their beautiful melanin, be disrespected, neglected, and told they weren't worthy. He had watched life beat them up so badly. He had watched men use them as personal trophies, never truly valuing their worth. He had painfully sat by and watched them be drawn toward superficial love like moths were drawn to flames. He feared that it was a curse for black women, like a generational pitfall that was the result of not being loved enough, not being told they were worthy of more...of everything. Then, there was Alani, and she was greater than the three combined, yet he had become that curse to her. He had decided that love wasn't destined for everyone, especially him.

"Come over here, Bella," Ethic said.

Bella looked up from the book that she was reading, some urban fiction novel that Alani had introduced her to. Remnants of Alani had been retained by his child and it only made him miss her more. Bella came to him. She was a beautiful girl and he feared her growth. It was the only thing he feared in his life. More than bullets, more than his own demise, Ethic feared the day that Bella blossomed, and a young nigga came to pick her out of his garden. He promised himself that he would build her emotional fence as high as he could, filling her with affirmations of her worth to keep the snakes from destroying her soil. Her roots had to run deep. As a father, he had to make sure of it. They had been on troubled ground, as of late. She barely spoke to him. She was still so angry at him, but today he didn't care. He was going to force her to be his little girl today because this ceremony symbolized a maturation, one that he wasn't ready for.

"I need to hear you say it. What are you?" Ethic asked.

"Aww, Daddy," Bella moaned. It was another sign that she wasn't little anymore. Things that she used to love to do, she now considered embarrassing.

"I just need to make sure you know," Ethic said. His voice was low, as if he were depleted, as if the idea of her not knowing injured him.

Bella sighed and rolled her eyes.

"I am woman and woman is beautiful. We are expected to be beautiful, so I will be what people don't expect. They don't expect intelligence, they don't expect grace. I am strong, and even when others have the ability to physically overpower me, mentally, I am stronger. I am a queen on a throne, and a place next to me must be earned. When I find my king, his power doesn't erase my own. My crown is not a man's to repossess. I was born in regality. I am kind, but naivety does not dwell within me. I am woman. I am the origin. Everything begins and ends with me. No man is worthy of my worth. I cannot be bought. I will not sell myself short. I do not give discounts. I am woman. I demand respect. I respect my dignity. My presence is a revocable gift, rented with effort and good intention. I am woman."

Ethic felt a bit of relief, as he kissed Bella on her forehead and sighed. She had been listening over the years. "Always remember that."

"I will," she promised.

He held up his pinky. It used to be their thing. They hadn't done it in a long while, but they meant the same thing. Pinky swears were like the ultimate contract that he only entered with the ones he loved. Bella released a stubborn smile, as she looped her pinky with his.

"Now, you repeat after me," Bella said. "I deserve to be happy too."

Her words hit him, harder than she intended.

"I'm happy. I have you, and Eazy, and Morgan," Ethic said.

"I want to see you happy like when you're with a woman you love. Like when you were with Raven. You were happy with YaYa. You were happiest with Alani. You were different with her. Your eyes looked different. You smiled when she was around. You make everybody happy except yourself. That's not fair."

Ethic hated that his daughter sensed his disposition. Men and women were created in pairs and roamed the world searching for their match. Man was made to hunt, to find nourishment not only to feed the hunger in their bellies but the hunger in their souls. Ethic had been eating for years, he had no problem with the hunt for wealth, but his soul was starving. Until he found his match, he would always feel incomplete. He was a king without a queen, a man without a rib, and it kept his heart vulnerable to melancholy. It was a part of him that was unfulfilled, one that he thought he expertly kept hidden. *Apparently, not well enough.*

"Leave the worrying up to me, a'ight?" he reassured. "Go get your brother and let's get going," Ethic said. "We've got to be out of here in the next five minutes, if we're going to make it to your ceremony on time."

"But I'm going to be the only person there without a mom. Can't I just skip it? I don't have to participate. It's stupid anyway," she said.

Ethic hated this affliction she was plagued with. There were times in her life that Ethic could distract her from the fact that she was a motherless child, but today, on the day that she was stepping into the next phase of her life and being honored for becoming a young woman, he wasn't enough. Only a mother would do. Bella had even turned down Morgan's offer to stand in. She wanted a mother, a real mother, whom knew what it felt like to have life growing from the inside out. She wanted Alani, and it was the one thing that Ethic's riches couldn't buy.

"I know it's hard to look at other girls with their mothers and not have that. I'm sorry, B. I can't replace that, but I will always stand with you as you feel the hurt. I'm not your mother, but I'm your father, and I will be up there today feeling incomplete with you. I can't erase that void, but I will try to fill it as much as I can."

She nodded, and he knew that she was on the verge of tears. "Don't cry, baby girl," he said. "It's going to be a beautiful day and you're going to be the most beautiful girl in the building. With all this handsome up there with you, everybody's going to thank you for bringing some testosterone into the room," Ethic said, playfully flexing his muscles and then making a body builder's pose and silly face to make his daughter laugh. It was a humor he reserved for her only and it could usually brighten her darkest day, but today the clouds didn't dissipate so easily.

Bella gave him a half smile that ripped a hole through his chest and hollowed his gut. He never wanted her to do anything with half her heart, but he knew that it wasn't full enough to exude true happiness. He stood to his feet, and then retrieved the jacket to his grey, Tom Ford suit before corralling his children.

"We're going to be late," he called down the hall. Eazy came flying out his room dressed in a black, Ralph Lauren suit that wouldn't stand a chance against his childish antics. There was already a chocolate stain on his lapel. Ethic wasn't the chastising type, however. He simply shook his head and rubbed the top of his son's wild head, as he said, "Go hop in the backseat, Big Man. Leave that video game here. We're focusing on your sister today."

"Aww, man!" Eazy shouted, as he ran back to his room to store the handheld system before bolting down the stairs for the door.

Ethic helped Bella down the stairs, as he took her in. She was a vision in her white, satin, debutante, ballroom gown. A silver tiara sat atop her head. She was a bit wobbly in the three-inch heels that he had been dead set against, but he was there, arm extended to keep her steady on her feet. He shook his head as he saw her pretty toes peek from the bottom of her dress in those damn shoes. She had begged him and begged him until he had finally given in, but the sight of her in heels stabbed at his heart. He wanted to lock her in her room for the rest of her life. Little, nappy-headed boys couldn't corrupt what they couldn't find, but it was a part of life, a part of growth and Ethic was being forced into acceptance.

"Where's Mo?" He asked, aloud. She was supposed to meet them at the house an hour ago. He picked up his cell, noticing that he had three missed calls - all from Morgan.

He dialed her back.

"Finally!" she shouted, as soon as she answered.

"Where are you, Mo? Ceremony starts in 30," Ethic said.

"I caught a flat on the highway," she explained. "I had to call Messiah. He came to change it, but the rim is bent. He got it towed and is bringing me to the church."

Ethic's jaw tensed. He didn't even like the thought of Messiah escorting Morgan to the church. He had been invited anyway,

41

but this sounded like a date.

"Ethic?"

Ethic cleared his throat. "Yeah, alright, Mo. We'll see you there."

Ethic attributed his suspicions to his foul mood. Messiah had never given him a reason to discount his word and Morgan was family. He trusted her. They both knew his rules. It was just a car ride. An innocent phone call because Ethic had been preoccupied and couldn't get to her first. It was what he had given Morgan Messiah's number for to begin with, all those years ago. He took a deep breath and walked Bella to the car, feeling like he was getting ready to give his little girl away.

CHAPTER 5

The parking lot to the church was filled with cars as Ethic hustled his minions out of the backseat. They stepped inside the building and Ethic could tell no expense had been spared.

"Mr. Okafor, it's nice to see you, again," Alicia, church ho extraordinaire, spoke.

He nodded. "Likewise."

"I'm really glad that things worked out. I'm sure the ladies would have loved to see you participate, but…"

"But, what?" Ethic asked.

"Alani!"

Ethic's eyes were literally ripped from Alicia's direction and fell onto her, as Bella let go of his hand and ran to the love of his life.

Stun wore him, as Eazy followed suit, running up to her. The way she embraced them both, then rolled her beautiful eyes up to him, took his breath away. He had to remind himself to close his mouth, because it was catching flies from the shock of it all. Church ho was still talking but it was muted, everything around him was reduced except her. She was magnified, as she stood in front of him, brilliantly displayed in a black, floor-length dress. Her hair was short and in soft waves, giving her a classic, 1920's, flapper's look. Her make-up was dark, alluring. She resembled Dorothy Dandridge and he wished she would say something because her words would surely sound like a song.

"Excuse me," Ethic said, distractedly, walking toward Alani. His eyes prickled. Damn, what she did to him was amazing. Not seeing her for months had made her presence that much more alluring.

He walked into her space, not caring that he felt her cringe, not caring that curious eyes of his children and the members of the church were watching.

"You don't know how fucking good it feels to see you," he whispered, unable to help himself from swearing, unable to stop himself from telling the truth. Staying away when she was across town had been a challenge, so having her within arm's reach, he didn't stand a chance. She lowered her head in discomfort and placed a hand to his chest, before taking a step backward. She was fidgety, nervous, perhaps even afraid.

"What are you doing here?" he asked.

"Just because you're a liar doesn't make me one." Alani whispered that part, so his children wouldn't overhear. Her words were meant to injure him, but Ethic just felt a stir in his soul from the melody of her voice. He would rather take the stab from her insult than the silence that accompanied her absence. Compared to not having her at all, her verbal jabs felt like foreplay. "I'm here because I made a promise. A motherless child and a childless mother. I would never not show up after telling her that I would be here. Just do me a favor and stay away." Her eyes burned with malice and resentment.

She had him up like a love-sick teenager, every crevice of his mind had been filled with her for the past 61 days. There was unmistakable fear in her eyes. Her hands trembled, as she gripped her clutch so tightly her fingertips turned red. Ethic's inner being crumbled, wounded by the revelation that when she looked at him she didn't see life. She didn't see the future in his eyes. She saw death and his presence reminded her of a past she desperately missed. He reminded her of pain. He was the source of her agony and within her he didn't even recognize the want to forgive him. She hated him, and he felt it. He watched her walk back over to Bella and knew better than to address her further. He wanted her in this moment, but Bella needed her, and if he pushed too hard, Alani just might flee. Placing the needs of his daughter before his own, selfish ones, he retreated to his seat.

"Eazy," he called out, grabbing his son's attention. He smirked, watching Bella's friends dote over his charming, young son, who wore the expensive suit well, as he soaked up all the attention. "Let's take our seats, Big Man."

The church was elaborately decorated for the occasion and Ethic took his seat, front and center, as the ceremony began. Morgan and Messiah filtered in just as the lights dimmed. Ethic stood, hugging Mo and shook hands with Messiah. Mo sat next to Ethic and put Eazy between her and Messiah. There wasn't much room for conversation. The sound of music playing began and the rear doors of the sanctuary opened.

On one side, the young girls were aligned. On the other side, the mothers entered as they strolled in unison down the aisles. Ethic's eyes naturally found his baby girl and a sense of pride swelled within him as she gave him a smile. She had grown up beautifully, even though she didn't have a woman to guide her through the confusing transitions she had made, and the even more confusing ones that were to come. He winked at her and nodded his head in approval, as she daintily strolled toward the front. He felt Alani's energy trying to pull his focus from Bella. His attraction to her was that strong that he knew exactly where she was on the other side of the room. His sweet Bella wouldn't let him go, however. Her pull was stronger on this day and he had to squeeze the bridge of his nose to stop himself from becoming emotional. Morgan looped her arm through his elbow and rested her head on his shoulders.

"She's so pretty," Morgan whispered. "You're such a good dad, Ethic." She hugged the arm she had taken tightly, and Ethic sniffed as he kissed the top of her head.

When Bella and Alani met at the front, Bella curtsied, spreading her gown and bowing her head. The sight of Alani lighting his daughter's candle forced Ethic to blow out a hard breath. He was overwhelmed. It was like someone was unbuttoning his insides, exposing him. Bella handed the candle to the pastor and the pastor added it to a chalice of candles, all flickering. Bella's shoulders hunched, as she began crying and there wasn't a dry eye in the house when Alani took her into her arms. Ethic stood from his seat, Bella was bawling so badly. He wanted to go to her, but somehow, he knew Alani had it under control. He remained standing, as Alani whispered in Bella's ear. His daughter nodded, repeatedly, agreeing to whatever gospel Alani spoke and then she lifted her head. The church clapped. Alani held out an open palm and Bella hung onto it as the pair made their way up the aisle. Everyone was on their feet, clapping, and hollering, catching the holy ghost, and crying. Everyone knew that Bella was orphaned, and that Alani's child had just died. This looked like God's work, like healing right in front of them.

"Ayyeeemen," the pastor said, as he clapped. "Ain't God good?" he began. "Ain't God great? Where God sees a need he fulfills!"

Ethic's throat was constricted, as he absorbed the words of this man in the long robe up front. He had always thought pastors to be frauds, but something this man was preaching about was reaching him. The mothers and daughters sat in the last pew and it took everything in him not to turn around to search for Alani's face. He was grateful when the program ended. "The reception is in the banquet center. Eazy, follow Mo and Messiah. I'll catch up," Ethic said.

Morgan followed Ethic's stare to Alani and she rolled her eyes before ushering Eazy out into the aisle. Her nostrils flared, as she looked up to Messiah who held out his arm for her to go first.

Ethic walked up the aisle to where Alani stood behind Bella with her hands on her shoulders. She beamed like a proud mother, as she smiled and accepted compliments from the people passing her by.

Ethic paused, as he watched Bella turn to Alani. They did some dance of celebration that, apparently, they had done before. It made him smirk. Then, Alani gripped Bella's chin between two fingers and gave a lingering gaze. So many unspoken words were shared in that look. It spoke volumes.

I'm proud of you.
You're beautiful.
We did it.
I love you.

Bella fell into Alani's arms and Alani held her so tight that it made Ethic's eyes wet. Ethic couldn't witness this type of personal interaction. Alani was so well versed with his child, so in tune with her needs. It made him want to hunt her. She

47

was prey and Ethic was a lion. He wanted to reign king over her entire existence. A woman had never been sexier. He had never loved one more. He licked his lips as he stepped up, this time respecting her space. Alani's smile faded. He felt childish to be jealous that Bella was a part of Alani's inner circle and he was standing on the outside. It was obvious she had a wall up when it came to him. Even her stance changed, growing defensive, as if she was full of tension and waiting to react.

He wanted to say so many things to her, but he couldn't get pass the sentiments blocking his throat and holding his stomach hostage. He felt like a middle school kid who had his first crush. He was nervous. Cool, calm, collected, Ethic Okafor was wound so tightly that he had butterflies. *Ain't that a bitch?*

He wondered if it was a sin to think curse words in church. If the curse words were a problem, the rest of his thoughts would condemn him straight to hell. Alani spotted Alicia behind Ethic.

"Alicia!" Alani called, as if they were old girlfriends. She hated this church ho, but she was her only escape and Alani was taking it. Alicia turned around and gave Alani the phoniest smile as she placed curious eyes on Alani and Ethic.

"Beautiful job, Bella," Alicia complimented.

"Thank you." Bella was beaming. "I'm going to have to get with your handsome father here to discuss joining the church. We'd love to see you guys around here more often."

Alani's brows lifted, as she placed astonished eyes on Ethic. Ethic fisted his beard. A quick glance to Alani and then a polite nod to Alicia.

"Alani has extended the invitation. We'll visit a few times before deciding. I really appreciate you welcoming Bella into the debutante program. It was beautifully done," Ethic stated.

Alani rolled satisfied eyes back to Alicia.

Bitch, she thought.

Yep, the devil was in her tonight. She was going straight to hell if she kept up this attitude. Deciding that Alicia was not her scapegoat, Alani turned on her heels. "Come on, Bella. Let's head to the banquet," she said. She and Bella walked side by side and Ethic trailed them, taking slow steps as he watched them from behind, taking in their dynamic. He wasn't quite sure where he fit in to it all. How Alani was boxing him out of his own daughter's celebration he didn't know, but he didn't mind. Bella was on cloud nine and it was all that mattered.

CHAPTER 6

The banquet center was professionally designed and sparkled beautifully as Alani and Bella walked into the room.

Alani paused at the entrance, when she noticed that each seat had a place card in front of it. Each mother was seated next to their daughter and each family had a table.

"We're over here," Bella said. Bella sped up, but Alani halted. She recognized Messiah from the beating that he had bestowed upon Cream. She didn't know if she could survive a dinner at the same table as them. Then, there was Morgan. No formal introduction had taken place, but she knew her as Ethic's oldest daughter.

The one my brother raped.

She tensed when she felt him beside her, and to get away from him she decided to hightail it to the table. Her place card was luckily between Bella's and Eazy's. She took a deep breath, as she sat.

Ethic joined them and everyone took their places, but no one spoke.

"Isn't this a family table?" Morgan asked, shooting daggers at Alani, as she stared at her without caution.

Everyone at the table looked on in shock at Morgan's uncharacteristic frankness.

Ethic leaned over and whispered in Morgan's ear, "Everybody

at this table was handpicked by your sister. Let today be about her, Mo. Everything isn't about you."

Morgan snatched her cloth napkin from the table and snapped it open before placing it in her lap.

Alani's hands shook, as she reached for her water goblet, but she forced herself to calm down. It felt like it was all of them versus her and it was so awkward that she just wanted to leave. She had shot their father. She understood why they hated her, but she hated them too, everyone except the two, little people at the table.

Just focus on them.

"I never got to thank you for the beautiful necklace, Eazy," she said, as she looked down at him. *She fingered her neck. It hung there every day.* "I love it."

"You're welcome," he said. "Thank you for the video game. It's my favorite one!"

Alani smiled. "The guy at GameStop thought you might like it. I'm glad I picked a good one."

"I wanted to give you my gift myself, but Daddy said you and Bella needed girl time! How is that fair? Bella always comes over to do cool stuff with you and I am always left out..."

Alani smiled.

"You're right. That doesn't sound very fair at all," Alani agreed.

"Bella won't be going anywhere anymore, Eazy, the pageant is over," Morgan cut in.

She was sickened by Alani and she wasn't into hiding it.

"Mo," Ethic stated, losing patience. Morgan felt Messiah's hand on her thigh. He gave it a gentle squeeze to calm her.

"What? It's over, right? That's the reason Bella was always there," Mo defended.

"Yeah, you're right, Morgan. I guess we will be seeing less of each other now," Alani whispered.

"But we can still talk, right? It's been so long since I've seen you. I was really worried about you," Bella said.

Alani didn't want to go down that road. "I'm fine, Bella," Alani said, as she touched her cheek. "I promise."

Alani avoided Ethic's eyes, but she could feel them on her, analyzing, picking her lies apart. No, she wasn't fine, but what else could she say? She couldn't admit that she cried herself to sleep at night, so she faked it. She pulled herself together to show up for Bella, but every day before this one had felt like she was dying.

"Welcome, families. We'd like to ask the mothers and fathers of these lovely debutantes to join us on the floor for a dance," the D.J. announced.

"Daddy, you and Alani have to get out there," Eazy said.

Alani felt Bella and Eazy's eyes on her, pressuring her, as they waited for her to say something. She had never felt so cornered in her life and she looked to Ethic for the first time since sitting down. *Help me*, she thought. She didn't want to be the one to say no.

"Daddy ain't much of a dancer, Big Man," Ethic rescued. "I don't want to step all over Alani's toes."

"But Dad! You have to! They're calling all the parents up to the dance floor," Eazy urged. "Look!" Eazy turned to motion at the floor. "Bella is the only one without somebody up there."

Alani's throat constricted. It was already painful enough, being in his presence, but the way his children were goading her with their glossy stares, ogling hopefully, made her lift from her seat. He looked up at her in shock and she shrugged, lifting her shoulders and letting her head fall to the side as if to say, *why not?* He pressed back out of the chair and stood to his feet and her legs turned to noodles when he took her hand. His aura was so strong that it swallowed her. She had wanted to keep a room full of distance between them, but the assigned seating arrangement had squandered that and now, somehow, she had been talked into following him to the dance floor. She flattened the wrinkles from the front of her off-the-rack, formal, floor-length, black gown. The way the bodice fit her curves all the way to the ground made a beautiful visual, but it was almost impossible to take normal-sized steps to meet his long stride. They made it to the center of the dance floor and white balls of light bounced off the walls from the strobe light. She felt like the introverted girl in high school who was about to dance with the prom king. Alani cleared her throat, as she stood in front of Ethic, her hands nervously straightening the front of her dress, the wrinkles from where she had sat no longer visible, but she needed something to focus on besides him.

"We don't have to do this," Ethic offered. *Of course, he notices I'm uncomfortable. He notices every damn thing.* His voice was solemn, dark. *Does he pity me? Am I pitiful for being here? Playing a role for his child. This isn't my family. Bella isn't mine...and who the hell am I to mentor anyone? I'm a mess.* Alani's thoughts were jumping her, double-teaming her with confusion and indecision, making her good deed feel foolish.

Alani glanced over at the table where Eazy and Bella looked on. They were watching them, and for the first time, Alani questioned if her relationship with Bella was appropriate. *She is not my responsibility. She's not my daughter. God, MY daughter.* Alani couldn't stop looking at Ethic's children. They were motherless. She was childless. So much hurt sitting at one table.

"It's just one dance, right?" Alani whispered.

The music began, but Ethic and Alani stood there, his serious glower looming over her as his height dwarfed her. Alani's focus was locked in on her pair of Aldo heels. They were modest, and although gorgeous, there was nothing premium about them; much like herself, they were regular. Ethic was the only person who made her feel like Aldo somehow belonged on the same shelf as Louboutin. What she didn't realize is that with everybody choosing Red Bottoms nowadays, sometimes simple matched better. When she was able to block out the circumstances surrounding his introduction into her life, she remembered that he made her feel extraordinary. She couldn't meet his stare because she was afraid of getting lost in the darkness of his gaze. Anthony Hamilton's soulful voice crooned from the speaker and Alani's back stiffened, as Ethic wrapped his right arm around her. He took her left hand in his.

I can't stay away from you too long
Even if I do, I'll always call

Alani's rigidity only allowed her to sway side to side, as a space large enough for Eazy to fit through, remained between them. Ethic felt her hand shuddering in his as he respected the limits she was putting up with her body language. Just her dainty fingers cupped inside his palm was enough contact to make him grateful. This woman had knocked down every guard he had built over the years, she had remedied every wound that life had put on his heart, and in return, he had destroyed her. He had come into her life like a wrecking ball and demolished her world. He understood why she cringed at the feel of his hands on the small of her back. It broke him, but he knew how they had gotten to this place. He felt lucky to be touching her at all, to be laying eyes on her even. He was lucky she was here, not only at the ball, but here on the other side of the dirt, because his actions had almost driven her to end it all. Ethic wasn't the typical man, selfishly blind to the inner battles of others. He knew the turmoil she felt, and it pained him to know he was the cause of anything other than her happiness. For her to still embrace his daughter the way she did showed he hadn't misjudged her character. She was even greater than he had suspected. She was one of those angels on Earth people spoke about. That was Alani.

Checking on you, make sure you're okay
Be the one to brighten up your day.
Yeah, yeah

Alani stared forward at his chest. *Don't look up at him. Don't. Do. It. How long is this song? Why did they play THIS song?* Her heart was uncertain, and she was fighting her natural instinct to run away from danger because that's what Ethic was... dangerous. Every innate alarm in her body blared, warning her that this was trouble...that this one dance wasn't just some dance and that it would lead to catastrophe. Her stomach was in distress and she felt hot, weak, as the room began to spin a little. *I can't breathe. Why can't I breathe?* Her grasp tightened in his hand. She felt like she would pass out.

And the point of it all. I love you.
Yeahhh
You know I love you baby, oh, oh, oh--

Alani stopped swaying and closed her eyes, as she took a step back from Ethic. She wrapped both hands around his forearms for balance. More space. She needed more space between them. Just to breathe. She inhaled, deeply sucking it in through her nose, blowing out through her mouth. *God, why does this feel like this?*

"I can't breathe," she whispered.

Her neck tensed, and Ethic could see her suffering. She felt like she was about to have a full-blown panic attack.

"You don't have to do this. We can stop," his baritone was deep, strong, but the way he said it told her that his words were only a nicety. Stopping was the last thing he wanted to do. She glanced over at Bella who was watching them. She was smiling, beaming, in fact, as she rested her head on the back of her chair, her entire body pivoted so she could have a good view of the dance floor. Of the parents on the dance floor. Her parents. That's what this dance represented for little Bella.

Just make it through this song. Alani shook her head and stepped into Ethic, resting her forehead against his chest. She felt his chin on the top of her head and the rise then fall of his chest as he sighed in relief. There was no space. He pulled her in and she let him because if she didn't her legs wouldn't allow this dance to continue. She wasn't even sure they would carry her out of the room without giving out, so she stayed, in his embrace, trembling as Anthony Hamilton filled her ears.

My days seem long whenever we're apart

Ethic released his grasp on her hand and wrapped both arms around Alani's waist, locking one hand around the opposite wrist. He was surprisingly smooth on his feet, as he led her through the beautiful song. Alani was enveloped in love. Love amidst the hate she felt. It was overpowering. All-consuming. Suffocating. The yearning in this song was almost as strong as the yearning in Ethic's embrace. The feel of his growing beard against her neck, as he buried his shame there, the roughness of his skin as his fingertips graced the small of her back, the tension of his muscles as he led her, swaying, forcing her to follow his steps without forcing her at all. The smell of him, not just his cologne but the way it mixed with his natural PH. It was all too much. It was an overindulgence in all things Ethic and Alani was drunk. Drunk in an emotion so strong she couldn't see straight, so she closed her eyes. There had been a change in him. She could sense it; a flux, a lessening of strength. *He's weak. I weakened him.* Tears filled her closed eyes. *He is killing me. He has murdered me. I am a carcass depleted from a lack of him, a loss of life. He's a murderer. Kenzie's killer.* The notion caused her back to stiffen and she turned on her heels to run, but Ethic's hold was like a leash. When she got too far away, she was pulled back. Her dress spun, as if the move was intentional, and then she heard applause. People were clapping for this tragic scene because it was beautiful. She wanted to run. He wanted her to remain. They were at an impasse, as her glare met his stare. His wrinkled forehead, brooding eyes, thick brows pushed together in torment… they all came together in a silent plea. Just one dance. He was asking her for this one song without even moving his lips. She knew him that well. Alani stepped in with reluctance as her heart thundered. She was so damn angry. Hurt beyond human comprehension. He had invented a level of pain that surpassed all others, with his deception, but still she allowed him this one dance. Alani forgot there were other people in the room, as she sucked in a baited breath while he pulled her even closer. It was like he was trying to pull her into him, because being apart as two, separate entities didn't allow them to be close enough. It didn't allow him to keep her forever. When the song ended, she would walk away. His strong embrace caused tension in his upper body and she felt the definition of his muscular arms, even through the expensive suit. He tightened his hold around her. He didn't want to let her go. She wasn't sure what she wanted. Then again, yes, she was. She wanted her daughter back. *He took her.* She had to keep reminding herself to stop her natural affinity to this man from taking over. She closed her eyes, tears teasing her lashes, as the words of the song shot an arrow straight through her.

It's like someone has stole away my heart

She wrapped her hands around his head and her fingertips tapped the back of his neck, as she kept the beat as their swaying relaxed, the formality melting between them. Him in his gray suit, her in her black dress. They looked like a couple in love. From the outside looking in, one would never guess the obstacles that kept them apart.

You're a major part of my li-i-ife

Alani pulled Ethic's head down, into the groove of her neck, like she was consoling him. Once again, he pulled her closer, as he breathed in the honey scent that rested on her skin. One of his hands slid up her back until he was holding the back of her head, cradling it like she was a newborn baby, while that one, strong hand never left the small of her back. The clean scent of his cologne enveloped her. It wasn't his usual fragrance and it reminded her that she hadn't been around him to notice the small things about him that had changed. The beard. The cologne. New details. Choices that he had made in her absence. The insignificance didn't matter. It still saddened her to think that there was evolution in his life and that she was missing it, but there was no way that she could be a part of it. Time was inevitably moving on without them, leaving their short union in the past. The emotional fortress he wrapped her in protected her from everything that was outside their circumference. He was good at that, keeping the world out, keeping her untouched, filling in the holes that marred her past and making her feel complete. *He loves me. The devil loves me.* The one thing he couldn't protect her from was himself. He was like the tide, rushing toward her, heightening her depths, filling in the footprints that people left when they walked all over her, restoring her. Oh, but when that tide receded. When Ethic pulled away, he snatched everything that laid in the sands of her heart along with him. He carried her out to sea to drown her. Yes, Ethic was her ocean, beautiful, deep, one of God's great mysteries, and deadly. Still, Alani clung to him as they swayed. She remembered when she had learned to swim. They told her not to swim against the current of the tide. Not to fight it. She would lose, and she didn't know it to be true until this moment. She was losing this fight, so instead of resisting the strength of the ocean, of Ethic, she submitted to it. Letting him carry her side to side to the music. *Just for one song.*

And no matter what the storm may bring, I'm fi-i-ne with youuu

Alani felt Ethic's lips on her neck. He was buried there so deeply that she felt him mouthing the words and she couldn't help but release the tears that she had been holding back. They fell, gracefully, down her face and landed on the jacket of his expensive suit, one after another.

And the point of it all, is I love youuu
And the reason for it all, I love youuu

Alani was wrecked, as she felt him, singing silently, his lips to her skin, his hand desperately holding her in place, his strength the only thing keeping her from becoming a pretty heap of lace, silk, and tears on the floor. She could feel his anguish and she shared it because it was theirs to behold. They had birthed it, it was theirs to raise. It was the only baby they still had to connect them; their hurt, and neither could let it go. Ethic was completely buried into her, as they two stepped, Alani's fingertips holding the tempo to the song as Anthony Hamilton put into words everything Ethic was too considerate to put on Alani's heart. He knew if he said the words, she would listen. If he made this song, his words, from his tongue, to her ears, she would hear him, but he wouldn't. He knew she needed to hate him for what he had done and a small part of him hated her for the way she had reacted, the way she had kept him away when she was pregnant. That part was so minuscule that it almost didn't exist, but it was there, and it was what made it easier to respect her request for space. Their love somehow produced tragedy to their offspring and he couldn't take any more of it. He didn't want to be selfish enough to expect her to stay. This song, however, this song was theirs. These three minutes and fifty seconds that he had been counting, belonged to them and reminded them both what a lifetime together could have been like.

I love you girl
Oh I love you
I love you girl
Ohhh I looovvvee
I love you girl
Oh I love you girl
Yeahhh, ohhhhh, ohhhh-oh
I can't stayyyyyyy

Neither spoke. Words weren't necessary. Mr. Hamilton was saying it all and only in song could their feelings be masked so beautifully that it felt acceptable. Only through this dance could Alani allow herself to feel for the man that had committed the ultimate sin against her. This wasn't real. *It's just a dance,* she thought, but she knew that he knew that it was so much more.

I can't stay awayyyy too longgg

Ethic felt her chest spasm.

I can't stay away from you baby

His gut tightened in angst when he heard a single sob escape her. She tucked her head into him, hiding her face from the rest of the room as she cried. He felt her trying to plug the hole that would allow her to appear weak. She was stubborn that way, too strong to yield to what being in this moment was doing to her. He wouldn't address the wetness he felt on his shirt because he knew she was trying with all her might to control her emotions. *She's probably pissed at herself for breaking down.* The thought made his chest go heavy because none of this was her fault. It was all on him; but somehow, just like a black woman, she was internalizing his wrongdoing, blaming herself, shouldering the responsibility when it should have been his. He couldn't bring her closer, only hold her tighter, and she reciprocated by adding a second hand to the back of his head. *Motherfucking God, I love this woman. Something got to give. Who got to die? Who I got to pay to keep shit just like this?* Ethic was tortured. This woman may as well have been the one to birth him. He may as well have been nurtured in her womb for 40 weeks because she felt like home. She felt maternal, like she had grown his heart on the inside of her body. Alani had taken the place of the mother he had figured out life without. He had imprinted on her in that way, that deeply, and pulling away from her was like pulling a baby from the nipple - unnatural. Unloving her was aberrant, unfathomable, and Ethic was dying. *Ma, I love you.* Ethic felt the sting and he snapped his eyes closed. He had done more crying in his short time of knowing Alani than he had his entire life. At times when his stomach touched his back in hunger as a young boy, he hadn't cried. When he saw his mother's body lying cold in her casket, he hadn't cried. He had endured things that would obliterate the average man and still only a handful of times had his eyes leaked tears. Alani…simple, pure, domestic, nurturing, Alani caused him to bleed emotion. She just opened him, like she was the keeper of keys to his sentiments and she alone decided which one to unlock whenever she was around. She was life, but he was death, and the two never co-existed. They only passed the torch back and forth, never intersecting because they didn't belong together. Ethic regained his composure, quickly, but didn't open his eyes because he could tell by the crescendo of Anthony Hamilton's soulful crooning that the song would soon end. When it did, Alani would let go and he just wanted to feel her a while longer. This gangster, this father, this king, this little black boy parading around, masking himself inside a grown man was cut in half like Alani was the fraction bar that ordered his reduction. He just wanted to feel whole, but every time she left him, she divided him and took half with her. He wondered if she knew she owned that half, if she was aware how she took shards of him with her. She was the best kind of thief. The one you never saw coming and who took the most valuable pieces in the room upon her departure. Ethic wished he had never met her, wished he had never known what loving her was like because he had developed a tongue for her, no other woman would ever be able to satisfy his tastes.

I can't stay awayyyy too longgg
Don't want to be with you
I needddd youuu
I can't stay awayyy too longgg
Why don't you stay around for awhile
I can't stay awayyy too longgg
And the point of it all
And the point of it all
And the point of it all
And the reason for it all
And the point of it all
Is I love you

Whenever we're apart. It damn near stops my heart....

The song faded to its end, and as other couples left the floor, they stood there, holding one another, grasping one another... seeing, smelling, breathing one another. Ethic had her hand, holding her over the boat as the ocean churned violently below her. They could both feel their hands slipping. He was about to let her go. Alani gripped the lapel of his jacket, as Ethic rested his chin against the top of her head. The entire room stared, wondering why they hadn't taken the cue to exit the dance floor. The energy between them was Shakespearean. Beautiful, passionate, yet tragic. When Alani finally pulled away, Ethic let her go and she plunged into that ocean...drowned. The room went back to black and white. The only color in his life was walking, damn near running, as quickly as she could toward the door. As much as Ethic wanted to go after her, he didn't follow.

CHAPTER 7

Morgan sat, one manicured hand covering her mouth as she held it agape while watching Ethic. *He really loves her.* She discreetly squeezed Messiah's hand under the table, as she turned misty eyes his way. "Did you feel that?" she whispered.

Messiah turned his attention back to Ethic who had returned to his normal, stoic, self. Any other day of the week and Ethic would have been unreadable, but today, Ethic wore melancholy all over him. He made his way off the dance floor, headed in the opposite direction of their table, as he rubbed the back of his neck. Messiah knew Ethic was in search of a place to restore his composure. "I think everybody in this room felt that shit," Messiah replied. "Damn." It was all he could mutter.

"I want that type of love one day," Morgan whispered.

"You got it today," Messiah said, as he leaned into Morgan, nipping her ear with his teeth, causing her to quiver. "And I ain't gon' fuck it up. I'm telling him tonight."

"No," Morgan whispered, as her eyes caught a glimpse of Ethic's back as he disappeared behind the door of the men's restroom. Tears burned her eyes. She hadn't seen Ethic this torn up since her sister was killed all those years ago. Somewhere deep down, her loyalty to Raven caused her to dislike Alani. *He can't love her like he loved Rae, can he? But what I just saw... wow.* It was like the couple had put the entire room under a spell. She shook her head. "Give him tonight," Morgan said. "That conversation will go badly tonight, but soon. I promise we can tell him soon."

She watched Messiah rise from the table.

"Where are you going?" she asked, her brow creasing at his sudden departure.

He stood behind her chair and leaned down to whisper in her ear. "I ain't in the mood to pretend like what's mine ain't mine, shorty." Goosebumps formed on the back of her neck. His lips on her ear, faintly touching it as he spoke, made the seat of her panties wet. The hint of displeasure under his raspy tone was sexy, angry, but sexy all the same.

She turned her body in the chair, bringing sad eyes up to meet his.

"I'ma pull up on you later," he said, expression still stern. He was angry. She could tell, and it put an instant burden on her heart. Not ever wanting to leave her with uncertainty, he took two steps away before he turned. "Aye yo, Shorty Doo-Wop?" he called. Morgan was spoiled and not used to things not going her way, so she simply folded her arms across her chest and didn't acknowledge him.

"A nigga ain't touch his plate. So, I'ma be starving later. You got any recommendations of something good I can eat?" The lewd comment came out with such arrogance that Morgan's entire face warmed and then turned red. He spoke openly, knowing the kids wouldn't catch the innuendo. *So damn cocky.*

"I can think of a thing or two," she answered, knowing that when Messiah feasted on her, he left no part of her neglected. The thought of him sucking on her clit until she screamed his name and then moving onto her other hole, while exploring her depths with his fingers made Morgan's womanhood clench in yearning. No part of her body went undiscovered with Messiah. He gave attention to every inch of her being. He was nasty, only with her, only ever with her. His. That's what Morgan was, and he worked to prove it with their every interaction.

Messiah licked his lips, as he eyed the way she squeezed her thighs together, applying discreet pressure to what he knew was wet and swollen in the center. His dick jumped, and he could feel it hardening by the second. He was addicted to this young girl. There wasn't one risk he wouldn't take for her. There wasn't one person he wouldn't send to their maker over her. Man, woman, child...shit, he wouldn't even carry the remorse Ethic did over the little girl. Not for Morgan. For her, any-motherfucking-body could catch bullets. He was unapologetic in the way he loved her. He wanted all the smoke. He knew it was fucked up, but he had come to terms that he was just a fucked-up individual, one that she saw fit to still love. For that, she would always have his loyalty. "It's really not good to go all day without eating," she said, lowering her long lashes to her lap before batting them up at him.

"Yeah, Messiah, my teacher says you should eat three full meals and two snacks every day," Eazy chimed in from across the table where he sat beside Bella.

"Is that right?" Messiah asked, his eyes never leaving Morgan. "I think I better eat now then," he added. "Aye yo, Mo. You'll do me a favor and fix me a plate?"

Morgan arose from the table. "Yeah, sure. Come show me what you want, and I'll wrap one up for you before I leave. I was headed out anyway," she said, coolly. "Bella, you killed it, per usual." She walked around the table and kissed the kids goodbye, before stepping in front of Messiah to lead him out.

She knew where his eyes were. They naturally gravitated toward her ass. She didn't even put a little switch in her step because he told her he preferred her without the extras. Effortless, was what he called her beauty. *Shit's effortless.*

"Yo, shorty, you got it," he admired, lustfully, as they stepped into the kitchen, disregarding the *staff only* sign that hung on the double doors. She giggled, as he gripped her waist and pulled her into his hardness.

"I did all that?" she asked, with intrigue, as she felt him pressing into her from behind. She was still amazed at the powers of womanhood. She could take Messiah from zero to a trillion anytime she desired. His loins, his temper, his pulse...it was all hers to control, like she had her foot on the speedometer of his emotions.

"All 'at," he drawled, as he kissed the back of her neck. She grabbed a strawberry that sat on one of the leftover trays and then pulled his hand as she walked further into the kitchen. "On some real shit, Mo. I just want to put my face in it, shorty. Where we going?"

He was crass, unrefined. He was a hood nigga in all his hood nigga glory and Morgan loved him. She figured one day they would mature into a lovely, established couple. One day when she was out of college and he was out the game, maybe they would travel the world or go to picnics in parks, have Sunday family dinners at a house they built together. She prayed they made it to those days when they were someone's couple goals, but today, they were young, and their love was brand new. All they wanted to do was eat good, spend money, and fuck. It was bliss. It was enough, and Morgan didn't want anything more. "Just nasty, Siah," she laughed.

"Shit shouldn't be so fucking sweet," he said, biting his lip, as he reluctantly allowed her to pull him further toward the back of the kitchen. "Now, I got a sweet tooth. Where you going?" Messiah asked. "You playing." Irritation frolicked in his tone. *Fuck this girl do to me. I ain't never wanted something as bad as this.* Pussy wasn't new to Messiah. He wasn't the type of man who had to search for it, it just found him. Everywhere he went it was available. The cashier at the grocery store threw it at him. The time he got hemmed up for driving with a suspended license and had to go to court, the stenographer gave him the 'you look like you got a big dick' eyes. Even when he went to the gym, the white girls on the treadmill hinted at liking chocolate. He had more pussy available to him than he could ever handle, but having the privilege to partake in Morgan put all the others to shame. He didn't know how she had infiltrated his life so drastically. It was like one day he was living just fine without her, getting money, enjoying women, building his name in the streets, and the next minute she was there, making it all seem pointless if he couldn't seek out her company after it was all said and done. He no longer even had the interest to entertain another. If it wasn't Mo, it wasn't for him. Even on nights when he was in Flint and she was away at school, he would need a release. His dick would be harder than those tests she always studied for and he never reached out to the many jump-offs in his phone. He would go to bed frustrated or FaceTime Mo on some chump shit and watch her play with it while he wrapped his hand around his strength until he came to the sound of her moans. Yes, Morgan Atkins had him on some other shit. On some faithful, do anything for her, sick-to-his-stomach type shit. On some fall-asleep-on-the-phone-so-I-can-hear-you breathe type shit. *Who would have fucking thought?*

She found a pantry filled with canned goods and an old,

wooden chair. A long string hung from the single lightbulb above. "Nobody should interrupt us back here."

Pulling him inside, Messiah looked behind him to see that no one had followed them into the kitchen. Before he could turn his head back around, Morgan was on her knees, fumbling with his Hermes belt. Holding him in her hands, she could feel the heat radiating in her palm. He was black and strong, with a wide mushroom head that always stretched her when he entered her. He was curved slightly to the right. Morgan had learned to master that curve at high speeds; because before she had learned to arch her back deep into the bed, he used to murder her little pussy.

She wet the tip of him and gave him one, long stroke.

"Ssss. . ." Messiah placed a hand on the back of her neck.

"I love this dick," she whispered, as she ran her tongue along the vein that protruded from underneath the shaft. He tensed, and Morgan grabbed his strong behind, pulling him into her warm mouth, forcing him deep down her throat. She removed it and it was so big that it made a *POP* as she pulled him from her mouth. She wet him, licking him more, focusing on the head and that vein. She knew he hated when her tongue got to the base of him, where his seed dwelled. It was where he housed her future babies. It was where their future lied, waiting to be released. *God, I want to have all his babies.* She wanted to run her tongue all over that spot, but Messiah had clear rules in the bedroom. "It's too close to my ass, Mo. Quit bullshitting," he would say. Morgan chuckled at the memory.

"Don't even think about it," he groaned, knowing where her mind was going.

"I bet it feels really good," she whispered. "When you do me it's mind-blowing."

"Then let me blow your mind," Messiah said, pulling her to her feet, as he claimed a seat in the only chair in the room. She stood between his legs and he slid a hand up her dress to discover she wore no panties. "You wild, you know that?" He admired her swollen clit, as it peeked out of her moist lips and she nodded while biting her lower lip, smiling down at him. "She so pretty, baby. I want something shiny on it. Something I can play with. You gone get it pierced for me?" he asked, as he blew on her clit, teasing it.

"I'll do whatever to make you happy." He wasted no time, as he leaned his face into her stomach and kissed her navel before going lower to slurp her clit into his mouth. Morgan was new and barely touched, and not a living soul could say they had experienced what he now possessed. All others who had taken it from her were no longer breathing. The penalty for hurting her would always be death. He was judge, jury, and executioner when it came to Ms. Atkins. If he was honest with himself, he would admit that he was killing any nigga walking who had experienced her before him, just so he could be the only man to say he'd had her. Thank God she hadn't been loose before him because it would have been hunting season. *My name all over this,* he thought, as he admired the tattoo she had gotten, right in the crease of her thigh. Messiah had been filled with jealousy when she had shown him because he knew whatever tattoo artist had done it, had enjoyed the view. *Shit, he probably did the shit for free.* But he couldn't help but love the sight of his name in such an intimate place on her body, hidden from view from everyone except him. *Damn, she know how to make a nigga feel like a god.* And to her, he was. He was the sun, moon, and Earth. For him, there was nothing Morgan wouldn't do. He was a beast in every other aspect of his life, but when he was with her, she tamed him. She was the leash on the aggression that he displayed in the streets. He intimidated most people…everyone except her. Beauty. Beast. Fairytale shit. Whenever he walked through her doors, she took the burdens from his shoulders, giving him a temporary escape and letting him know that there was at least one person who cared if he lived or died. Before her, he moved through the world uncaring that any day could very well be his last. Since her, he put a little more effort into making it to see the next day, just so he could see the smile that spread east to west on her face when she saw him.

"Ugh," she moaned, as he sucked on her with aggression, having no mercy for her little bud as his full lips devoured it.

Zadddyyyyyy. I swear he's the best.

She grabbed his locs and pulled at them to get him to lift his head.

"Wait…wait," she moaned. "Didn't anybody ever teach you table manners. Don't stuff your mouth," she teased. She lifted the strawberry she swiped from the kitchen and a mischievous leer danced at the corners of his mouth. He plucked it from her fingers and took a bite, exposing the pink flesh inside. He circled it on her southern lips and then licked the sticky juice off with one, long, flat swipe of his tongue. "Hmm," she moaned, closing her eyes. She felt him spread the strawberry all over her once more and then tensed as she reached for his hands when she realized what he was doing. "Siah, nooo!" Her eyes widened when he pushed the strawberry up into her wetness. "How am I going to get that out?" Her tone was panicked a bit and he licked his lips.

"You not, I'ma get it," he said. He pulled her onto his lap and pulled her face to his, kissing her lips. She tasted herself on his tongue and the sweetest hint from the strawberry he had mixed her with.

"You're crazy," she said, between kisses.

"Than a mu'fucka and only over you," he replied. "Lean back." He used his hands to push her gently backward until the palms of her hands were touching the floor. She looked like she was halfway through a back flip.

"Messiah, what are you..." her words caught in her throat as she felt him lift her hips, pulling them up toward his mouth. "Oh!" she screamed, as he stuck his tongue deeply in her love, while his nose rested on her clit, moving his head in circles. He held her ass in the palms of his hands like he was in a watermelon eating contest, as he dove in. His fingertips kneaded her ass, as he ate the strawberry right out of her. He had to go so deep with his tongue that he had to curve it to reach the fruit. He was sucking and pulling and licking, and gnawing and...*Oh my fucking God what is he doing?* Her juices mixed with the extra nectar from the berry and Messiah lapped at it all, alternating between burying his tongue in her and playing with her clit. The sound of him enjoying her, moaning gutturally sounding like a lion enjoying his meal. She wasn't his prey, but he was king of this concrete jungle and he knew how to command her. Only he could have her in a public pantry, on a handstand, neck crooked and aching with his face between her legs. He just couldn't get enough of her and she hadn't reached her fill yet either. Gluttony was a sin that they committed on repeat. The flavor of her was exotic, it melted on his tongue like chocolate. It didn't matter if Morgan was fresh out the shower or if she basted in a pair of skinny jeans, hopping from class to class all day. Whenever Messiah ran up on her, he had to have her. *Three squares and two snacks. Eat it, baby. Eat it all. God, what is he doing to me?* Morgan felt bad for the day Messiah tried to leave her alone. *He bet not ever.* The way Messiah was locking her down, Morgan knew her head would be gone if he ever took his love away. She could feel a bit of his crazy rubbing off on her and a bit of something else…

"Oooo, shit!" she creamed, as her orgasm caused her to spasm and she forced her love into his mouth harder, throwing it at him. She was surprised she didn't knock out any teeth, she bucked so hard. "Messiah!" He didn't stop, he merely caught what she was throwing at him until she was spent; and even then, he licked her clean. He pulled her body up so she was sitting back in his lap, straddling him. His strong arms wrapped around her back as he rubbed her, soothed her, as she caught her breath. They were face to face, so absorbed in one another, always present, mind and body.

"If you ever leave me, I'm going to die," she whispered.

"I'm never leaving," he massaged the back of her neck, as their foreheads met.

"Why not?" she asked. "I've seen you switch out these hoes like you do your cars. Why am I different?"

"You know why," he answered, pecking her lips.

"I know, but I like to hear you say it. I have my insecurities. I need to hear it first from you sometimes, Siah," she whined.

"A nigga will tell you what you want to hear every day and go out and do some bullshit that proves he don't fuck with you at all, Mo. I'm not that nigga. If I told you once that was for life. It's some shit attached to those words for me. Some heavy shit. I barely even like to hear it from you because it just brings up bad shit in my head. It's a lot you don't know, yet. Some shit, I'll never share, but just know what it is between me and you. I ain't got to say it every day, but I show you. That's all you need to worry about."

She pouted, displeased with his answer for so many reasons. Morgan closed her eyes and behind her lids she saw her five-year-old self.

"Mommy, why Daddy always tell you he loves you a million times?"

"A man who loves you will never be afraid to tell you," Justine Atkins had said.

Morgan heard the words as clear as day, as if her mother was standing and breathing right in front of her. *What does he mean he has some shit he'll never share? He knows everything about me. Why can't he share it?*

He trapped her chin between the 'U' that formed between his thumb at the rest of his fingers, commanding her from her thoughts. He was frustrated. She could see it in the lines that creased his forehead. "You keep bringing this up. Don't I show you? Cuz let me know if I'm lacking because I will tighten my shit up. I know what I got, so if I'm not doing what I got to do to keep you locked down, let me know. I don't want to leave opportunity for the next nigga to take what's mine. I show you, right?" Morgan could feel the tension in his shoulders. He was concerned. Over-analyzing. Apprehensive. About losing her. About someone giving her something that he wasn't. About another man taking his spot. *Impossible.*

Morgan nodded and reached for his handsome face, her delicate fingers caressed him, soothed him...something only she had mastered in all his years. She was medicine to all his ailments. The intensity in which he cared for her was terrifying to him yet gratifying for her. It was the love she had been searching for since the day her father died. "You show me, baby, and I feel it. I'm just a girl that isn't accustomed to hearing, Siah. I couldn't hear shit my whole life and the person I want to hear say the thing that means the most to me, hardly ever says it at all," she whispered. She wondered about the parts of him she didn't know. He never mentioned his past. He never talked about his family or where he came from and her heart ached at the thought of who could have hurt him so badly that he feared the words 'I love you.' It was a sentiment she had been comfortable receiving ever since she was born. First, her parents. *God rest their souls.* Then, Raven. *I miss her so much. I could have told her about Messiah. She would have understood. She would have helped Ethic understand.* Then, Ethic. He had told her more than everyone else combined in his attempt to make up for the life she lost when her family disappeared. She was never short on love. There was always someone in her life to remind her of it. She looked into the abyss that he called eyes. They were so dark, so pained and cold, but she could see the flickers of warmth that were trying to ignite as he looked at her. Messiah was fighting his instincts, just to be with her. He was trying to be what she needed, thawing a frozen heart just to place it in her possession. She could see the battle he was fighting just by staring in his eyes. *Has no one ever told him before me? How could anyone not love him?*

"I'm never leaving you, Mo," he signed. Morgan's heart skipped a beat because there it was clear as day. A *show* of love. He was still learning to sign and getting better every day. He said it was her first language, one that she shouldn't abandon just because she had learned another. "Let me hear you say it? It's important that you believe that," he continued, his hands speaking fluent sign language. *Damn, he's getting really good.*

"You'll never leave me." She both spoke and signed the words as he stood with her in his arms. He placed her on her feet, removed the jacket to his Gucci suit and placed it over her arms to hide the red strawberry stains that he had gotten on her dress. He adjusted his clothing, untangled the chains around his neck and opened the door. "Go home. I'll be by later for that snack." She turned to him, mouth agape, wearing shock as he shot her a charming wink.

She snickered and only shook her head in disbelief as she walked out. *Messiah, my Messiah. What am I going to do with you?*

CHAPTER 8

Alani laid in the middle of the floor of the darkened sanctuary. The only illumination in the room came from the giant cross that hung above the pulpit. The room was so silent that it felt creepy. She remembered when she used to play in between these pews as a child while Nannie attended Bible study. She would find a spot on the floor and stare up at this very cross with not a care in the world. Times had been much easier then. What she wouldn't give to go back. As she laid there, eyes on the cross, she prayed for a little reprieve. Everyone else was in the banquet hall next door, but Alani just couldn't keep up the act much longer. With so many eyes on her, with Ethic and his family present, she felt like she would suffocate. The dark halls had led her here, her torment had pulled her to the altar, fatigue had taken her down to her back. Sleep was a thing of the past for her but in this room where the Word of God had healed worse souls than hers, it felt possible. "God, help me," she whispered.

"Does it work?"

The sound of his voice startled her, and she rushed to her feet, dusting off her dress in embarrassment, as she turned to find him. Ethic stood at the end of the aisle. She cleared her throat, as she picked up her clutch from the front pew.

"Why don't you come and see?" she asked.

He lifted his eyes to the cross behind her and then stared directly at her. She knew when his gaze was on her, even in the shadows of the darkness. His stare was like the sun. It warmed her. She felt it. It even tanned her like the sun, leaving her Ethic-kissed long after his gaze was gone. He came down the aisle, neck tie undone, top button loosened, sleeves rolled up to the elbows.

"I hope I didn't embarrass Bella by running out," she whispered, as she took a seat. Ethic joined her, purposefully taking the end seat in the front pew on the opposite side.

"She's happier than I've seen her in a long time. I could never thank you enough. I sent her and Eazy home with Lily," Ethic answered. "I stayed behind to..."

"To what?" she interrupted.

"I don't know," he said. "This felt like a place I could think clearly. Shit's been real foggy lately. I can't see above the clouds."

Alani closed her eyes and exhaled deeply. She nodded but didn't offer a verbal response. She could relate.

"Do you pray, Ethic?" she asked. "I mean," she paused and steadied her voice before continuing. "Do you believe in the power of prayer?"

It was his turn to sigh. He rubbed his hands together, as he leaned forward, elbows to knees, head hanging in despair. "No. I used to pray a lot when I was a kid. I needed a lot. Didn't have anybody else to ask but some imaginary man in the sky. Things never got better. No one ever answered, so I stopped praying. I prayed the day I told you what I did. You're still absent from my life, so apparently, that one didn't work either."

"So, you don't believe in God?" she asked.

"Can't see him, can't hear him. I trust the tangible."

"Can't see love, can't hear love...and you believe in that," she said.

"I'm looking at it right now," he whispered.

Alani placed her eyes in her lap. "How can you still see love when you look at me after I kept my pregnancy from you? After I shot you?"

He intertwined his fingers, steepling his pointer fingers as he brought them to the center of his forehead. He closed his eyes. He didn't like to think about that.

"At you're worst, you're still love. Living and breathing right in front of me. I questioned it for a long time after I lost Eazy's mother. Did it ever even exist? Was it real? Then you..." Ethic shook his head.

"Me?"

"That night," he answered. He drew in a deep breath, his chest filled, as he reminisced. "Inside you. Was love. I could smell it on your skin. Taste it on your lips. I could hear it in the tone of your voice..."

Alani went inside her head.

This is too good, Ethic—

Her desperate pleas, begging him, then calling out his name for doing her body so right, flashed in her mind as she recalled the passion behind his love making. Just off the memory alone she felt her clit respond. Her pulse was back. "Stop," she whispered.

"I'ma forever believe in that," Ethic stated.

She didn't look at him. She couldn't bear to be captured by his glower, but her heart thundered in intensity. Instead, her eyes were on the light...on the cross above. She stood, and as she bypassed Ethic, she felt him, tugging at her hand. Alani sighed. She wanted to run but her feet defied her mind and stopped in front of him. He rested his bowed head against her stomach and Alani closed her eyes. She trembled. Every single touch was always so intimate. She refused to touch him back. She fought the urge to hold him. Her arms felt heavy at her sides, but she kept them there. To hold him would be treasonous, against her own flesh and blood. It was the most restraint she had ever had to show.

"I'm so alone," she murmured.

"I'm sorry," he whispered. Alani was amazed at how this powerful man, this undeniable king, submitted to her...always her...only her...never showing his weaknesses to anyone else. He was never too stubborn to apologize. Never too right to be wrong. Never too angry to love. Not with her, anyway. So, did it really matter how he was with everyone else? She wanted to say that it didn't. She wanted to give in to the thought that as long as she never met the murderer... the gangster... as long as he was always the gentleman with her then she could turn a blind eye. Only she couldn't. Her daughter had met the version of him that was capable of killing. So, yes, it mattered. The parts that he showed the world mattered as much as the ones he reserved for her. He was too damn good to do the bad things he did...too reminiscent of God's image to work for the devil.

"Who broke you?" she asked.

Without hesitation. Without taking a beat to reflect. He replied, "You."

The answer knocked the wind from her lungs. She had recognized the woe inside him at first sight. She had tried to guess the events that could have occurred in his life to make him so dark. Never would she have imagined that the moment he defined as most damaging as the moment he lost her. The revelation rattled her. They were two halves trying to be whole apart. It made no sense.

"That's not fair." The frog in her throat barely released those words.

"I mean no offense. I know you only returning the energy I gave you," he clarified. She sighed and took a seat beside him. She relented and rested her head on his shoulder. "A woman only hates a man as passionately as she loved him. I lost you. Now, all I get to experience is the hate without ever knowing what the love felt like. I have resentments about that…with God…within me…none with you, though, never with you."

"Your resentment with God didn't come from losing me. That was there before me. What happened to you?"

She felt him stiffen. She had hit a nerve.

"This isn't the place to talk about that," he answered.

They both sat, side by side, looking straight ahead. She turned her face and then placed her hand on his cheek, forcing him to turn toward her.

"Then take me to a place where you feel comfortable talking about it, because I need to know," she said.

He held out his palm and Alani stared at it for a few awkward seconds before placing her hand inside it. Her fingers slid through his and he closed his fist, connecting them.

Without words, he stood and led her out of the church.

CHAPTER 9

They drove without speaking and Alani was filled with discomfort. A knot of apprehension aligned her spine and made her sit up straight in the seat, as if she were waiting to react to any sudden movement. She was afraid of Ethic, not of the man she knew, but the one she didn't. He was clearly a man who compartmentalized himself and only exposed certain parts in certain situations. She knew he wouldn't hurt her, but something about being in this metal box, driving at high speeds, with such heaviness thickening the air made her feel like prey he had captured. She had to remind herself that she had come with him willingly. He hadn't forced her. This was her idea.

Relax.

She studied him. One hand wrapped around the leather steering wheel. Strong veins sprouted from his hand up his forearm that was exposed because his sleeves were rolled up to the elbows. Tattoos over dark skin. Fixated eyes on the road, as he gave the slightest nod of his head to the crooning that oozed from the speakers. It surprised Alani that it wasn't rap. Her every experience with other men accompanied a hard soundtrack. Jay-Z, Nas, or Jeezy, seemed to be a hood nigga's repertoire of preferred musical selections. Beanie Siegel, if he was really street, but not Ethic. Ethic didn't feel the need to be overtly masculine because he felt no need to prove his manhood to anyone. It was there, undoubtedly strong, undeniably street, so he didn't mind vibing to something soft. His reality was hard enough. Soft was needed. Soft was appreciated. Musiq Soulchild.

Someone who will put up with the things
Loving me can bring
And still be there to see us through
Someone who will put up with the strange and complicated things
Because I will do the same for her too

His other arm rested on the center console, as he rubbed his lips with his thumb. He was brooding. A haunted soul.

Like me.

His presence even when silent was loud. He overwhelmed her. He was a king.

And a killer.

She blinked wet eyes away from him. He always extracted tears from her. It never failed. She just turned into a crybaby-ass bitch around him. She sighed, as she let her back melt into the seats. Release. Relief. She felt a myriad of things when in his presence, but she couldn't acknowledge the fear, the hatred, and anger without admitting the good too. It was just complicated. *They* were just complicated. A complicated love song like the one playing on the radio. When they pulled into the parking lot of a hotel, she tensed.

"I need four walls and no interruptions for what I'm about to tell you," he said.

She nodded, but inside she was screaming. Every internal alarm inside her went off. Stop. Go back. Run. Don't. You. Fucking. Dare.

He wouldn't hurt you. If you want answers, you got to woman up. She coached herself.

Did she want to know his story badly enough? Did it matter what his story was? Insight didn't change anything. He was still deadly. It was all Alani could see when she looked at him. He was a constant reminder of the hardest day of her life. She didn't even remember who she used to be before that great hurt came over her life. Things she had thought were catastrophic before were so minuscule in the grand scheme of things. She would pay to have those problems. Late bills. A failing car. A knucklehead brother. Those things had stressed her so badly back then. She had struggled over them, prayed about them, cried. Then, a real challenge had struck, and she was left unarmed to fight the emotional battle. She was losing. Every day, she was sinking further into a depression that would cripple her. Ethic opened her door.

All because of him.

She climbed out and followed Ethic into the hotel. With every step, she wanted to turn around. His tall stature, strong build, and broad shoulders filled out the suit like a Wilhelmina male model, but Alani could see that he carried something with him…something inside and it was heavy. Her curiosity fueled her forward. She stood off to the side, clutching her small handbag in front of her body, as Ethic paid for a room. Even the girl at the front desk was taken by him. Alani smirked and rolled her eyes because she knew exactly what the young girl saw in him. The magnetism, the authority he exuded, the charm. He didn't even have to flirt. It was effortless. He turned to Alani and her heart stalled, the exact same way her car used to. There was dread in his eyes. He looked like a boy who was preparing to tell his mama what he had done wrong in school that day. It was an innocence in him, a vulnerability that she had never seen before. Apprehension squeezed her. *What has he been through?*

He led the way to the penthouse suite, because well, it was Ethic and she just didn't expect anything less. Not that it made her any difference, but the man was a standard. He just indulged in the highest level of everything, even heartbreak.

He held open the door for her and she halted.

"We don't have to talk," Ethic offered. "I can take you back to your car."

"We do," Alani said. "We should," she corrected. She entered the room. She was grateful for the full living area. She didn't need the intimacy of a bedroom. She found a seat on the couch and Ethic leaned against the back of the door.

"You're uncomfortable," he observed.

Her body language told it all.

"I'm fine," she lied, as she tucked a fingernail under the neckline of her dress to pull it out a bit. It was so damned hot in this room.

Ethic removed his cuff links and then relieved himself of the entire jacket. He pulled the neatly tucked shirt from his pants. Snatched it, in fact, with a face pulled tight in a grimace, as if he had been dying to do so all day. Like he was filled with exhaustion and he was stepping over the threshold of their home to unload his burdens after a long day of work. He was the type of man she would have waited at the door for, with a warm plate and wet womanhood, to help him unwind. How could such a perfect love go wrong? As she stared at him, she couldn't help but wonder why God would bring him into her life. Why couldn't they have met under different circumstances? Any situation would have given them better odds than the one they found themselves in. She sat wringing her fingers, pondering this...the why of it all because it was said that God always had a plan...one too grand in scheme for human comprehension. One simply couldn't peek at the blueprint for understanding, you had to walk the path, step by step...often not gaining clarity until after you've already maneuvered through the confusion.

Ethic cleared his throat and sauntered to the other end of the couch, giving her space. He sat. Dragging two hands over his face, he released a sigh. It was like the prelude to his life story...that sigh...that torment...she heard it.

"You know I don't think you can say you love someone until you love the darkest parts of them," Ethic said. "It's easy to love when everything is good, when everything feels easy. It's the darkness that tests true love."

Alani was silent, but lines of contemplation creased her forehead.

"I know that to be true because of my mother," he continued. "She was a beautiful woman, even through her darkness."

"Where is she now?" Alani asked.

"Dead."

He offered nothing further and Alani didn't want to

push, but she had to, she needed to pry into his mind. She needed to know.

"How did she die?"

"She died of a broken heart long before the day she was murdered," Ethic said. "There's a moment... When our soul dies, but we're still breathing, still here, but we're gone. I've seen that. I'm living that."

"Me too," she whispered.

"I remember the last time I felt whole. Some people can't remember too far back. They were too young to process the insignificant things. I remember it all because it was the most normal time of my life. Before..." Ethic cleared his throat. He stood and crossed the room. Her eyes followed him to the mini bar. He opened the mini refrigerator and poured one of the little bottles into a glass. Liquid courage because his was fleeting.

"Before what, Ethic?" she whispered.

"Before he left us. My father. He was my mother's whole being. I remember she would iron his favorite dress every Friday night. I never understood it. It would take her hours to put these big curls in her hair, make her face up extra special, and she would iron razor sharp creases into this black dress. She would get all dressed up and they wouldn't even go anywhere, but when he came home she would be wearing it and he would call her beautiful. She did all that for one word," Ethic whispered. "I was only a kid and I would tell myself that I wanted a wife who took out that much time to get beautiful for me one day."

I would have.

She wouldn't dare let the thought float from her lips,

but it was true. "Then, one Friday, he didn't come home. She waited hours. She pulled me out my bed at midnight. I remember, because it was to the minute. I remember my eyes focusing on the red clock on the side of the bed. I marked that moment because, somehow, I knew shit was about to change after that. We went to the hospital and I remember thinking she was sick. She had to be sick because that's where we went the time I was sick, and my stomach was so tight. I knew something was wrong. Even at five. My mother got out the car and was moving so fast that I could barely keep up. The snow was almost as tall as me that night. I was freezing because she didn't even take the time to put a coat on me before we rushed out. She ran through those halls screaming my father's name. Then, he stepped out into the hallway from one of the rooms carrying a new baby in his arms."

Alani's eyes watered, not because of the events that had occurred, but because of the poignant way he shared the story...like it had affected him.

"I remember feeling this crushing feeling. Like somebody balled my little body up and threw it away to replace me with this little baby in his arms. I mean, I couldn't breathe. Couldn't inhale one sip of air. My mother crumpled. I tried to pick her up from the floor, but I was only five. 'Help me, Daddy. Help me'." Ethic stopped to shake his head. "I begged that nigga to help me pull her to her feet and he just stood there. Then, a woman in a hospital gown was at his side and he walked back into the room and shut us out. We didn't see him after that. My mother didn't get out of the bed for weeks. I was cleaning up soiled sheets and shit because grief wouldn't even carry her to the bathroom. She did a lot of yelling. A woman who had never spoken to me above a whisper, now screamed everything at me. 'I hate you and you look like your fucking father. Your black, ugly-ass was the worst thing to ever happen to me.' Just vile shit that you don't say to your kid. She no longer cooked, no longer cleaned, until she met a new man. I thought things would get better. The yelling stopped, but something else started. The nigga turned her out. She healed her heart with crack, and when she didn't have it, couldn't afford it, she would go dark...get real mean. She asked me if I wanted to know what it felt like for a man to hurt a woman's heart. I did. I wanted to know what type of pain had changed her. So, she told me to sit between her legs and grab my knees. She put cigarettes out on my back. An entire pack. She lit them, took a puff and put them to my skin..."

"Ethic," Alani gasped. She closed the space between them and placed a hand on his back, as he leaned over, his hands on the top of his head, his elbows on his knees. Alani lifted his shirt without permission. He was covered in ink, but as she worked her fingertips over his canvas, she felt them, raised scars, years healed, but they were there. The burns.

"It felt like I was on fire and then she ordered me not to cry. When I did, she beat my ass. Beat me until the belt tore through my skin and welts turned to bloody wounds. She screamed my father's name the entire time." Ethic closed his eyes, as he continued. "Ezra, how could you? Ezra, you said you loved me." His voice was a ghost of his normal baritone, barely audible, as he recalled his mother's screams. Alani's tears ran, as an unstoppable sadness choked her. How could a woman ever? How could a mother? "She was my mama. All I had left. All I knew; and even after that, I loved her still, but the beatings only got worse. The addiction got worse too, but as long as she was high, she was too giddy to beat me, so I started begging the local dealers for free dope. I'd work it off. Ride my bike to deliver their packages, be their lookouts, whatever it took to feed my mama's habit. All so she wouldn't beat my ass. My own mother. All she saw when she looked at me was him. I wasn't her son. I was the nigga that left her, and she wanted to fight him, but instead she fought me. What else could I do? I stopped going to school because social workers started coming around, asking questions. I didn't want to be taken from her. She needed my father and I was all she had left of him. Then, one day, she came to my room, dressed real pretty in that dress she used to wear for my daddy. She had lost weight, so it didn't hang the same, but she was still so fucking beautiful... the prettiest girl in the world to me. After all the beatings and cursing my name, I still idolized her. She said she was going out for a little while and she would be right back, but I knew. I don't know how I knew, but I knew it was the last time I would look in her eyes. I begged her not to leave me. I mean, I cried, held onto her legs, tried to glue myself to her waist. She promised she would stay, put me in the bath tub, and sang me my favorite song, before putting me to bed. When I woke up, she was gone. I prayed she would come back. Every day. Every fucking day, I asked God to bring her back. I was seven years old when they found her body. My first heartbreak. I've had many since then. None like that, until you...losing you feels like that."

Alani's heart pounded, as she saw him clasp his hands in front of him, his head hanging in defeat. He was beaten. Broken. He was a boy in a man's body searching for a mother's love.

"Your father? What happened to him?"

"He's where he is. I'm where I am. The two places never intersect. That's probably for the best," Ethic stated. "I'd kill him."

Alani reached for his hands, wrapping both of hers around his.

"I'm sorry," she whispered. "God, you were a baby. You were innocent."

"Don't pity me. It was a long time ago. Shit happens. I'm sure worse shit has happened to far better people," he said, regaining composure and beginning to lay the foundation of the wall he had sealed those memories behind.

He turned his head to her and looked down at her. His gaze scattered across her face, as hers collected details of him. His eyes, fighting emotion, were red. His nose twitched. His jawline pulsed. He was so damaged. He didn't even see how much he was worth, how much he deserved that apology.

Alani felt herself becoming distraught and she didn't want to embarrass him. It was evident how much it had taken him to even share this story with her.

"Excuse me," she whispered, as she stood and headed to the bathroom. Alani had to grip the sink to stop from falling to the floor. She opened her mouth and her face crumbled into a silent cry, shedding tears over the history of his life. How tragic it had been. He hadn't stood a chance. She could still feel the indentations of those burns under her fingertips. The abuse, the absolute disregard of caring for such a phenomenal human being, it was disgusting. Did losing a man do that to a woman? Make her hate his child? Destroy her soul? Would it have happened to her if Love was still alive? Alani swallowed her torment and wiped her eyes. She turned on the water to pretend that she had really needed to use the bathroom. She looked at herself in the lighted mirror. She was beautiful. Dressed up in a black dress, just like his mother had done for the man she loved. She slipped the straps from her shoulders and let the dress fall to the floor. Black, Victoria's Secret lay beneath. She stepped high heeled feet out of the pool of fabric. She opened and closed her fists, nervously trying to contain her trembling hands. Yes, he had done the unforgivable, but he was owed an apology as well, not from her, but she would give it to him anyway tonight…in the form of fulfilling that childhood dream. He wanted a woman in a black dress.

Here I am.

CHAPTER 10

Alani stepped out of the bathroom. He was in the same place, legs wide, head bowed, hands to the back of his head. So solemn.

When she didn't return to his side right away, he rolled troubled eyes up to her. She was less than confident about her physique, but the way need reflected in his eyes made her feel like a woman...like the type of woman that men lusted after. He sat back, and she braved the space over to him. Seven steps. That's all the distance she had to change her mind, but she knew she wouldn't. The way he was looking at her left no room for second-guessing.

When she was within reach, he placed a hand on her hip, then a kiss there followed. He came off the couch onto his knees in front of her and maneuvered her to sit as he kneeled in front of her.

Ethic knew what it felt like to be without her, so he took his time to wallow in her presence, drown in her essence, as he rested his head in her lap. Her hands circled his waves, his calloused fingertips gripped her waist, then gripped the elastic sides of her panties and pulled them down. He reached around her and gripped the hooks of her bra. He paused, meeting her eyes, to give her a chance to stop him. She didn't, and he freed her breasts.

The art of a woman always took his breath away. Men rushed. Men forgot to marvel in the structure of a woman. Whether thin, voluptuous, svelte or thick, more than thick, the body of a woman was designed to be ammunition for a man's erection. Her pheromones filled the air, attracting him, encouraging him to hunt and capture the natural scent. Ethic understood, and he admired the view, taking his time as his body reacted exactly the way it was intended to - just from sight alone. His manhood grew, springing in anticipation, coming alive inside his slacks, fighting to break free of the clothes that restrained it and he hadn't even touched her yet.

Power of a fucking woman.

Alani's insecurities sprouted. He saw them twinkle in her eyes, as she lived inside her head. *Insecurities of a woman.* He smirked. *Silly shit that silly-ass niggas done put in her head. Shit's perfect.* He licked his lips. It was like he was at a buffet and he needed to decide what delicacy he wanted to try first. He shook his head. Everything looked so motherfucking good. *God damn perfection.*

"What?" she asked, slightly irritated. "You're staring." Her nude color fingertips spread across the front of her body, as she tried to cover her flaws. He even found that shit sexy. The subtlety in her choices. The way her nails blended into the color of her skin.

"I'm appreciating," he groaned.

He saw the marks on her belly from where it had stretched, a sign of womanhood, an indication of motherhood, a club of which she no longer belonged - thanks to him. If his remorse was a measure of his love, no man had ever loved a woman greater. It was moments like these that he would constantly have to endure, punches to the gut that reminded him he was a monster in her story. He was lucky she was present at all. He placed a hand on her stomach and he felt her breath catch.

So fucking insecure. I'ma have to love that shit away.
He knew it came from a fuck boy, maybe a couple, not loving
her right before him. Her eyes closed, and she placed a hand
on top of his as she released a long, slow, sigh. "They're ugly,"
she whispered, as if she was making excuses for her body being
exactly what it was supposed to be, a home for seeds to grow.

"My baby grew here," he said, softly. His words caught, like
a hang nail on a pair of panty hose, fucking up his cadence,
revealing anguish. "These marks prove that he existed. That
we existed, Lenika. Nothing about that shit is ugly," he said,
his forehead wrinkled, his heart heavy. He was a man who
could carry everything in his life but carrying this discord he
had created between them was so fucking hard. "These marks
remind me that you loved me once. After I did the worst to you,
you loved me enough to carry my seed. You're beautiful. Never
knew anyone prettier."

He always did the right thing, always said the right thing,
except when it counted, except the one night she needed him
too...the night he killed her daughter. He was so wrong that
night that it didn't even seem like the same man could have
done the heinous act. She stiffened at the thought.

"You want me to stop?" he whispered. He didn't miss a beat
when it came to her. He was receptive to the things she said and
those she couldn't speak. She was uneasy.

Alani nodded. Obediently, his hands retracted.

"Not touching me," she spoke. "Loving me. Stop loving me,"
she whispered. Tension lived in her neck and collarbone as he
saw her swallow down a ball of emotion. He couldn't breathe.
The air in the room was too thick. She was a victim to the crime
he had committed. The guilt in that was like a noose around his
neck, forever choking him...forever enslaving him.

"I can't do one without the other," he admitted, as he planted his lips on her stomach. She gasped, as her brow pinched, and her mouth slacked in disbelief. He loved her so wholly. She felt it. She missed it and it saddened her that she couldn't allow him to do it forever. It just wasn't right. As his lips puckered against her skin and he dipped his tongue inside her belly button, she submitted. *Just one night,* she thought. *He can love me for one night.* A little sin never hurt nobody. A little wrong...shit, she could pray that away in the morning. Ethic picked her up and she wrapped her legs around his waist as he carried her to the bedroom. She was in need of so many things. He could feel it. She was dripping emotion, the wetness he felt against his stomach gave her away. He set her on the bed and made his way between her legs. He stared up at her. Her pain was beautiful. Even the hatred he detected was like art. She tried to conceal it, but it flashed in her eyes like lightning sporadically illuminating the sky. Her pain was brewing a storm inside her and he was about to make it rain. He had never seen a pair of eyes go darker than the ones he stared into. So much sadness was buried in those orbs of resentment. He could disappear in her darkness. No one weakened him like this woman. Her desolation pulled the strength from his soul. She was in complete control and didn't even know it, or perhaps she did, but was too weak to take advantage of it. She placed her hands on the sides of his face and rubbed her thumbs back and forth, gently, slowly. He steeled. Her scars were internal, his were visible, and she was reminding him. It was hard for him to think of the day he had gotten those scars without thinking of Raven and he didn't want his mind to wander there in this moment. He had rehashed enough bad memories. That was a story for another time. He took her hand and kissed her inner wrist before removing it from his face. Alani's mouth opened like she wanted to speak. He could see her grappling in her mind over what she wanted to slip from her mouth. He shared her struggle because there was so much he wanted to say, but no words could fix the things that were broken between them.

He gripped her thighs and pulled her forward, causing her back to fall onto the bed. She didn't resist. Alani offered no protest, as he stood to undo the Hermes belt. He stepped out of the slacks and halted. He wanted to give her time to say no...to reconsider. If she was depending on him to press the brakes, she was getting fucked tonight, so he wanted to go slow...give her time...to voice her rejection. Alani lifted onto her elbows and as soon as she saw him she shook her head. Such a shame. To have a man like that want a woman like her and she couldn't even have him. *Under different circumstances I would treat this nigga so good. Every day, cooking, cleaning, pleasing. God...* Her mind was screaming, as the definition of his body was displayed in front of her. Her heart sank at the scar in the middle of his chest. She had put it there and guilt seized her. The black Versace underwear was the only thing concealing what she was dying to get a peek at. *Such a high-quality man. Even his drawers.* She knew it wasn't because he was flashy but because it was his standard. It made her wonder if she was of a certain caliber to even garner his attention. The thought gave her confidence and she laid back down and placed one hand between her legs to take her clit on a test drive. It was unspoken acquiescence for him to continue. He stepped out of the underwear, lifting toned legs and sturdy thighs. Her compliance was unexpected. Everything about her was bewildering. Her presence in his life went against every code he had ever lived by. She made him break rules, she required that he move in a way that made him uncomfortable, a way that made him relinquish control, a way that forced him to trust her even after her rage had caused her to put a bullet in him. It was illogical, and Ethic was a man of deep contemplation. With her, he acted from a place of emotion. It was dangerous. It was irresponsible, yet here he was. He stood and the sight of the king heritage that hung between his strong thighs made Alani's stomach tense in anticipation. Ethic lowered his body on top of hers. Her thighs opened for him, he was sure out of instinct, because the reluctance in the stiffness of her body told him she was uncertain. She didn't trust him. He hadn't earned it. He wasn't afraid of the work it would take to dismantle the walls she had built around her heart. A woman multiplied what a man gave her. He had given one brick of discord, of mistrust, and she had built the wall of China around herself. A defense mechanism. He would have to navigate around it to touch her in a way that would penetrate. A part of him wanted to taste her, but his dick had a mind of its own. Teasing the apex of her opening, Ethic knew he was about to fight a losing battle. She was soaking wet. For him.

Mine.

The thought wasn't arrogant...merely fact. A woman didn't nectar for a man that wasn't meant to pick her fruit.

One thrust, and he was inside her.

"Agh!"

Ethic invaded her body, like a disease, spreading rapidly, multiplying, making her sick...love sick and Alani closed her eyes as she gripped his strong back. He was overwrought with frustration. She could feel it sitting on his shoulders like boulders. His strokes were slow and intentional. Hard and deliberate. Desperate and grateful. Every single inch of him entered her, exploring her depths, before withdrawing to the thick mushroom tip, only to do it all over again.

"God," she whispered. Tears rolled out the sides of her eyes. This connection to this man was going to kill her. Never missing a beat, Ethic slowed his pace, planting himself deeply, before taking pause to look her in the eyes. His face was inches from hers. His exhales became her inhales. He was teaching her to breathe. If he had to breathe for her forever he would.

"I can stop."

She shook her head, as her chest quaked in resistance. She was trying her hardest not to let these tears burst the levees that were keeping them at bay.

"Lenika," he whispered. She could feel his heart beat in the pulse of his manhood. That's how connected they were. The steady throb between her legs came from him, from his anxiety, from his fret over what she was feeling. He wrapped one arm around her back and rolled back onto his thighs, dick still rooted, always rooted, in her soil like a 100-year-old tree…like he had every right to grow there. She locked her feet around his back and they just sat there. Seconds passed, then minutes, as she sobbed. That arm never left her back, the other hand fisted the back of her head as he kissed her lips softly. Alani wound her hips, her stomach rolling to a slow rhythm as he took her bottom lip between his teeth. The subtle bite he gave her made Alani gasp in surprise as she picked up her pace. The hand on her back slid down until he gripped a handful of her ass and pulled her down onto him with aggression.

She felt a tap on her backside and Alani lifted, taking the silent instruction. They didn't need words. Their bodies spoke a different language, one that they were both fluent in. She turned and got on all fours, her arch like the biggest dip on a roller coaster. Ethic looked forward to the ride, as he entered. The position gave him control. She was giving him access to parts of her he hadn't touched before. Alani's hands were above her, gripping the edge of the mattress and accentuating the feminine muscles in her shoulders. Her ass sat high and round. The view was spectacular. She coated him like baby oil, shining his wood as she sucked him in. He was planted behind her, one knee in the bed, one foot sturdy on the bed and his hand on her shoulder pulling her back when she tried to run.

"Ethic!" His name bounced off the walls. Ethic's body tensed as the familiar tingle that came with eruption overcame him. He slowed. He wasn't ready yet. He wanted this moment to last because once it passed he would have to let go again.

He pulled out, replacing his dick with his tongue and she cried out. Alani was sitting on gold. "Hmm," he groaned, as he kissed her ass, grazing it with his teeth before running his tongue down her crease and working his way toward her clit. He could tell it had been neglected. It was swollen and ready, waiting for him to tend to the garden he had left vacant. He told himself to go slow, as he opened her peach more, like he was trying to finesse a Laffy Taffy from the paper. He swirled his tongue around it once before blowing on it. A warning shot for what he was about to do.

"Ethicccc..."

His lips pulled at her swollen sex. Alani was amazed at the way he made love to her. Another man could never. Ethic kissed at her clit as naturally as if he was kissing her red-painted lips. There was no reluctance in his exploration of her body, like he was well acquainted with pussy. The thought of the women he had gifted this tongue to before sent a streak of jealousy coursing through her, but he sucked the thought right out of her with his next slurp. Nah, this wasn't universal love making. This was for her. This was about her. Her pussy was his pacifier and the way he was moaning at her flavor told her that only she could satisfy him in this way. Alani may not be able to have Ethic, but she was sure if she ever saw him out with another she would slap the shit out of him. The day she had to witness that she felt sorry for everyone involved. He brought the crazy out of her. She couldn't have him, but still she owned him. Alani creamed all over his tongue when he beat it up with the tip. Like a boxer hitting a speed bag, he pulled her first orgasm from her soul. She tried to scoot away, but he pulled her back, lapping at her until he ate up every drop. Ethic couldn't keep his face out of her. He opened his mouth wide around her clit, sucking it in, not caring how tender it was, as he pulled all the flavor from the tiny bud. His dick was hard and growing harder with every taste. He planted a final kiss there. When he was done, he stood, gripping his insane erection. The black skin of his dick was pulled so tightly over his need that veins drew crooked lines down his length. It looked edible and she wanted to taste him, but before she could make a move, he lowered on top of her. Ethic planted himself so deeply inside her that he danced on the line of pleasure and pain. No condom. No need for one. Neither wanted a barrier between them.

"I can't," she whined. "God, I can't."

"You can't what?" he whispered in her ear, his chest to her back, as he rolled her onto her side, spooning as he fucked her soooo fuckinngggg slowly. Her eyes rolled to the ceiling.

"I can't let this goooo," she cried out.

He didn't answer because there was nothing to say.

He held one leg, lifting it so he could go deeper, and Alani gasped. She clenched the sheets with her left hand and reached backward to grip the back of his neck with her right.

"You have to pull out," she panted. "Ooh, Ethic, please. Pull out. We can't...agh..."

She was so close. He could feel the change in the way she gripped him, it was tighter, wetter. She pulled him so close that his lips were on her neck. With other women, he might have asked them whose pussy it was, but with Alani, it was an unspoken ownership, an entitlement that he didn't deserve, and one she was ashamed to give. It was his pussy. She was his soul mate. Her heart was trapped in his possession. It had nothing to do with the two of them making a choice. It wasn't about ego or self-proclamation of loyalty. It had been assigned like a test they knew they would fail. From the very first time he had seen her, he had felt the pull of gravity in her direction. The last thing he wanted to do was pull out but the wounds of the baby they had lost were still fresh. A trap wasn't the way he wanted to hold onto Alani. It had to be her choice and that was one she would never make. Even if she gave him access to her body, she would never give him free reign of her heart again. With his mind plagued and his heart bleeding out, he was going harder than he intended, hitting it so hard that ripples waved through her flesh as he connected with her ass. "It's so good," she whispered, her eyes pinched, as she pulled her bottom lip in. Another woman wouldn't be able to handle it, but she took it. She took all of him because she knew she couldn't have it again. The aggression, the regret, the love, the pain, the sorrow he poured into her, she absorbed it. It was almost better than the first time he had made love to her. This mixture of pleasure and pain felt right for them. That's what they were…it's what made up their connection, an amalgam of bliss and agony. He was tearing her pussy up and Alani bit her lip as she endured. They needed this. "God…Ethic…" Her pleasure slipped out in whispers of disbelief. Never had she ever had a man work her body over so thoroughly. The hand on her shoulder rounded to her breast, filling the palm of his hand with mounds of her flesh, as he trapped her taught nipple between the slits of his finger. "Goddd," Alani was breathless, so she didn't scream, but the passionate moans escaped her like a plea. Sex wasn't supposed to be this good. Ethic's strength made everything effortless. There were no tired thighs and cramps with him. He did all the work and allowed her to reap the benefits. He entered her, not stopping until he connected to her center, then pulled back, stretching her with his length, opening her with his girth. There was so much of this man to take in. His dick inside her, the look of adulation on his face, the appreciation in his touch… it all filled her up, reconditioning her soul, making her feel…making her remember that she was a woman and she didn't have to carry it all. With a man like Ethic, she didn't have to carry anything. Her burden became his to resolve because he didn't come with any shorts in his manhood. He was both the rock that crushed her and the one to keep her sturdy. The fact that he could never be hers to keep brought tears back to her eyes. Her legs shook, her perineum stretched and her clit throbbed. This was the devil's play.

"I'm…agh! I'm cumming!"

He pulled out, barely escaping before spilling his seed.

As soon as the bliss was over, a heaviness returned to the room.

Alani kept her back to him. "What kind of mother am I?" Her words were laced in discontent. "I'm in bed with the man that..." She choked on the rest.

"Come." It was the order she always followed. Like a puppy he had trained well. This time was no different. She turned toward him, and her red eyes tormented him.

"Focus on me," he said. His deep voice was so soothing, but she felt guilty for obliging. She blinked away tears. She may as well had been in chains. She was enslaved to this love she felt for him. Sure, she had left, but still she ended up here in bed, his dick buried in her womb, his name lived on her tongue like she had created it herself, so did her leaving ever really count? She hadn't told Cream about Ethic's involvement in their child's murder, she hadn't contacted the police. Sure, she had shot him, but somehow it wasn't enough. If she was honest, she wanted him gone so that she wouldn't have an option to come running back. It wasn't about revenge. Shooting him had been about release.

Her eyes were like faucets, the kind without the lever so you had to use pliers to shut off the leak, only she had no tools. Her tool box for self-control, for emotional stability, was empty so the tears kept coming.

"Breathe," Ethic said. She lay on her side, staring at him. He lay on his side, staring at her, only a small space between them. She couldn't help but think of the baby that was supposed to fit between them. Love Okafor. Their son. Would have fit perfectly. He would have glued them back together.

"I can't," she whispered. Her chest caved, as she hyperventilated.

Always receptive to her needs, he closed the space, pulling her into him. He rested his chin on top of her head as she laid underneath him.

"Breathe. Focus on pulling in new energy and blowing out the bullshit," he whispered, as he massaged her scalp with the pads of his fingertips. Alani drew in air and let it out slowly, as her heart slowed. "Focus. On me. My breaths."

She did, and she calmed. It didn't surprise her anymore. The way he was able to manipulate her emotions so effortlessly.

"You didn't come to Love's funeral. I was alone, and I needed you. I was ready to forgive you and then you didn't show, and you didn't call. You just disappeared from my life. You pulled Bella from my life. You left," she whispered. "Everyone I love leaves."

Regret gripped his stomach as he pressed his fingers into her scalp, rubbing, soothing. "You buried him next to your daughter. I couldn't face you there. I couldn't look you in the eyes at her grave. I was there, though. I was watching and when you left, I buried him. I put the dirt over his casket," Ethic whispered.

Alani released the angst that had been inside her over that. It came out in a sigh, as she held him tighter. "I'm sorry. I didn't think about how you would feel. About him being buried there. I just wanted them together."

"They should be," Ethic said. "I was selfish. To take Bella. I was angry."

"I should have never asked her to lie to you. I should have never lied to you. If I had told you, Love might still be here. He would probably have healed us. I would be with you, loving you, watching you love our baby. Love would have fixed it all."

"Hmm," Ethic offered. His mind went to that place she spoke of. Where they were a family. It was the sweetest fantasy.

There was a pause and Ethic knew what she would ask next.

"Is he dead? Did you kill him?" Alani asked.

"Don't ask questions you don't want the answer to, Lenika," he whispered.

She nodded and went silent again. He was relieved when he didn't feel her tense. She knew what he had done, and she didn't pull back. It was progress. It was acceptance. She was taking him for exactly who he was in that moment. She was loving the darkest parts.

"Oh, and Ethic?"

He looked down at her.

"Thank you, for Christmas. I'll never have to work another day of my life with the type of income those homes will bring in," she whispered. She had been too angry to tell him that before, but she appreciated him.

"They're coming along? The crew isn't giving you a hard time?" he asked.

"No, they're great. The inside of them is done. I'm starting landscaping soon, now that the weather is breaking. I want to do it myself."

"On the whole block?" Ethic asked. "That's a lot of work."

"It will fill my days. I have a lot of lonely ones," she whispered, but her voice was fading. He heard the exhaustion in her.

Alani's eyes were heavy, but she didn't want them to close. They only had this moment. She didn't want to miss a beat. She wanted to love him like tomorrow wasn't an option, until the reality that came with the rising of the sun interrupted this Heaven they had carved out on Earth.

"You need sleep," he hummed.

She shook her head. She hadn't slept in months anyway. What was one more night? "I don't want to spend my time with you sleeping," she whispered. "All we have is tonight."

He pulled back and looked into her eyes, as the tip of his nose met hers. He kissed her, invading her mouth, bullying her tongue with his. So dominant. So, Ethic. She tasted herself as she kissed him back. So sweet. So, Alani. When he broke the kiss, he left her breathless. This man was 100 proof.

"If I could take it back..."

She didn't even let him finish. She placed four fingers over his lips. "I know," she interrupted. She moved her hand to the side of his face, intertwining her fingers in his beard. She loved it but hated what it signified. She had missed time with him. Months had passed without her being privy to the inner workings of his life. She missed him, no matter how much she tried to deny it. She captured his gaze. "I know," she repeated.

"I'm dying without you," he admitted. The vulnerability she heard made her feel sympathy for him, her perpetrator, her offender. Love was a paradox. It didn't go away no matter how much hate it was mixed with. Like a stubborn stain, she couldn't bleach him away. No matter how much she tried, she couldn't rid herself of him.

"I know." Again, it was the only answer she had to give. She sighed, as she gave him a little more. "I'm dying too."

She moved her head to his chest and closed her eyes. The last thing she felt was a kiss to the top of her head before she drifted asleep in his arms.

"I love you."

She was already halfway in a dream when she heard the words. She wasn't sure if he had whispered them or if she was just that disoriented from the lull of exhaustion. She couldn't will her lips to move to say it back. Even if she were wide awake, she wouldn't say it, but the sentiment lived in her bones.

I love you too, she thought. Then, the lights went out.

CHAPTER 11

Alani slowly drifted into consciousness, but she fought it. She wanted to bask in the afterglow of her night with Ethic for as long as she could before the devastation of morning ruined it. When she opened her eyes, he would be gone, and she would retreat to loneliness. She was weighed down by extreme guilt, but if she had to do it over again, she would. She had needed that night. She had needed to feel him. Yes, her hate for him burned at the highest intensity, but her love also shined equally as strong. He brought out the very best and worst parts of her. Days were getting darker and darker for her. The night had rekindled a light that reminded her that life could feel good…that it would eventually feel good again… perhaps not with him, but one day with someone else. Alani sighed. Who was she kidding? Never with anyone else. That type of connection was rare, but she hoped to find half of him one day…someone good, someone dependable, someone safe. *Safe is the one thing Ethic is not.* She opened her eyes and looked at the crumpled sheets. Her stomach sickened at the vacancy beside her. Even though she expected him to be gone, it still hurt. She could still smell him. The tumbler and champagne glass on the night stand proved she hadn't dreamt the entire thing. She shook her head, as a resistant smile danced at the corners of her lips. *Like this sore-ass* *pussy ain't evidence enough.*

She felt her face warm at just the thought. She tucked her adoration and restored her hate, as she climbed out of bed. It took so much effort to hate a man like Ethic. It was so unnatural that she had to remind herself every second of his trespass against her. Her bare feet crossed the carpeted floor and she went into the bathroom. She hesitated before stepping into the shower. She didn't even want to rinse the scent of him down the drain. Her need to feel close to him was a borderline obsession. She turned the water on and stepped under the stream. Her legs were weak. Her stomach was in knots. She reached for the tiled wall in front of her and lowered her head under the stream, wetting herself, drowning her sorrows as the water covered up her tears. Alani sobbed. How had she gotten so lost? She didn't even know who she was anymore. Before Ethic, she had been a mother. She was a single woman raising a child, doing her all to put food on the table, but that was her role…a mother. It wasn't who she was. She couldn't remember the last time she knew…the last time she could identify who Alani Lenika Hill was. After being stripped of that title she had fallen so hard for Ethic that he gave her a new purpose. She lived to love him, but now that she couldn't do that…she was just floating, directionless and so damned grief-stricken. She had tried to write the pain away, but there was so much that it just kept coming. No book should be so solemn. There was no happy ending, every sentence was heavy. Every sentence made her ache.

"Get your shit together," she whispered, as she lifted her head. "Fuck him."

She washed her body and then walked back into the

bedroom. Dressing quickly, she didn't bother with her hair. She simply blow dried it straight and slicked it all back, tucking it behind her ear. She took the walk of shame, dressed in last night's clothes. She was overdressed for the morning hour and it seemed to garner her more attention. She kept her head down, as she stepped through the doors to the Marriott hotel. *My car is at the church. I need an Uber.* Just as the thought crossed her mind, she looked up. She stopped walking so abruptly that the couple behind her crashed into her.

"I'm so sorry," she said, distractedly, as she bent to pick up the old woman's things, while stealing glances at Ethic. He stood against his Range, feet wide, his left hand gripping his right wrist. She scrambled to help the old woman, apologized once more, and then stood.

Alani was confused. Their night wasn't supposed to spill into the next day. She didn't need to see him. She couldn't handle this. She did the only thing she could think of and turned on her heels, headed back into the hotel. He came off the car in pursuit.

"Alani!" That wasn't his voice. He didn't have the privilege of calling her that anymore. That was...*Eazy?* She paused and turned back toward the car.

"Hey, Alani!" Bella shouted, as she leaned over the center console to roll down the driver's side window. She waved, and Alani returned the greeting, awkwardly, waving a hand of her own. Ethic crossed the street and Alani looked at him incredulously, shaking her head from side to side.

"What are you doing?" she asked. She mean-mugged him while sending a fake smile and a wave in the direction of his kids.

He took his time responding, massaging his bearded face

and looking off to the side, as if he hadn't thought this whole thing through yet.

"I woke up this morning with you beside me and I left. You cried about being alone last night, about not having anyone, no family and then I left you this morning. You told me once that every man in your life left you because you were too much work. I'm not leaving," he said. "I'll fix what I broke and what they broke too."

Alani saw red. "That's not your choice to make!" she caught herself and lowered her voice because they had an audience. "And then you bring your kids here? Why? To pressure me into loving you?"

"I ain't gotta put pressure on you for that. I already got that," he said.

Alani's eyes widened. *Arrogant son of a bitch.* If Alani was biscuits, she would be burnt. He had her that heated. She looked to the truck and then back at him. She pointed at him. "You. Inside. Now."

She stormed through the doors of the hotel and over to the private handicap restroom before strolling in. He was on her heels and she turned to face him. "I don't know who you think you are, but you don't get to just decide my life for me. You didn't cheat on me. I didn't catch another bitch calling your phone. Because I would probably be able to get over all that. I would put my independent, strong, black woman shit to the side to keep the type of dick that you have. Because my God, it's so good and you make me feel so good," Alani closed her eyes and shook her head, as if it was a shame to be so skilled, but she popped them back open, instantly. "But we're not talking about something as trivial as that, Ethic. You ain't a cheating-ass nigga that I'm

118

letting walk all over me. You're not the boyfriend with no job, sitting at home playing Xbox all day! I wish I had those problems! That shit is child's play compared to what I'm going through. You killed my baby. You shot…" She gripped the sink and her legs loss strength, as she dipped slightly. She leaned over the porcelain, trying to bring her temper down, trying to regroup because she was so angry that she was a little lightheaded. She should have never let him back between her legs. One night was too much because now he wanted more, now that she knew he wanted more, she needed more. "You don't get to show up here with your cute-ass kids! Your breathing, living children and tell me that you aren't letting me go!"

She pushed him, his sturdy frame barely budged.

"Why would you do that?" she screamed, as she pushed him, again. Hot tears burned her eyes. "I'm so fucking tired of crying over you. We're done. Last night was a mistake. I don't want to see you. I don't want to feel you. I don't want to talk to you. I don't want to know you!" Alani raised her hand to slap him and Ethic caught it and pulled her into his body. She was heaving, she was so livid. A panic attack. That's what this had to be. Like the one last night in bed. Ethic made her panic. He made her so irrational and emotional. She couldn't think with him in her face. She couldn't deny the cuteness of his children. She couldn't not want the security she felt when in their presence, like she was Mama Bear to those two cubs, and if she couldn't handle it, Papa Bear was on the ready.

"I hear all that and I'm not leaving," Ethic stated, simply. "You're not alone, Lenika. My children love you. They love you like I've never seen them love anyone before. I don't speak to them about you and they can sense that I love you. You carried their brother in your womb. That makes you connected to them, and I know that hurts because they're connected to me and I've taken so much. You're family. My family. I've searched for you. For a long time..." Ethic cleared his throat, stopping vulnerability from spilling from him. Alani lowered her head to his chest and gripped his shirt, as her tears fell. *Stop all this crying and tell him to kiss your ass.* "I'm not trying to pressure you. I'm just letting it be known that I'm right here. I don't run when shit gets hard. I tried to walk away. I tried giving you space, but last night—" He stopped talking, at a loss for words, as he cupped her face and forced her to look up at him. He was a man that didn't usually fluster, but she frustrated him. The unsolvable problem between them angered him. He had to remind himself that she had every right to deny him. He was asking for more than she could give, more than he would be willing to give. It was the double standard that men lived by. They expected women to accept what they, themselves, would not. He decided to take a different approach. He couldn't bully his way back into her heart.

She wasn't that type. Conceding. Easy. Compromising. "Can we just take you to lunch? Bella wants to thank you for being her mentor at the ball."

"Ethic," she paused. "I can't," she stressed.

"You got to eat," he sighed. He wondered if she was this difficult under normal circumstances and then remembered the battle it took for her to accept a ride to school. He smiled. "You fed me last night, it's my turn to feed you."

She turned hot and lowered her eyes in embarrassment. He was cracking through her anger. He had to find a way around it, because when it reared its ugly head, he couldn't get to her heart.

He smirked, enjoying her discomfort. For her to be such a willing participant in bed, she was uncharacteristically demure out of it. Her eyes misted.

"We would have been so good together."

He nodded but didn't speak because she was speaking hypothetically, and he was still working on making it their reality.

She lifted those eyes to his and he got lost. *I got to fix this shit*, he thought.

She shook her head. "No."

CHAPTER 12

Alani sat on the floor of her living room in Indian-style with praying hands in front of her. It was a position of rest and she pulled in a slow breath through her nose before pushing it out of her mouth.

"I don't know why you're down there fake meditating," Nannie said. "All that yoga mess you been around here doing. You need some good, old-fashion prayer and an ass whooping."

Alani opened one eye, as she peeked at her great aunt. She was so glad that Nannie was getting around better, but today she wished she could transport her back to that bed upstairs. She was disrupting her Zen. Alani closed her eye and took another deep breath.

"You ate a whole pack of pork bacon this morning, now you acting healthy," Nannie said. "You're stressing over that man because you're stubborn. Just let him love your behind. You shot the man, Alani, and he's still sniffing around. I'd say it's safe to say he's crazy about you."

"Mind your business, old lady," Alani said, playfully. She stood to her feet and rolled up her yoga mat.

"The contractors are coming inside here today. This is the last house on the block that needs to be renovated. We're starting on the landscaping, now that the weather's breaking. You want to help? The gardening will be good for you."

"Growing something is good for the soul. It's your soul that's unsettled. I'll be right here watching my stories while you're out there getting dirty," Nannie fussed. She was so cranky these days...bossy too, but Alani was just grateful that she was here to be any of those things.

"Love you. Let me know if you change your mind," Alani said. "My blue tooth is on, so if you need me, just call. I'm right up the block."

The doorbell rang and she rushed to it. She pulled it open expecting to see a crew of contractors, instead, Eazy and Bella stood on her doorstep. Ethic was parked curbside. A trailer was attached to the back of his Range Rover.

"Heyyy, guys. What are you doing here?" she greeted, in confusion. She embraced them and then stepped out onto her porch, holding a hand up to shield her eyes from the sun. Ethic stood, unloading flowers, plants, shrubbery, soil, and everything she needed for the landscaping job at hand.

"Child labor," Bella complained. "Daddy says we have to help. We're on spring break."

"Who do we have here?" Nannie asked, as she wobbled toward the door, using her walker to assist.

"Oh, um, Bella, Eazy, this is my aunt. We call her Nannie," Alani introduced. "Nannie, these are Ethic's kids. I'm not sure what they're doing here."

"That don't make no never mind, come on in," Nannie ushered them inside and Alani was grateful. It would give her time to confront Ethic without his children overhearing. She took him in. Nike, sleeveless tank that barely covered his muscular upper body, with grey, Nike sweats that covered everything but defined the print that she knew for a fact could change a woman's life. He was a whole whore out here in these streets. The way the defined muscles in his arms and chest bulged. The way his three, diamond chains rested against his skin. The brand-new sneakers on his feet and the Detroit Tigers baseball hat on his head. She had never seen him this casual, not out in the world. She had only seen him this relaxed while working out. The jealousy that tore through Alani, as she devoured him with her eyes, was almost crazy. She trembled thinking of what he had done to her body just a week prior. They hadn't spoken since, however, and this visit was unannounced. *What the hell is he doing here?*

"Landscaping," Ethic said, as he continued to dump supplies on her curb.

"Ethic," she whispered. "I said no."

"And I said I'm not leaving," he stated. There they were at this impasse, again. It was a frequent stop on the Ethic and Alani train. She didn't feel like arguing.

"Fine. I've got a whole block to work on. You pick a house over there. I'll pick a house over here. You stay on your side, I'll stay on mine," she warned. "Oh, and the kids are mine," she said.

"I'll take Nannie," he countered.

"Good luck with that." Alani smiled. He winked, and she shook her head, blushing, slightly, as she backpedaled up her driveway to retrieve her helpers. Ethic followed.

"Hey, Lenika!" her neighbor, Connie said, as she smoked a cigarette on her porch.

Her ass ain't spoke all year and now she wants to say hi.

Alani waved for the sake of peace. If she didn't, she would be all types of stuck-up bitches in the neighborhood grapevine.

"You got a new man, Nika? Or nah? Cuz he fine. If he ain't your man, put me on," Connie called out, with pure thirst, as she blew out smoke from her cancer stick while ogling Ethic with no shame.

Ethic chuckled and shook his head.

"At least somebody want a nigga," Ethic mumbled. Alani shot him a *boy don't play with me* look but kept walking toward the porch.

She entered her home and he lingered on the porch. When she turned around and noticed his hesitation, her heart ached because she knew why.

"I'll get them," she said.

Alani walked into the living room and Nannie had Eazy and Bella right under her on the sofa as *'Days of Our Lives'* played on the television screen.

"What y'all doing? I need some help outside. Come on," Alani corralled. The kids groaned but climbed up and headed out the door. "Ethic would like to speak with you, Nannie," Alani added.

Nannie climbed to her feet and made her way outside.

"Hey, beautiful," Ethic greeted. Alani was halfway down the steps when she stopped and glanced back. Nannie took Ethic into her open arms, as she chuckled. When had they gotten on, *hey, beautiful* status? Alani was floored but she kept walking, heading to the supply truck with the kids.

Alani, Bella, and Eazy worked all day, pulling old shrubbery, digging up weeds, and turning over old dirt. Ethic kept his word and worked across the street. To Alani's surprise, Nannie stayed over there all day with him, sitting in a lawn chair, watching him work. She was talking and laughing so loudly that Alani had wondered what he could possibly be saying that was so damn entertaining. A whole slew of neighborhood women had joined Connie on the porch, as they sat around drinking, smoking, and ogling Ethic because, of course with all the sweating, he had come out of the shirt. Alani stayed out the way and just enjoyed her time with Eazy and Bella. They followed her every direction and never complained. She was impressed. Ethic was truly doing a great job raising them.

"Are you coming to my birthday party this weekend?" Eazy asked.

Alani was on her hands and knees, digging and sweating, but she took pause to converse with him.

"Birthday? How old will you be?" she asked.

"Seven," Eazy answered.

"It's a pool party," Bella added. "At the house."

"Can you please come?" Eazy asked. "You always show up for Bella. Please, please."

Alani smiled. It felt good to be wanted. It felt even better to be needed. "I wouldn't miss it, Big Man."

As soon as she said it, she took pause. It was the nick name Ethic called his son. Eazy didn't seem to mind. It wasn't even a big deal, and Alani warmed at the thought that she had been comfortable enough with Eazy to use it.

"I don't have a lot of friends. People don't like me like they like Bella, so I hope you mean it," Eazy stated.

That statement stopped Alani's hands and she pulled back out of the flower bed she was working. There was sadness, comparison, and insecurity dripping all over his phrase, like someone had told him these exact words before.

"Hey, why would you say that? Of course, people like you," she said.

Eazy sat Indian-style and looked at her with wrinkles in his forehead.

"No, they think I'm weird. My teachers call me hyper and they always call my daddy to complain. They yell at me every day. The kids at school don't even play with me."

Alani was incensed. "Who yells at you, Eazy?" There was a tremble in her voice. Since when was being hyper a bad thing? What kid wasn't hyper? Especially, a little boy? Who had told him this was wrong?

"Mrs. Solo," he said. "She doesn't like me very much."

"Well, I don't like her very much," Alani said. *Ethic needs to talk to her. He spends most of his day with her and she should be pouring confidence into him. She's chipping away at it. Old bitch.* "Eazy, your energy is beautiful. Every time I've ever seen your face you have made me smile. I have a lot to be sad about and you make me feel happy, every single time. You're supposed to be hyper, baby boy. You're young and you're full of life. Your father makes sure you have no reason to feel any other thing besides happy. Your teacher probably feels bad about her life, so she takes it out on you. That's not fair. Somebody's going to set her straight, I promise you that. And those kids that don't play with you. You avoid them. Some of them don't have what you have at home. Some of them have never seen love a day in their life. You find the nice kids at school. There's this thing about friends. You don't need a bunch of them. If you can find one good one, that's all it takes to make a good friendship. You're beautiful, Eazy. Just the way you are," Alani said.

Eazy leapt into her arms, hugging her so tightly that Alani teared a bit.

"Yo, thing one and thing two," Ethic called from the street. "We've got to get going," he announced. He helped Nannie up to the porch, as his children begrudgingly followed his directions.

"Aww, man," Eazy groaned. "You messing up my green thumb, Dad."

"That thumb is as black as black can get, boy, come on," Ethic stated. Alani chuckled. She liked this. It was an easy day...a family day and it felt good. Plants weren't the only thing growing out here.

"We did all the hard stuff first. We want to help plant the flowers," Eazy added.

Nannie took a seat on the porch, resting her old bones.

"Plus, Alani promised us spaghetti and homemade cheese bread," Bella added.

"Can we stay? Please, please," Eazy begged.

"They're more than welcome to stay," Nannie offered. "You're a single father. I'm sure you can use the break. They're in good hands."

A break was something he had never been offered - ever. He wouldn't even know how to fill the time. He looked at Alani. He didn't want to bombard her with this responsibility.

"They're always welcomed here," she confirmed.

"So, we're staying?" Bella asked.

"I guess so," Ethic answered.

"Yay!!" Eazy yelled.

"Go get washed up. You guys can help me cook," Alani said. They sprinted for the house.

Ethic watched them disappear inside and he couldn't help

but feel left out, as he stood near the bumper of his car. Nannie stood and made her way up the porch steps at a snail's pace, before joining the kids inside. Now, it was just the two of them and silence filled the air.

"I'll take good care of them," she whispered.

"I have no doubts," he answered.

Alani turned to walk away but was half way up the driveway when she turned. "Hey!"

To her surprise, Ethic hadn't moved. He stood there, watching her, as he held dirty working gloves in his hand.

"Eazy's teacher. You should talk to her. Black little boys have it rough in elementary school; especially, the type of school he goes to. He's a minority there with white teachers, white students. You have to advocate for him. That has to be tough," Alani said, her brows pressed together in concern. "I'm not saying you don't, but that bitch of a teacher of his can damage him."

Ethic's dick hardened. The concern. The fact that Eazy had obviously shared something with her and she hadn't brushed it under a rug. He could see the fight in her coming out. It was in her eyes. Whatever Eazy's teacher had done, it had offended Alani. Ethic would find out later and put his lawyer on it. All of his children had lawyers who specialized in educational law for purposes just like this one, but he only needed them because they didn't have a mother. Alani had picked up on an injustice and she was reacting like a woman who loved her son. Ethic was sure that he had found the person he was supposed to marry, the missing piece to his entire family, only she didn't want him.

"I'll make sure I have a talk with him," Ethic said.

"Not with him," Alani said. "I don't want him to feel like

he can't come to me...like I'm going to run back and tell you everything. You have a talk with his teacher."

She was bossy, stern. Like a wife putting down a game plan for her husband to follow regarding children they shared. Ethic would be taking a cold shower tonight because his natural affinity for this woman made him crave her sex. He wanted to be deep in her womanhood, soaked in her passion. He wanted to make babies with a woman who protected them like this. She was awakening him, and if he didn't leave, she would notice soon.

"Got it," he answered. She nodded and then turned; this time, it was his beckoning that stopped her.

"Lenika. The water thing," he said, motioning for the house.

"Oh," she answered. She had gotten so used to having lead water running out of her pipes that it didn't even seem like a big deal to her. Of course, he was concerned. His children were there. "We don't cook or bathe with it." She explained.

"You can now," Ethic said. "I paid your contractors to install a commercial purifier first. It'll remove lead and anything else from the water coming into your home. Into all these homes." He motioned for the block.

Alani was floored. He hadn't even known his children would be staying. This wasn't about them. It was about her. "I'll come for them in the morning. You have a good night."

He climbed into his Range and pulled away, feeling like he was leaving something behind.

CHAPTER 13

"Renege, nigga, your ass just cut diamonds two books ago," Ahmeek stated.

"That's three books," Morgan said, as she held out her pretty, manicured fingers.

"Run that shit!" Meek shouted.

"Yo, when did I cut diamonds? Y'all cheating like a mu'fucka," Isa protested.

Messiah sat atop of Morgan's kitchen counters, as he watched her. She was in the mix with his crew, holding her own, as she partnered with Meek on the card table. Aria and Isa had been losing all night and losers took shots after every game. It was like Morgan had been a part of his circle her entire life. The banter, the comfort level, it was impressive because she was sitting at a table with two shooters and she showed no intimidation. Messiah pinched a blunt between his fingers, as he placed one hand on his strong thigh. Morgan was green when he'd first met her. Even the first time he'd been intimate with her, she had possessed a naïveté. Dealing with him, she had matured. She was gamed up now and it showed. She wasn't a pampered princess anymore. She was a queen, his queen, and she knew it. It exuded from her like she knew she had a gang of young wolves behind her, so one better think twice. It was an arrogance. A confidence. He loved it. He dug the shit out of Morgan Atkins.

With her pretty-ass.

Morgan was like a chameleon, blending into his gutter world and then going right back to her college girl vibe with ease. It was impressive because she played both roles so well.

"I'm done. If I take any more shots, I won't make it to class in the morning," Aria said, folding her hand and lifting from the table and ending the game. "I'm not sure I can even make it home."

"Grab your stuff. I'm headed out. I can drop you," Isa said.

"Nigga, you can't make it home. You had just as much to drink as she did," Ahmeek said.

Morgan stood and approached Messiah, standing between his legs, as she buried her face in the side of his neck.

She rested her head on his shoulder, as she looked at Aria. "There's blankets and extra pillows in the closet. "Y'all can stay if you want. The couch pulls out and the spare bedroom is furnished."

These people had become her people. She had adopted them into her life from association with Messiah alone. They were the ones she felt free around because with them she didn't have to hide whom she loved. These late nights and early mornings of her freshman year in college felt like ones she would remember forever.

"If that's cool with bro, that's a bet," Isa stated.

Messiah hopped down off the counter. "Yeah, make yourselves comfortable," Messiah co-signed.

Morgan nodded and rolled her eyes. "Umm... my say so is all that's required. Messiah don't pay no bills in here."

Isa chuckled but Messiah's body stiffened. Morgan was so in tune with him that she felt his energy shift instantly. He kissed the nape of her neck and grabbed her hand.

"We'll see y'all in the a.m. We gon' break out early to handle that business," Messiah said.

"Yup," Isa replied.

"I'ma get out of here, bro, just hit me in the morning when you're ready," Ahmeek said.

Messiah nodded and pulled Morgan into her bedroom.

She was on top of him, as soon as he closed the door. Her lips to his, her body leaving no room for separation. She had issues with space. She gave him none; lucky for her he didn't require any. Connected was all he wanted to feel when it came to her. His hands rounded her waist, scooping up two handfuls of flesh before running up her dress so that he could feel bare skin. He groaned. His hands, so coarse, as he slid them up her back, the dress she wore sliding up with them until he pulled it over her head. Their lips never missed a beat. He had never seen the point in kissing before her. It felt juvenile, childish, but with Mo, the foreplay was the best part. The kisses were not to be rushed. Her tongue was like candy and Messiah overindulged. On days when she was studying and didn't want interruption he would come anyway, because he was hardheaded that way. He would race all the way up the highway to taste her lips. Morgan was the shit and she had his nose wide open. She stood in front of him, panties and bra, body thickening up by the day and Messiah shook his head. If she was older and he were different, he would marry her right there, on the spot.

"You staring, what you gon' do with it?" she asked.

"Not a mu'fucking thing with my nigga in the next room," Messiah said. "With ya loud-ass."

She pouted and pushed him toward the bed. Messiah leaned back, as she climbed on top of him. The seat of her panties was super soaked. She was always saturated with need around him.

"You might as well climb your ass off, Ms. Y'all Can Stay the Night. Messiah don't pay no bills around this bitch," he said. "You're getting no dick tonight. That nigga will be hearing ya sexy-ass in his dreams and then I'll have to kill him."

Morgan put her hands on his chest and did a dirty wind on his hardness. His mouth was speaking a different language than his body. Morgan wasn't looking for consent. She reached inside the band of his Gucci sweats and gripped him in her hands.

"Go'n, shorty," he grunted.

"Just let me kiss it," she whined. "It's mine, ain't it?"

A stubborn smile pulled at the corner of his mouth. "Get your pretty-ass on somewhere."

Her brow creased in actual annoyance. "Is it mine or is it not mine? Simple question."

He licked his lips, as he stared up at her. "It's yours, shorty."

"That's what I thought," she said. Her head lowered, her ass lifted, and Messiah's eyes closed.

Good girl Mo was gone. He had turned her into something else. As she wet his manhood and made his toes curl, Messiah's mind drifted. He didn't want any other man taking care of a woman he called his. Ethic or otherwise. Father or not. Morgan was his responsibility. The way she put her mouth on him, without hesitation, with much appreciation, was so intense that he felt like she was claiming his soul. He had to claim hers as well. He had to claim her fully and take care of what belonged to him. It was how a man ensured that a woman remained his. He kept her. He provided. It didn't take long. It never took long for her to satisfy him because he was on a constant orgasm with her. The tingle that pulsed in him was something he had never had before…genuine happiness…if he died tomorrow, he would be satisfied, and it was only because of her. She came up for air and laid down on top of Messiah.

"See, I'm a giver, not a taker. I don't even want to do anything else," she snickered. "You were tense. I just want you comfortable."

"I'm comfortable, shorty," he whispered, kissing her forehead. She laid on him, one leg draped across his belly, head against his chest.

"Why don't you ever ask me for shit, Mo?" he asked.

She frowned. "I don't need anything," she answered. His silence, paired with the tension she felt in his rippled abdomen, caused her to look up.

"What's wrong?" she asked.

"I want you to move in with me," he said.

"Messiah," she whispered.

He picked up her hand and twirled the diamond ring he had purchased her. It was almost as flawless as she was. Almost.

"You don't want to?" His brows pinched, as he lifted his head off the pillow slightly. She sat up all the way, but Messiah put his head back against the bed and moved his hands behind his head. "Hmmph."

He hadn't expected her to not want to. What did that mean?

"Of course, I want to, Ssiah, but Ethic will never allow that," she said. "He tracks my locations."

"So, turn 'em off," Messiah countered.

"It's not that simple. He worries. He just wants me to be safe."

"Exactly, safe is with me," Messiah stated, as he sat up, suddenly feeling antsy, like this question was about to open a can of worms in his relationship that should have remained sealed. "Fuck what Ethic think. You grown or you a kid, Mo? Cuz you been acting real grown? Doing grown-ass shit to a nigga and I want you home. I want you every day. Every night. I want your tampons on my credit card bill, that's how much I want to take care of you, Mo. I'm your man, so I should provide. Fuck this back and forth bullshit. Fuck Ethic."

"He's my father!" Morgan hissed. "I can't just say fuck him."

"That nigga ain't your daddy," Messiah mumbled. He didn't even see Morgan's hand coming. She slapped him and then pushed him and then thought about the shit and pushed him again. Her eyes glistened.

"Why would you say that?" she shouted.

Messiah had let his frustration get the best of him.

"I'm sorry, Mo," he whispered.

His possessiveness had caused him to overstep. He could see her feelings on the floor around her feet he had crushed them so badly.

"Since when is it fuck Ethic? Since when do you even disrespect him? First, the gun at Alani's that day! Now, you speaking like it's animosity in you. Who are you right now? Don't ever, ever, ever in your life disrespect him. Not if you want me. Pulling me away from him is not the way to get me closer to you. You'll lose me."

Messiah reached for her and pulled her fingertips, forcing her to take reluctant steps toward him. He sat on the edge of the bed and she stood between his legs but didn't touch him. Her hands were crossed over her chest and she looked aside, angry, heaving, as tears fell down her cheeks. He buried his head in her stomach. She could feel his regret, but she didn't care.

"You should leave, Messiah," she whispered.

He looked up, in shock. He wasn't used to her rejection. It felt like a fist to the stomach.

"I was out of line, shorty," he said. "Just come to bed."

"I'm coming to bed. You're going home," she said, as she took a step back.

She wasn't normally the one pulling away. He was now in the position he had put her in one too many times. He was the yo-yo on her string and it didn't feel good. He nodded and stood to his feet. He dressed slow than a motherfucker, trying to give her time to change her mind. She didn't. She didn't even speak. She just leaned against her wall, scrolling down the screen of her phone. Leverage. She had it and he didn't like the shit one bit. He wondered how far she would take it, but when he ran out of excuses to leave and she didn't say a word, he knew the night was over. He walked over to her and pulled her into him. She pulled away, but he kissed the side of her head anyway, before sauntering out the room. Morgan didn't move until she heard the sound of his bike roar outside her window. Then, and only then, did she fall to her knees and cry. Messiah didn't realize the magnitude of his words. She had always felt like the step-child in their family, not because of how Ethic behaved, but because of the circumstance. She wasn't his. Not by blood, and somewhere in her she felt his love was manufactured. How could he love her like he loved Bella and Eazy? They were blood. She wasn't. Messiah had dug up old wounds that she had never spoke of to anyone, and now he was gone and even that hurt. There was nothing left to do but cry. The soft knock at her door caused her to stifle herself. Aria popped the door open enough to peek inside.

"Mo? Is everything okay? Messiah just left here pretty upset. I just want to make sure you're good in here," she said.

"You can come in," Mo whispered. "I'm fine."

Morgan remained on the floor and put her back against the bed, as Aria sat beside her.

"I'm sure whatever you two are fighting about won't last. That man is crazy over you," Aria said.

Morgan chuckled. "He wants me to move in with him."

"Your fine-ass daddy don't even know about y'all yet, though, right?" Aria asked.

"A) Eww," Morgan commented. "B) No, he doesn't know. He said some really fucked up things and I don't know...I probably overreacted but I just wanted space tonight."

"Messiah has to understand, you're young. What he might be ready for, you might not be. He'll wait for you, though, Mo. No way that man will let you go over something so trivial. This is nothing," Aria said.

Morgan nodded, hoping Aria was right, but still feeling the sting behind Messiah's words.

"So, you and Isa, huh?" Morgan asked.

"There is no me and Isa," Aria said. "That's the type of nigga that wants you just because he can't have you. Just because you're something he's never had before. Then, he gets you and rips your heart to pieces. I see the way his phone blows up when he's around. Bitches. He has an entire roster of them. I don't want to be added to it. He would never do right. I know his type. He's fine as fuck, he'll make you feel like you're the only girl in the world, have you crawling up the wall in bed, buying you this, flying you here and there, then when I'm pulled in, I'll find a phone number, some bitch will DM him a pussy pic, or I'll smell a woman's scent on his clothes. Something will happen, and I'll be devastated. No, ma'am. Isa can go'n somewhere. With his fine ass."

Morgan laughed but she wondered if that was exactly what Messiah was doing with her.

CHAPTER 14

Morgan was uncharacteristically disheveled, as she traipsed across campus for her morning class. Her hair was braided back in two with a part down the middle and she was in sweats and sneakers. She wasn't the typical college student. Her fashion choices were on a level of their own, but after a sleepless night, Morgan had no energy. She would have skipped all together, but attendance was mandatory in her Chemistry class. If it wasn't for Aria sharing the same course, she probably would have stayed stuck to her tear-soaked pillow. She was half-engaged for the entire two hours. She was grateful that it was her only class for the day. She gathered her books and walked out into the hall. She was so distracted she bumped right into Bash. Her things spilled all over the floor. She hadn't seen him since the previous semester. She had all but quit his class when Messiah had come back to her. She never attended. She only got the reading and writing assignments from a classmate and delivered it directly to the professor, bypassing Bash altogether.

"I'm sorry! I didn't see you," she exclaimed, as she bent to pick up her things and help gather his as well. Her hands were shaking, and her eyes were blurry. She was having a shitty day and it showed.

"Hey? Morgan?" Bash lifted her chin and frowned when he saw that she was emotional. "You good?"

She wiped her tears away, quickly. "Yeah, I'm fine."

They stood, and he looked down at her, admiring her. "It's been a minute, huh?" he said.

"Yeah, I guess it has," she whispered.

"I assumed ol' boy's back. That's the reason you've been MIA," he said.

He was always a straight shooter and Morgan scoffed.

"He is," Morgan confirmed. "I'm sorry if I was rude or if I just disappeared. I just didn't want to blur any lines."

"Friendship blurs lines?" he asked, frowning.

"I think a friendship with you might," she answered, truthfully. He was boring. Messiah was butterflies. Women were supposed to marry the boring ones. Build a life with the boring ones. Bash was as good as any, probably even better than most. He was handsome, educated, intelligent, and pedigreed, according to Aria. Bash came from a long line of money and was grandfathered into a successful family business. He had the gift of gab, was full of compliments and positive energy. He was the type to take you on picnics and choose the book store for dates. He was a good guy and Morgan enjoyed spending time with him. Yes, a friendship with him would complicate things.

He smirked and rubbed his lips, pulling her eyes to them, focusing on those light, full lips as he licked them. There was tension in her belly and confusion hit her. Why was boring now turning to butterflies?

Stop, she thought. *You're just mad at Messiah right now.*

"When he hurts you. When you want somebody to fix what he tears down, you know how to find me. I hope he doesn't. I hope I'm wrong because you're amazing, Mo; but if I'm right... If it ever happens, don't hesitate to use my number," Bash said. "There could be an entire girlfriend on my arm and I'd leave her standing right there to shoot my shot with you."

Morgan smiled and shook her head. Yes, the boring boy was definitely giving her butterflies. On a day when Messiah had left her open to insecurity, Bash was walking right in on his territory. It was the ultimate finesse and Morgan felt him putting a Band-Aid on her emotional wound.

"Where'd you park? I'll walk you to your car," he said, as he grabbed her books from her hands. He held no pretenses. He was just a gentleman and a gentleman walked a lady to her car.

Morgan nodded and led the way.

"You know I'm organizing a trip at the end of the semester. It's a summer abroad program. You should think about going. I'm partnering with Cambridge University," Bash said, as they stepped out into the sun.

"That's in England, right?" she asked.

"Yeah, it's going to be pretty dope. You know England is a hop away from France and Italy. It's easy to hop from country to country in Europe, so there will be a lot to see and do on down times. London, Paris, Rome," Bash stated. He pulled a flyer from his messenger bag and handed it to Morgan.

"Hmm," Morgan breathed, as she read the details.

"I don't know. A few months is a long time. Plus, Aria has some auditions lined up. Some rapper is going on tour. It's a paying gig and tons of exposure, so I don't know. I'm thinking about auditioning for that," she said.

"Yeah, I've been following you. A half million followers. You're getting too big for the little people," Bash said.

She laughed. "Yeah, okay."

"It's probably for the best anyway. You being here and me being there," he said, as they finally made it to her car. She hit the unlock button and he opened her door for her, motioning for her to get inside. He leaned down to kiss her cheek. "You wouldn't come back thinking about a boyfriend."

Morgan heard a small beep of a car horn and when she looked up her heart plummeted. Messiah sat across the parking lot, leaning against the hood of his car where a two-dozen bouquet of long stem roses sat. He was rubbing his thumb and middle finger together and she knew his trigger finger was itching. She had seen him do the same gesture while watching her shoot targets at the gun range. When he had been dying to take the gun and just put a bullet through the center of the paper man in the distance, he did it, he rubbed those two fingers together...

God, please.

She wanted the ground to open up and swallow her whole because she knew this looked bad. She knew it *was* bad.

Bash's eyes followed hers to Messiah.

"You should go," she said. "Like, now."

Bash shook his head, noticing the apprehension that lived in her eyes.

"Are you afraid of him?" Bash asked.

No, but you should be.

"Does he hurt you?" Bash pressed. Bash took brazen steps toward Messiah who didn't move. He sat there, arrogantly, poker face strong, despite the fact that the scene in front of him wrenched his insides.

Morgan frowned, as she chased after Bash. "What? No! Bash! No!"

"Better listen to her, college boy," Messiah warned, as Morgan placed sturdy hands on Bash's chest. Messiah cringed at the sight of Morgan, his Morgan, hands pressed to the chest of another man. Begging. But why? He couldn't decipher her intent. Was she begging Bash not to confront Messiah? Not to hurt Messiah? Nah, she knew better than that. But why was she so afraid for Messiah to hurt Bash? Did she care? What was it to her? Did she love this nigga? Had she *fucked* this nigga?

"Bash, just go, okay? I'm fine. Please," she pleaded.

Bash shook his head. A small crowd was taking notice and he wasn't into scenes that tarnished his name.

"You deserve better, Morgan," he said, before walking away.

"Pussy," Messiah scoffed, as he stood in the same spot, one hand clasping the opposite wrist. Morgan crossed the parking lot with urgency.

"Messiah, it's not what it looks like. He was just being nice. I dropped my books and he carried them to the car for me."

Messiah didn't speak but she could see him weighing the situation in his mind. He remembered the pretty boy from the club. The one who she had smiled at, the one who had kissed her in the parking lot. His stomach clenched.

"You know you just murdered that nigga, right? I told you. NOT. TO. FUCKING. PLAY. WITH. ME."

There was no yelling, just a pure threat.

"The first time the nigga put his lips on you, you told me you didn't ask for it, that you didn't want it. That you weren't feeling it, but I didn't see you pulling back just now, Mo."

"Messiah, it was innocent," she whispered.

"You know what, Mo? You were right. You moving in is a bad idea. All this shit is a bad fucking idea." The titter came off his lips so condescendingly that it made Morgan's eyes mist. He slapped the flowers off the hood of his car, and Morgan jumped in startle. He opened the door to his BMW.

"Messiah. It was nothing! I told him I had a boyfriend. He knows!"

"You told him wrong. You got a shooter. You got a nigga that will send bullets in his direction. Should have told the nigga that, then maybe every time I see you with this nigga his lips won't be on you. Can't believe I asked you that shit last night. You ain't mine. You ain't even ready, shorty."

"How am I not yours?" Morgan shouted, as she stormed toward him, standing in his doorway to stop him from pulling it closed and driving off.

"Move, Mo!" he shouted, trying to close his car door. Several students slowed in passing to witness the drama, but Morgan didn't care.

"No!" She protested. "Tell me! How am I not yours? Because I don't want to move in with you? I'm 18, Messiah! Why do we have to rush?!"

Messiah turned toward the windshield and tuned her out. He just went deaf, ignoring her, which only upset Morgan more. He had to zone out, because if he kept playing the kiss over and over in his mind the way he was, he was afraid of what he might do.

"You right," Messiah stated. "Let's not rush, Mo. We ain't got to rush shit. Let's slow this shit all the way down. Let's freeze it," Messiah said. He snatched his door so hard that Morgan was forced to move to avoid it hitting her. Still, she reached for it, snagging her finger on the metal. Pain throbbed in her hand, but she didn't care. She beat on his window, as she stood outside his window, locked out of not only his car, but his heart. She felt it. She felt the disconnect as soon as he made it. "Messiah!" He didn't even look at her, as he put the car in drive and drove off, running over her flowers as he departed.

Morgan couldn't even drive. She sat in her car sobbing so hard that she made herself sick. Her pointer finger on her left hand was purple and swollen. She needed help. She had called him 18 times, according to her call log, but he never answered. He sent her to voicemail and her texts were read but ignored. She wanted to call Meek or Isa and tell them to calm Messiah down, but she was afraid that they would take his side. They were just as ill-tempered as Messiah. Their opinions would only escalate the flames. Aria wasn't answering the phone. Ethic would kill Messiah, so she couldn't call him. The only other person who knew him, the only other person who might empathize with her, was Bleu. She was so desperate that she dialed her number. She couldn't even stop herself from crying long enough to take the call without causing alarm.

"Morgan?" Bleu answered. Morgan could hear Bleu's surprise. They had never spoken on the phone. They barely talked in person.

"Bleu, I messed up. Messiah's going to leave meeee." Her chest rocked, as she gripped the steering wheel.

"Mo, where are you?" Bleu asked. Her voice revealed sympathy but not shock. It was like she had been expecting some type of blow up between the two passionate lovers.

"I'm at school. I can't breathe without him. It feels like he's killing me." Morgan was hysterical. Her entire body ached. It pulsed from the inside. "He hurt me so bad, Bleu."

"He hit you?" Bleu's voice was angry.

"No, no," Morgan corrected. "I wish he had. It would be better than this. At least I'd know he still cares. He just drove away, Bleu. He left me."

Morgan's poor heart had the concept of love all twisted. She craved the abuse, she desired a reaction from Messiah. She didn't care if it were good or bad, she just wanted him in her space, instead of wherever he was, doing whatever he was doing with whoever he was with. Her mind imagined the worst and it was tearing her apart.

"Drop your location, Mo. I'm on my way," Bleu said.

Morgan sat there for an hour. She didn't even realize how much time had passed until she heard Bleu's hand tapping on her window. Morgan hit her unlock button and Bleu opened the door.

"I'll drive," she said. "My son's father will follow me to your place."

Morgan was silent, as she lifted from the seat and walked around to the passenger side.

"Now, what happened?" Bleu asked.

"I kissed a boy," Morgan whispered. "Or a friend. A guy," she said, continuing to correct herself, trying to find an explanation that sounded better. "A guy walked me to my car and kissed me on the cheek. He's kissed me before and Messiah thinks something's going on. He was waiting for me in the parking lot with flowers and he was so mad. He just asked me to move in with him last night."

"He did what?" Bleu asked, her neck snapping toward Morgan and eyes widening in shock.

"How did I mess this up?" Morgan asked herself, as she shook her head. "I love him so much, Bleu. I've never loved anyone like I love him."

Bleu looked on in sympathy and then noticed Morgan was holding her hand gingerly. Bleu turned on the interior lights and her eyes widened when she saw Morgan's finger.

"Did he do that?"

Morgan shook her head. "It was an accident."

They pulled up to Morgan's apartment and a Cadillac pulled in beside them.

Morgan looked over and saw a handsome man sitting behind the wheel.

"That's my Messiah," Bleu said. Morgan looked to her in surprise. "His name's Iman. I love him like you love Messiah. It's all-consuming, it's passionate, it's all I can think about when we're together and that's why we aren't together," Bleu added.

"Why? If you love him, why is that wrong? Why not just be with him?" Morgan asked.

"Because I had to love me more. Iman made me feel sick to my stomach when I first met him. I was so nervous and so intoxicated by him. I lost myself in his world. I became someone I wasn't, trying to keep up with his lifestyle, trying to live up to his expectations," Bleu explained.

Morgan held her breath because it sounded so familiar. Bleu was explaining something so reminiscent of her relationship with Messiah that it scared her.

"I had to let him go, and when I did I found something very real, very solid. Love is safe, Morgan. It makes you feel secure and it's patient. It listens. It never hurts. I'm not saying you don't love Messiah and I know that he loves you. You're the only woman he's ever loved, but you're young. You have your entire life to be in something this heavy. It doesn't have to be now. So what some guy kissed you?! You're a college freshman. There's nothing wrong with that. Messiah's world demands loyalty, and if it's questionable, his world requires separation. That's not fair. You're living in a different world with a different set of rules. College is about experiences. It's about finding yourself and connecting with different people, figuring out what type of people you enjoy being around. You're trying to limit those connections because you don't want to upset him. Don't lose yourself in him. You can love him, and you can even keep him, because as much as Messiah likes to think he's in control, you have him so confused on the inside that you call the shots. Just make sure you take care of you first. I made the mistake of loving a man more than I loved myself and thinking that the measure of love he had for me would be more than enough. It never is. Self-love is the greatest love of all, Morgan."

Morgan's lip trembled.

"I have to love him more. He's never gotten it from anyone. He needs me. If I love me first, it'll feel like I'm abandoning him," Morgan cried. "That's why he's so mad. I hesitated about moving in and then he saw the kiss and...God, he's going to leave me."

She was hyperventilating and so destroyed that Bleu reached over and grabbed her hand. "I'm going to stay, okay? Give me one second. Let me speak to him and we'll go upstairs, okay?"

Morgan nodded.

Bleu exited the car and stood outside Iman's window.

"You good?" he asked.

"Me, yes, her..." Bleu shook her head. "She reminds me so much of myself that it's scary. College girl trying to love the wrong man. It led me to a dark place, Iman."

"Hey," he said, jarring her eyes to his. "You're not there anymore. You're here. I'm here and you're better."

Bleu nodded. Iman motioned his head toward Morgan.

"Don't nobody see the problem with this but me?" Iman asked.

"We all see it, Iman, but he loves her. I don't think he meant for it to be this way, but it happened; and if this girl ever finds out..."

Bleu's words broke, as she sniffed away her own tears.

Iman reached through the window and pinched Bleu's chin.

He pulled her near and kissed the corner of her mouth where the tear had pooled.

"I take it you're staying," he said.

"Yeah, Saviour's with Noah's mom anyway," she said. "I hate being at home alone."

"You're alone by choice," Iman said. "I'd gladly be there with you, if you let me, but go ahead, take care of your friend. If you need me to come scoop you tomorrow, I got you."

"You're perfect. Thanks."

Bleu turned and opened Morgan's door.

Morgan sat with her face in her hands.

"Come on, Mo," Bleu said.

Morgan flipped her hair backwards out of her face and reluctantly got out. She went inside, showered, and then curled up on one side of her couch while Bleu took the other as they watched old movies. Sometimes, they spoke. Sometimes, Mo cried in Bleu's lap, while Bleu stroked her hair and told her it would be okay. Other moments, they were just silent. In those wee hours of the night, a friendship was forged and now Morgan not only had Aria, but she had Bleu. Two girlfriends. More than she had ever had. Heartbreak eventually gave way to sleep and Bleu was relieved because she was exhausted.

Bleu could predict the storm that was to come. She only hoped it didn't destroy Messiah or Morgan when it finally arrived.

BLEU

DID YOU HIT MORGAN? I'M HERE NOW AND HER HAND IS ALL FUCKED UP. MESSIAH, I WILL LITERALLY MURDER YOUR MEAN-ASS IF YOU DID THIS TO HER. GET YOUR ASS OVER HERE AND TALK TO THIS GIRL. SHE'S TOO YOUNG FOR THIS. YOU'RE GOING TO BREAK HER. YOU'VE SEEN WHAT HAPPENS WHEN A GIRL LIKE HER IS HEARTBROKEN. STOP DOING THIS TO HER. LET HER GO, MESSIAH, OR DO RIGHT BY HER. YOU CAN'T DO BOTH.

Messiah got the text message at 5 o'clock in the morning. Morgan had his mind out of whack. He couldn't think because his thoughts constantly navigated to her. He had made up a million scenarios that involved her and Bash. He knew none of them were true, but still, the questions burned in his mind. He was so livid with Morgan that he thought he might put hands on her. His temper had never taken him there with a woman and it scared him that the thought had crossed his mind. Hurting her was like hurting himself, and the thought devastated him.

What's wrong with her hand?

He was out of control. He had lost his grip on the situation. He couldn't love her with limits. He worshipped her so much that the slightest slip felt like the end of the world to him. He showered and dressed, stepping out of his apartment at the crack of dawn. He couldn't wait until a reasonable time to pull up on her. He had to see her now. If Morgan had called Bleu, he knew she had been desperate. He had broken her, and he hadn't intended to do that. He recounted yesterday's events in his mind over and over, trying to make sure he hadn't touched her. Something had occurred if her hand was injured. Messiah prayed he hadn't blacked out and hurt her. Messiah had a way about him. He had a mean streak; and the fact that it had been put to use against her, bothered him. It had torn him up all night. Even the way he had snatched his door closed without regard for her standing there had him burdened with guilt. He never wanted to touch her with less than his whole heart and the way he had handled her was unacceptable. Right or wrong, kiss or no kiss, he wasn't justified in his actions. Yelling at her the way that he had. Slapping the flowers from the car. He had been enraged and he had promised himself he would never target that type of energy her way.

The flower order he had picked up had been custom. He couldn't replace them if he wanted to. It was too last minute, but he couldn't come empty-handed. He stopped by a 24-hour grocer and picked up a cheap bouquet, a snicker, and a pack of Twizzlers. It was her candy order that she put in with him monthly. Every time her period came, he was on the highway taking her the treats. He hoped she'd count the effort not the price. It wasn't smooth, but he had no time to be calculating, he had no time to put a game plan together. He just wanted to get to her, to breathe her and to apologize and to see... *What the fuck is wrong with her hand?* He needed her to hear the words, "I'm sorry," from his lips to her ears. He sped down the highway, and when he pulled up to her place his chest felt heavy, like maybe she would turn him away. He would deserve it if she did. If she knew her worth, she would. He had never prayed on her downfall before, but today, he hoped that a part of her was still the insecure girl who had vied for his attention. That girl would still want him. He needed her to still need him. He climbed out of the car and walked up to the door. His steps were heavy. His palms sweaty and his heart racing.

The fuck?

Messiah was nervous. He couldn't recall a time in his life where he had ever felt this way. It was foreign to him, to be anxious over the way something would turn out. She had him like a 14-year-old kid, nervous about getting his first piece of pussy. He curled a knuckle and placed it against her door. His hands rested on the frame and his head hung low. When she pulled the door open, he died a little. Morgan had placed an invisible fist through him and snatched out his heart. Mortal Kombat style. The sight of her finished him.

Her eyes were swollen from crying and her entire face was red. Her messy ponytail was piled on top of her head and sadness swallowed her. His eyes traveled south to her hands and her purple finger, double in size, and a little crooked brought tears to his eyes.

"Shorty," he whispered.

He turned away from her, as disappointment filled him and tears stung his stubborn eyes. How could he hurt her? Her finger was broken. He knew it. He had broken enough of them, purposefully as punishment, to spot it on sight. He turned back toward her, eyes burden-filled.

Her lip trembled, and she looked down, instead of at him. He had shaken her. He had stripped her of the confidence it had taken her months to build.

She can't even look at me.

He peered over her shoulder and saw Bleu sitting there, on the couch, shaking her head. Then, he focused back on Morgan. Moisture clung to her lashes. Huge droplets of devastation just rested there, and Messiah knew he had caused them.

"I'm sorry," he whispered. He touched her face, four fingers behind her neck and a thumb on her cheek. She melted into him, sobbing. So forgiving, without much effort from him at all. He would have to be careful with that. He understood now how Nish had taken advantage of her kindness. Morgan was a people pleaser. She just wanted people to like her, to be in a good place with her. Conflict was scary, and she avoided it at all costs, even if it meant forgiving what she should not. That kindness was a weakness. He didn't want her to get in the habit of overlooking his misdeeds. She nuzzled into him, burying her nose into his chest and weeping. He lifted her face and kissed her lips. Softly, softer than he ever had before, ignoring the snot and tears that covered her face. He would take all of that. He would accept the entire mess of emotion on her face because he had made it. "I'm sorry, baby."

"He's nobody to me. I'm so sorry, Messiah. I thought you were done. I didn't know if you would come back," she said.

"That'll never happen, Mo. Ever. I swear to God, if I ever disappear on you it means I'm dead and gone because nothing or nobody will ever keep me away from you. Even if I'm mad, even if we argue, I'll always come back. You hear me?" he asked. "I was wrong. I'm dead-ass wrong and I will never talk to you like that again. I will never treat you like that again. Fuck, your hand, Mo. I would kill a nigga for doing that to you and I did this." He choked on his words, as he pressed his forehead to hers.

"You didn't. I grabbed your door. It's my fault. I should have let you go," she said, taking the blame.

"It ain't your fault, Mo. It's mine. All this shit is my fault and I'm so fucking sorry," he said. "I'm a sorry-ass nigga for everything I've done to you. I ain't shit and I don't deserve you, but I want you and I can't let you go."

"I don't want you to let me go," Morgan whispered.

She closed her eyes, as he gripped her face and stepped over her threshold, taking her into his arms.

Bleu stood and cleared her throat, giving him a knowing look.

"I'm going to head out. Iman's outside," Bleu said. Morgan released Messiah and embraced Bleu. She held her so tightly that Bleu's eyes moistened.

"Thank you," Morgan whispered the words with such grace.

Bleu nodded and then pulled back, setting firm eyes on Messiah, warning eyes, before walking out the door.

Messiah lifted the cheap bouquet. "They aren't roses. They ain't shit, actually, just some cheap grocery store flowers, but I felt like I couldn't come empty-handed."

Morgan gave him a weak smile, as she took them, along with the candy from his hand. "I don't care how much they cost, as long as they're from you," she whispered. "I don't want anything or anyone but you. If you want me to move in with you..."

"Mo," Messiah interrupted. "Don't tell me yes because you don't want me to be mad. You said no, stick by that. I respect you and I respect your choices. Don't bend for me or nobody else. Mean what you say and say what you mean, even if I don't like it. I understand. You're young. You got your life..."

"You are my life," she interrupted.

"And I'ma be here. I respect how you feel. I let my temper get the best of me. It won't happen again. That's my word," Messiah whispered. "Your hand, Mo. What the fuck is wrong with me?"

She could see his remorse. He was dripping in disappointment, in self-hate, from the fact that he had hurt her. He had said it more than once, so she knew it bothered him.

"Nothing's wrong with you. You didn't do this. I did it. I should have just let you leave, Messiah. It was an accident," she defended.

"Accidents like this can't happen, not to you, not because of me," he replied. She placed a hand on the side of his face and kissed him.

"I will die without you, Messiah. I will endure whatever it takes to be with you. I know there is a lot of anger in you. I don't know why, but I know it's there. I can handle it. I can handle you," she whispered. "If it ever becomes too much. I'll tell you." She held up her hand. "This was an accident." He was in turmoil, as he lowered his head into the groove of her neck. "Just an accident," she whispered.

CHAPTER 15

Ethic stood, shoulders squared, as he gripped the semi-automatic handgun in his hand. His estate was massive and held its very own gun range in the back, with an arsenal so extensive it looked like he could arm a platoon for war. His finger curled on the trigger, as he sent bullets flying, hitting his target dead in the center with ease. When one clip was done, he reloaded, swiftly, expertly, as he re-centered his aim. His defined arms extended in front of him. Squeeze.

Bang! Bang! Bang! Bang!

There was no reaction to the sound of the bullets. Ethic didn't startle. He was built and bred in the streets. It was a sound he had heard many times.

He counted the shots. He had been trained to count the shots until the chamber was empty.

"Excuse me, Mr. Okafor?"

"I thought I said no interruptions," he said. "Where are my kids?"

Lily's voice filled the brief silence. He didn't turn to her. Instead, he reloaded. "I know you said you didn't want to be disturbed. The children are in bed, but there is a woman here and she says she isn't leaving until she sees you."

Ethic lowered the weapon to his side, before tossing it on the table beside him. His heart quickened, as Alani's face flashed in his mind. He knew anger was probably what had brought her to his doorstep, perhaps even revenge, but he didn't care. He would take her however he could get her. Ethic ached for her and it was unlike any void he had ever felt in his life. It reminded him of the heartbreak he felt after losing his mother. One woman had birthed him, the other had re-birthed him with her love and without them he felt hollow. He exited the gun shed, making sure to lock it on the way out, and then made his way across his vast, well-manicured, backyard. He could see her in the distance, up on the cherry oak deck, and he appreciated her from behind. Even her silhouette was breathtaking, and Ethic wanted to enjoy it because he knew when she faced him all he would see was heartbreak. He ascended the steps and walked up behind her, but when she turned to him he froze.

"Hey, you."

Shock seized his chest and his entire stomach churned, as he looked into those emerald eyes.

"YaYa." Her name slipped from his lips in a whisper of disbelief. "How are you here, right now?"

"I just felt like you needed me," she said. She placed a delicate hand to the side of his face, the injured side, her favorite side and she saw him weaken. The average person would never notice the change in his disposition, but YaYa did. He reached for her hand and kissed the inside of her wrist. Ethic pulled her into him, burying his face in the crook of her neck, as she massaged the back of his head. "It's okay. Whatever it is, it's going to be okay," she whispered. Ethic inhaled her scent and then cleared his throat, before taking a step back. He had to remind himself that this woman was not his, not to hold in this way, so intimately, not anymore, but YaYa closed the space between them. They had never followed any rules when it had come to their relationship. It was clear to him that she didn't plan to now. "You want to talk about it?" she asked.

Ethic nodded, knowing that he could trust her with his secrets. YaYa was the one person who would never judge him.

"First, I want to introduce you to someone," she said. She took his hand and led him inside, walking through his house, as if she were the queen of his castle. YaYa was a woman who knew her pedigree. She was royalty and she looked the part from her stiletto heels with the skin-tight denim, to the fox fur shawl that rested over her cream bodysuit. YaYa was perfection, but she didn't excite him in the way she used to. She led the way to his living room where a baby boy slept.

"Aw, man," Ethic said. He was rendered speechless, as he watched her pick up the baby. Their relationship was an unusual one, filled with love and respect, despite the other people in their lives. Somehow, the pedestals they had placed each other on had never fallen, even though they were no longer together.

"Is there any chance he could be mine?" Ethic asked. He had to. He always wondered if YaYa had been truthful with him about the results of the DNA test she had conducted.

YaYa looked up at him and then quickly back down to her son. "If I had a piece of you to keep forever, I would claim that. I would be grateful for that. He's not yours, Ethic. I thought he may be, we both know we put in enough work for him to possibly be. Even after we ended, we didn't really end." She chuckled, as she blushed from the memory of their slip up. She had flown to Flint just for a few hours with him. It was a secret she had told no one. "But he isn't. He's Indie's son."

Ethic nodded and then took the baby from her arms. He held him up in front of him, taking him in, before bringing him to his strong chest.

"He likes you," YaYa noticed, with a smile, as she watched Ethic sit on the couch with her son nestled against his shoulder.

"Yeah, well, he gets that from his mama," Ethic shot back. YaYa beamed, as she sat beside him. She leaned her head on his vacant shoulder.

"Where's Sky?" he asked. YaYa smiled. Ethic was that type of man. He took care of women and children, even those who didn't belong to him.

"She's home with her father," YaYa said. "I would have brought her, but she has a big mouth, you know? This trip isn't something Indie would understand."

Ethic chuckled but YaYa noticed there was no glee in his eyes. He was going through the motions but not feeling them.

"I suppose not," Ethic answered.

"So, start talking," she said.

"I fucked up bad, Ya," he admitted. "I hurt someone."

"A woman?" YaYa asked.

Ethic leaned his head back against the couch and closed his eyes. His lack of response was confirmation for YaYa. It felt like a punch to her gut. She hadn't expected a man like Ethic to remain single for long, but she knew him, she knew him like she knew her own man, Indie; and although she knew the answer to her next question, she asked it anyway.

"Do you love her?"

His silence again was his answer. YaYa's hand rested on his chest and she could feel his heart, hammering, racing. *He loves someone else*, she thought. She was both happy and saddened by that fact, because if anyone deserved love it was Ethic. He was the best man she knew, even better than the one she had chosen over him.

"You love her more than me?" Her jealousy caused that one to slip out, but she waited with baited breath.

"I love her more than everyone," Ethic admitted. YaYa sucked in angst, as his words cracked her heart like rocks to a window pane. "But I broke her and it's eating-me-a-fucking-live because I know where she is, and I can't go get her. I can't fix this and I'm a man that used to fixing shit, carrying shit on my back for everybody that I love. I'm empty right now. I can't even look at my kids without feeling guilty."

"Guilty? What do Bella and Eazy have to do with anything?" YaYa asked, genuine confusion shining in her green eyes. Ethic used to love those eyes. Once upon a time, he would drown in those emerald pools she called eyes. Now, they were simply a color because the brown eyes of another had given him a peek into a soul so genuine that everything else felt like a knockoff. Even YaYa couldn't compare and the pedestal he put her on was pretty high. Alani's was higher, however...Alani's was a throne.

"I killed her daughter," he barely said it above a whisper, but YaYa heard him. Her blood seemed to freeze, as a chill ran through her. She sat up and stared at him, but he couldn't look at her. His eyes were on the ceiling. Lines creased his forehead. His revelation explained his energy. He was in a dark place. She had felt it as soon as she saw him, but she could have never guessed this. She used her finger to turn his head toward her and her eyes watered when she saw the tears that fell from his eyes. Only gravity had freed them. Ethic had been holding them in since the moment he sat down. If he was honest, he would admit that he had been stifling them for 35 years. He doubled over, cradling her son in his arms like a football, as he sobbed, while kissing the top of his innocent head. YaYa covered her mouth with her hand, as she reached for Ethic's back, rubbing it gently as he wept. To see a man who was so strong, so solid, this weak was gut wrenching.

"I know you. You would never—"

"Her brother raped Morgan. I shot him. The little girl got caught in the fire. I didn't even know she was there," Ethic said, through gritted teeth, as he lifted his head from the baby in his arms.

YaYa sat, stunned. She blew an audible breath from her mouth. "Oh, Ethic," she whispered.

"How do you fix something like that?" He asked.

YaYa's forehead wrinkled, as he looked at her for answers. "Motherhood is a privilege. Once a woman has kids, it's like a light is flicked on inside her. It's a love that's consistent and pure. A connection that needs no explanation. It just fulfills you. I can't explain it. It's like it completes you. Your child is the one person that will never abandon you. You get to see the world through new eyes and it's so much better the second time around. You took that from her. I don't know if that's something you can fix," YaYa said.

He nodded. "I know."

"You're a man who is used to controlling things. Sometimes, as women, we don't want you to fix anything…sometimes, we just want you to be there while we figure out how to fix ourselves."

YaYa took her son from his arms.

"Now, show me where I'll be sleeping so I can lay my child down and come fix you a drink. It looks like you need one,"

YaYa said. "My bags are by the door."

Ethic shook his head and smirked. YaYa was the exact opposite of Alani. High maintenance. Bossy. A diva. Both women were beautiful but vastly different. YaYa was proof that he was an appreciator of all types. He had experienced quite a few YaYa's, never had he run into another Alani. He rose from his seat and headed to the kitchen, with YaYa on his heels.

"Lily, can you put the baby down in the largest guest room, please? You can call it a night after that," Ethic said.

"Yes, sir," Lily said.

YaYa handed her son to Lily. "There is a baby monitor in the diaper bag by the front door," YaYa instructed. "Could you set it on the bed beside him, please?"

"Of course," Lily answered.

"Thank you." YaYa pulled the other monitor from her handbag and set it on the counter. Then, she turned toward his cabinets. Ethic crossed his arms, as he stood and watched her move around his home, like this was her kitchen, like she had picked out the tiles and the cabinetry herself, like she had handpicked Lily out of a bunch because she was impressed by the resume. She was comfortable in his space...beautiful in it in fact. He didn't mind. He had once thought he would share it with her. It seemed like so long ago that he had planned to build a life with her. Alani had muddled his timeline, made him forget just how potently he had desired Disaya Perkins. Here in the flesh, this green-eyed beauty reminded him. She located a bottle of bourbon.

"Is this all you have?" she asked, grimacing.

"I'm not much of a drinker these days," he said.

"Un uh," YaYa said, with a pointed, stiletto fingernail. Another difference. Between YaYa and Alani... Alani's nails were plain, always muted in nude colors and always short, never fake. Although Ethic had no preference, he couldn't help but contrast. "None of that healthy mess you're on. You're hurting. You deserve a drink. Besides, you are not the only one nursing a heartbreak." YaYa pulled down two tumblers and poured a shot in each glass.

Curiosity broke through Ethic's solemn. "Married life not treating you well?"

YaYa shook her head. "Married life is fine. I'm not heartbroken over Indie. I just found out the man I love is in love with someone else."

She slid the glass over to him. Ethic sighed. "You left me, Disaya. You broke your own heart," he said.

"I know," she answered, her tone sad and laced with regret. "I'm a woman with not one, but two children. My choices are not my own to make. I had more than myself to consider, Ethic. Maybe if I was a selfish woman, I would have chosen differently. I would be here with you right now and this girl you love wouldn't even exist to you."

"You're where you supposed to be," Ethic said. "You're the woman who wants whatever she doesn't have at the moment. When you're with Indie, you want me. When you're with me, you want him. You know your power, Ya. You ain't slick." Ethic took the shot and slid the glass across the island. "Pour up."

YaYa refilled his glass and slid it back, then tossed back her own.

"You make me sound horrible," she whispered.

"If I felt that way, you wouldn't be under my roof while my kids are asleep upstairs," Ethic said. "There's nothing wrong with the way you move. The type of man I am, other women wouldn't have the privilege to hop in and out as they see fit."

He took the shot. "I'll take the time I can get with you." He shot her a wink and YaYa smiled, but there was no light behind it. She climbed on the bar stool with perplexity written all over her.

"I don't know why I can't leave you alone. It's like, I'm with him. I *chose* him, but I lay in bed at night and I think of you." YaYa whispered it like it was her darkest secret.

"You're just half filled. You attached yourself to a man that doesn't pour into you. Maybe he used to, but something has changed. I believe he loves you, because any nigga willing to war with me over a woman definitely loves that woman…" Ethic paused, choosing his words carefully because he was never the type of man to kick in the next man's back to gain leverage. "But because he's lost his focus, he forgot that the woman every nigga wanted is the one in his possession, so he's slipping. He's neglecting. I compensate for what he's not giving you and you love me for it. You want me for it, because you know that it doesn't take anybody else but me to keep you at 100, to make you feel secure, to keep you full. But you're stuck. You already chose him, you're already indebted to him, so there could never be an us. You're too honorable of a woman to let go of a man you feel like you owe. You have years in with him. You're invested, but you don't love him anymore. It took him too long to change into the man you needed him to be and you built up walls to protect yourself from the man he was. He damaged the best parts of you in the beginning. He's a different man now but, unfortunately for him, you're different now too. The hurt he put on you has changed you. That's why you're here because you trust me with the parts of you that he took for granted. You know what I do to you, how I would have made you feel before…"

"Before what?" YaYa asked, her eyes slightly misted from the truth he spoke.

"Before her," Ethic answered. He swallowed the bourbon. Her shook his head and massaged the right side of his beard before wrapping four fingers around his tense neck to rub there too.

"I love my husband, Ethic." Her words were defensive. Then, she added the sincerest, "I'm just so in love with you too. You have my heart, he has my soul. There are no winners in that." He believed that she believed what was coming from her mouth. He knew she meant no malice.

Ethic shook his head. Another difference. He was running up the score board with the comparisons. Alani was a woman who loved one and one alone. Him. He had just fucked it up. "Nah, that's not how it works, YaYa."

"You don't think you can love two people at the same time? You don't think you can love two individuals for different reasons?" she asked. "What about you?"

"What about me?" he asked.

"You claim to love this new girl," YaYa said. "But we weren't that long ago. You can't tell me you don't still have feelings for me?"

"I do. I would never deny that, but her..." Ethic paused to shake his head. She was floored at the regard he held for this woman. "I am in love with her. *In* love, YaYa. In. Submerged in. Dissolved in. Parts of her have melted into me so I couldn't separate the sentiment from her on the darkest day. She's in me. That means you and everybody else that was inside my heart before her had to get out," Ethic explained. "The way I love her doesn't leave room for anyone else."

"I want to beat her ass," YaYa muttered. Ethic's laughter

came from the pit of him, from a genuine place that had been hard to locate lately. She smiled, happy to see the clouds lift from him - even if only for a little while. She was only half joking, however.

"You know Eazy's birthday is tomorrow," Ethic stated, deciding to lighten the flow of conversation. He and YaYa could dwell in the past forever and he knew it would be easy to revisit that place...all it took was a few more shots. He didn't want to mix what he was feeling with Alani with what YaYa provided. He had his hands full with one woman. Alani was enough. He never understood how men felt they could handle two simultaneously. It was ego that caused a man to think he was functioning at a high enough capacity in a relationship to give pieces of himself to a third party. If a woman had even one complaint, one insecurity, one area in which she was unfulfilled, then her man wasn't doing his part. Ethic always believed in satisfying the one he was with. In his experience, when a woman was loved correctly, she would give a man all he needed to not stray.

"Of course I know, I come bearing gifts," YaYa said, with a wink.

"Expensive ones, no doubt," Ethic answered, with a smirk. "I'm glad you came, YaYa. I'd fly to the end of the Earth to come see about you. Feels good to know this thing between us is reciprocated. I question that at times."

"Never doubt that," YaYa replied. "I love you, Ethic. I'll do anything for you."

"Except stay," Ethic said, definitively.

She nodded. "Some people can stay in your heart but not your life," she whispered, sadly.

The poignancy of her words struck the core of him, as Alani

flashed in his mind. He wondered why he was only ever able to capture time in small increments with the women he loved. It was never lasting. It was always fleeting, and it always left him in pieces. Fragments of Ethic were in the ground with Melanie and Raven. He was sure YaYa's siddity-ass carried pieces of his soul around in the Birkin bag she owned, only taking them out when she needed them, as if he were an accessory. Alani was the latest to break off a piece of him. He realized he was busy trying to fix each of them, when it was he whom needed repair. He couldn't save anyone without saving himself first. He prioritized everyone around him, but there were things that haunted Ethic that blocked love from surviving in his space. Until he addressed what ailed him at his core, he would be reduced to pieces. He would never be whole. "I'm going to get some sleep," YaYa said, as she slid off the bar stool and collected both glasses from the countertop. She strolled to the sink and washed them quickly, before heading for the stairs. When she bypassed Ethic, she stopped and planted a soft hand to the side of his face. He appreciated her touch, but it paled in comparison to that of another. Still, it soothed some of his self-loathing. She leaned and planted a kiss on his wrinkled forehead. "Good night. Party time tomorrow."

CHAPTER 16

What am I doing here?" Alani whispered. She stood on Ethic's doorstep, hands gripping the gift bag in her hand, looking down at her feet. Nervous energy danced inside her, eating her alive. She didn't know how she had survived the morning. She had pulled everything out her closet, trying on outfit after outfit, searching for something to wear. While most women wanted to impress and allure a man, Alani tried her hardest to mute whatever light it was that drew Ethic to her. She didn't get it. He was a league of his own and she was just regular enough not to be an option for him. She should be one of the women he overlooked, like the decent cashier you saw at the gas station, or the okay nurse who checked a man in at the doctor's office. He shouldn't have ever considered her, never even looked twice, but somehow, he had doubled back…she had him hooked and she hated it. The way he looked at her, like she was the most exquisite version of a woman he had ever seen intimidated her. She wished she hadn't given her word that she would show. Alani was one of those people who wanted to be invited because it let her know that people hadn't forgotten her, but she didn't really want to show up. She had become a willing prisoner to the four walls of her home. Going out for recreation was a thing of the past. It didn't even feel like she was allowed to have fun. What woman sought fun after losing two babies? People would judge her if the smile on her face was ever too big. Grieving mothers weren't allowed to smile again. She forced her finger into the bell and heard it chime from inside the house. The door swung open and a presence so grand greeted her that she forgot to breathe. Ethic stood before her, casually dressed in Burberry-checkered swim shorts. Washboard abs and biceps chiseled like boulders were his accessories. The cologne that filled the air was a familiar one. It was different than the one he had worn to her house the other day. It was the one from the night of the pageant. The one that had taken her an entire week to 'unsmell.' He was infecting her air, again, and she wanted to run.

"Wow."

The words of stun fell off his lips, as he feathered his lips in appreciation. "I don't even know how you're standing at my door right now, but I'm grateful."

Only Ethic spoke like that, like being deprived of her presence caused him physical harm. Words from his lips were used differently than any other man she had ever encountered. It was like he only combined them if he could express exactly how he felt...if he could convey his desire precisely, to make her feel it too.

"Eazy and Bella invited me. I promised them I would come. I hope that's okay," she whispered. She could never quite find her voice around him. It always felt like a VISE-GRIP was around her heart, when in his proximity.

Alani had thought she was making progress. She had thought she was severing the connection that kept her slave to his affection, but as she stood under the intensity of his stare, his dark presence engulfing her, she realized that there was no progress to be made. You couldn't 'un-love' a man like Ethic. You couldn't unlearn the value he made his woman

174

feel. You couldn't stop the tickle that spread through your stomach under his scrutiny. His love wasn't the Indian giving kind. There were no take backs. Once he gave it, it settled in your bones. Not even the hate she felt could scrape the love from her existence. So, inside her lived both adulation and contempt. Once a woman experienced the presence of a real man, her life changed. So, no, progress she had not made; she had simply been avoiding him. She hated the resounding hurt that filled her when he was around. She was no longer cloaked in anger, but the resentment was forever etched in her soul. It was just another part of her now. It was as natural as saying, Alani with the curly hair? Alani with the brown eyes? She could now be classified as 'Alani with the bitter heart?' It was just who she was.

"I know you don't have to do what you're doing for Bella. Hell, now it seems that Eazy is a recipient of your time too. You'll never know how much it means to them."

"It's not just for them," Alani admitted. She wrung her fingers, unable to look him in the eyes.

"If this is uncomfortable for you..."

She shook her head.

"Life is uncomfortable. Breathing and putting one foot in front of the other is uncomfortable. It just is what it is now," she answered, with a shrug.

The lines in his forehead revealed his angst. "I'm sorry."

"I don't want to bring down Eazy's day. If I can just pop in and out, let him see my face and give him my gift, I can be on my way," she stated. She couldn't get into this emotional battle with Ethic. Every time she saw him it was so heavy, so daunting, it pulled her right back into depression. She just wanted to be a woman of her word and bring some love to two little people who had brought a little to her the other day. Fair exchange.

"I worry about you, Lenika." Those words were heavy, burdened, and the way his eyes shone down on her she knew that they were real.

"I'm fine. I just want peace. I'm trying really hard to attain that. I'm praying and doing yoga," she scoffed, as a slight smile spread across her face.

"Yoga, huh?" Ethic asked. Amusement played on his lips and he licked them. Did the word make him remember too? Did he recall the way she had ridden his face into the early morning hours that night? The licking of lips made her tremble. Those lips and that tongue were so talented. The simple gesture made her body ache.

She blushed because they both knew how she had been introduced to the practice. "And I'm writing. Putting what I feel on paper, so it doesn't build up, you know?" She shifted, nervously, looking down at her feet to avoid the magnetic pull he seemed to have over her gaze. "I try to keep my mind from spinning and I try to believe in something that makes me think my babies are okay. I pray for you, for me to be able to be around you one day without it hurting."

"If I believed in God, I'd pray for that too," he whispered.

Alani put sad eyes on him, they misted because, well, it was just what happened around him. They were a pair convoluted in emotion.

Ethic wanted to tell her he loved her, but he held those words. He could see she was barely keeping it together and he didn't want to be the one to unravel her. She was like an old sweater with a loose thread. It was better to let it be; because once you pulled it, the entire thing came apart.

Alani peered past him into the beautiful home. She hadn't

been inside since the day she found out about her daughter and he noticed her fret.

"It's just a house. Brick and plaster like everyone else's. I won't trap you here," he said. The corner of his mouth turned up into a smirk, as he rubbed his hand over his head before folding his strong arms across his broad chest. He had to trap his hands to stop himself from reaching out and touching her. She was known for taking her presence away from him. He never knew when she would pull back again, and he appreciated these moments she graciously spared to allow him to breathe her air. It was good air; pure, whenever she was around. He took her in, sweeping her over with his eyes, as he admired the beauty that was woman. He didn't want to scare her away or interfere with the connection Bella was making with her, so he didn't press her, despite the fact that he desperately wanted to fix her broken pieces...because he, in fact, was the one who had diminished her wholeness.

"It just feels weird that you would welcome me here and allow me to be around them after I almost killed you," she whispered. "I don't know forgiveness like that."

"You're not a threat to my children. I don't feel that from you. Me, on the other hand, I have to tread lightly. You just might wake up one day and decide I don't deserve to be here," he said, with a chuckle. "I won't ever test your gangster."

"That's not funny," she whispered. So many complicated things dwelled between them. There were so many sordid details intertwined in their short history. It only reminded her of hate. It was a pain she had been running from since she had buried their son. With Kenzie's death, rage had consumed her and pushed her into a darkness that had almost killed her. With Love's death, she was trying to stay in the light, fighting to make every day purpose filled to honor his memory...to honor both her babies' memories. They were her angels and she wanted to be a woman they would be proud of. She couldn't make light of what she had done, although she appreciated Ethic's ability to forgive.

"I'm fine, Lenika," he said, as he stepped onto the porch. "You're fine. We're both right here living and breathing. I hold no judgements about that day."

"I shot you," she whispered.

"I know. Believe me. I got the scar to prove it," he licked his lips. She closed her eyes, her brows dipping in longing.

I wish he would stop doing that. Then, she felt his finger lifting her chin. *God, no.* She rolled her misty eyes up to him and he sucked in a breath when she finally allowed their gapes to attract. He had to disconnect his skin from hers immediately to stop himself from crossing a line. Even something as simple as a finger to her chin ignited feelings of need within him. Restraint was a way of life for him, but with Alani, it was damn near impossible. "Breathing is an in and out thing," he reminded. Alani released the air in her lungs that she had been unknowingly holding.

"You suck the life out of me," she whispered. Her words were soft, but the blow behind them was mighty. Alani cleared her throat.

"If this is too much, I can make up an excuse with my kids. You're not obligated..."

"I promised them, and I don't break promises," Alani said.

Ethic nodded. She had no idea how her dedication to his children moved him, especially her interactions with Bella. He could guide Eazy. He could teach him how to be a man, but he could never fully do Bella justice. He could never fill the shoes that a real mother would. Alani's efforts were healing something inside his daughter. He could see it. Bella smiled differently, since having Alani in her life; and for that alone, Alani would always have his loyalty. "Come in," he invited, as he stepped aside to allow her entry. "Everybody's out back."

Alani made her way through the house, almost rushing so that the bad memories wouldn't ruin her mood.

When she made it to the back patio, she smiled, as Eazy came rushing up to her. "Alani!" he ran full speed, bulldozing into her. *Must be a quality of Okafor men, because his daddy bulldozed his way into my life too.*

"Hi, birthday boy!" she greeted. There was genuine cheer in her voice, as she embraced him in a hug. Ethic came up behind her, placing a gentle hand to the small of her back to move her out the way as he passed by. In a smooth gesture, he relieved her of the gift bag she carried.

"I'll put this with the rest of them," Ethic said. Alani nodded, but kept her attention on Eazy.

"We have a diving board. Are you going to swim with us? Please, please," Eazy pleaded. Alani laughed and patted the heavy tote that hung from her arm. "I have my swimsuit in my bag."

She looked up at the small celebration. She understood the intimacy, especially considering all that they had been through. Strangers couldn't be permitted to enter Ethic's space. Poor Eazy didn't make friends easily, so there were no classmates or neighborhood kids. Just family and close friends and...*who the fuck is she?* Alani watched as Bella played with a baby boy and laughed with the green-eyed, bikini-clad, beauty on the deck. They were familiar with one another. Bella was comfortable with this woman. Alani couldn't explain the knot that formed in her stomach. Jealousy. The green-eyed monster accompanied this green-eyed bitch.

"Yay! I want to have a cannon ball contest and a race and..."

Alani was only half listening to Eazy. Her eyes were glued to this mystery woman. When she saw Ethic bend down and scoop the bundle of joy from Bella's arms, Alani lost strength in her legs. Bile built in the back of her throat. Seeing Ethic with a baby in his arms reminded her of the one she had lost.

Is that his baby? No, it can't be. He would have told me. Alani was trying to use logic to explain the scene before her, but damn it if Ethic and this woman didn't look like a couple in love, doting over their new baby. They were so comfortable with one another. The baby was so comfortable in Ethic's arms and this woman was so freaking gorgeous, and she kept touching Ethic. A hand to his forearm, a finger to Ethic's eyebrows to smooth them out, a sip from the cup Ethic was drinking from. He was drinking after her and Alani knew then that he had tasted her pussy, because what was a little backwash compared to vagina juice all over your tongue? She was sick, and she was sure she was close to passing out because she was forgetting to breathe.

Who the fuck is this bitch?

"Alani!"

She tore her eyes from the trio and rolled them down to Eazy. Her smile this time was forced. Eazy wore Burberry swim trunks and a necklace where a small bell hung around his neck. He reached for it and rang it.

"Is that a servant's bell?" she laughed.

"Yep! It's Okafor tradition. The birthday kid gets the bell and when I ring it, whatever I says goes. Now, go change so we can swim!" Eazy urged, pushing her back toward the sliding door that led to the inside.

"Okay, okay, birthday boy, I'm going," she chuckled. She was grateful for the escape. A part of her wanted to run right out the front door, but she couldn't show that she was bothered. *She could be a family member or something.* Alani scoffed, as she entered the half-bath. *Bitch ain't no family member. He fucked her. I know what a woman looks like after she's been yoga fucked.* Alani pulled her black, one-piece from her tote. *What type of respectable woman wears a two-piece to a kid's birthday party?* She changed quickly and stared herself down in the mirror, adjusting breasts that she felt sagged too much and sucking in the lasting baby fat that Love had left on her mid-section. Her snap back hadn't quite snapped all the way back yet and the swim suit brought out all her insecurities. Or was it the new bitch in the backyard smiling in Ethic's face that did that? She didn't know. Either way, she was uncomfortable as fuck. Her thighs were too big, childbirth had given her a baby fupa that felt like a stress ball when she touched it, faint stretch marks covered the sides of her behind. *Fuck what he thinks and fuck that bitch too. You're not here for him. You're here for Eazy.* She tied the sheer cover-up around her waist, put her sunglasses on top of her head, and slipped into a pair of flip flops, before walking out.

Eazy and Bella had escaped to the pool and a threesome sat at the table while Ethic manned the grill. As if he could smell her presence, Ethic turned toward her. He nodded for her, beckoned her to him and she gave a flat smile, as she walked over to the group.

"Everybody, you remember Alani."

Alani's eyes bounced from Morgan to Messiah. She gave a polite nod, despite Morgan's obvious disdain regarding her presence.

"And this is my friend, YaYa."

Alani's eyes stuck on YaYa.

She's even prettier up close. What kind of friend? Friend from where? You ain't even that fucking friendly.

Her mind was spinning. She was jealous, and he hadn't even given her a reason to be, but somehow, she knew. Ethic and YaYa were two people who had made love before and were figuring out what friendship looked like.

"Nice to meet you," YaYa greeted. She was friendly, which forced Alani to be friendly too.

"You too," Alani managed. She couldn't lie and say it was nice because it wasn't. It was torture. She turned to Morgan and felt another type of pang in her belly. How could she be around the girl her brother had wronged? The girl whom had started it all. She understood Morgan's discomfort...her anger. Alani felt accountable for Lucas' actions. She felt like an apology was owed, but she was too afraid to deliver it.

Lucas, what did you do? Morgan was so pretty, but Alani noticed her uneasiness. There was a hint of emotion in Morgan's eyes. Most probably wouldn't see it, but Alani caught the wetness that pooled near Morgan's black-lined eyes. She wanted desperately to have a conversation with Morgan. She felt the urge to tell Morgan that Lucas wasn't raised to act like an animal, but the eyes of the others stopped her from doing so. She quickly looked away.

"You hungry?" Ethic asked.

She shook her head. "I'm fine."

"Alani!" She looked up, grateful for Bella. "Come get in the water!"

Alani handed Ethic her bag. "Take care of this for me?" she asked.

A similarity, Ethic thought with a smirk. Apparently, the women in his life thought he was good at handling baggage, emotional and otherwise.

Alani walked over to the pool and didn't shed the sarong until she was on the edge of the pool. She only gave a glimpse of her body before diving head first into the water. It was enough to awaken the lust inside Ethic. He turned away from the pool because she clearly wasn't present for him.

"So, that's her?" YaYa asked.

Ethic's stare pierced YaYa before he turned back to the grill. "Yeah, that's her," he replied.

"Why is she here?" Morgan cut in.

Everyone turned to Morgan. Ethic chose his words precisely. He had known that the dynamic between Morgan and Alani would be strained. Morgan wouldn't be as easy to woo as Bella and Eazy. He expected Alani to harbor reservations as well. "She's here for Eazy and B. They want her here, Mo. You only know the bad parts of her side of the story. It would mean a lot if you would give her a chance and get to know the good in her...there's a lot of good in her."

Morgan's nostrils flared, a tell that she had possessed since childhood and Ethic knew she was trying her best to control her anger.

"She doesn't belong here, and if she's going to be here, I won't," Morgan said. She stood so abruptly that she knocked her chair to the floor.

A tantrum. Ethic had seen her have them before. Mostly, when she was deaf, and her frustrations would get the best of her. He looked out at the pool where Alani was standing in the middle of Bella and Eazy, holding their hands as they counted to three before jumping into the water. He looked to Morgan who was storming away and then down at Messiah who was rising from the table.

"Make sure she gets back to campus safely," Ethic stated. He didn't bend when it came to Alani. Not for YaYa, not Morgan, not even for himself. She was welcomed wherever he was. Alani trumped all.

"You got it," Messiah answered. "Yo, when time permits, we need to chop it up about something."

Ethic nodded.

When Ethic and YaYa were the only two that remained, she folded her arms across her chest. "Hmm."

Ethic pulled out the chair across from her. "I see judgement in those eyes. You gon' speak your peace or just leave me guessing?" he asked.

YaYa held up her hands, in surrender. "No judgment here. There was just a whole lot of energy at this table. That's all," she said. "I'm going to make this easy for you and head out."

"You don't have to leave, Ya. It's always good to have you here," Ethic said. It never mattered how much time or distance was between them. Whenever they managed to come back together, it always felt good.

"I know, but me being here in your space will complicate things," YaYa said. "You're a good man, Ethic. You are worth more than the mistakes you've made. I love you with my whole heart, Mr. Okafor. I just want you to be happy." YaYa glanced toward the pool. "You know, hearing you talk about her last night... It made me jealous, but then she walks through the door..." YaYa paused and turned away from the pool and stared directly in his eyes. "I get it. She's your happiness. She loves you."

"It's complicated," he began.

"Love typically is, but she was devastated to find me here. I know she felt my energy because I felt hers. We are two women who have had the privilege of being loved by you. You've been inside me. Inside her. Those are roots no woman could ever pull and ones we recognize in each other. She and I have soul ties with you, which inadvertently connects us to one another. My presence made her sick, Ethic. I could see it in her eyes. A woman who doesn't want a man doesn't give off those types of vibes. She doesn't show up and play in a pool with a man's kids. I don't know much, I don't even know her, but I do know that she is 100 percent in love with you. And seeing her, meeting her, makes me feel a little better about going back home; because with her, I know your heart will be okay. Mine might hurt a little bit," she laughed. "Because I also know that because of her, this will be the last time I see you."

"You talking crazy," Ethic said, as he sat back in his chair, legs spread wide, hands behind his head, as he lifted his eyes to the sky. "I ain't going anywhere. I'm right here, always a phone call away if you ever really need me. You know that."

"You're a good enough friend to keep that promise and I'm a good enough friend to never abuse your loyalty. Don't let her slip through your fingers, Ethic. Take it from me, you'll regret it." YaYa stood. "I'm going to head to the airport and go back home to work on my own shit. Walk me to the door?" YaYa asked.

Ethic obliged, taking her son from her arms.

"You want to tell the kids goodbye?" he asked.

YaYa shook her head. "No, I don't want to interrupt their time with her. Kiss them for me," she said.

"I will," Ethic answered.

He escorted her to the rental car she had parked in his

driveway. He took extra care in tucking the baby in his car seat. He stared at the little guy long and hard, and then planted a kiss on his forehead. Something in him stirred. Something paternal. Something innate. He turned to YaYa. "And you're sure? He's not mine?" There was emotion glistening in her eyes.

YaYa nodded. "I'm sure," she whispered. "You are such a good man." She shook her head in admiration. YaYa wrapped her arms around his neck and he pulled her in, closing her in his embrace. He felt her body shudder and heard the makings of a sob. He held her tighter. "God, Ethic, I love you so much."

"YaYa, don't do this to me, ma." His tone was guttural... piteous. They had been here before. Their goodbyes were never easy... always weighted because Ethic would always love her too. In another world, some alternate universe, she would be his wife. Not this one, though. In this one, she was meant to pass through his life briefly and give him an experience that was full of passion, but not everlasting.

"Take care of yourself, okay?" she whispered. "Take care of her too." She pulled back and swiped away a tear, and then pursed her lips as she took a deep breath. YaYa loved two men. It just was what it was. She probably always would. He wrapped four fingers around her neck and used his thumb to swipe away her tears.

"So fucking beautiful," he complimented. She blushed. Then laughed. Nobody could big her up like he did. He just made her feel like the only girl in the world. She felt bad for women who had never experienced an Ezra Okafor before. The Ethic effect was amazing, and something no other man could ever make her feel. He was a gift and she was so grateful to have been on the receiving end of his love - once upon a time. Letting him go had always been her weakness. He could drop into her life whenever, however, wherever, no matter whom she was with and she would always welcome him. Into her heart, into her bed, into her soul with open arms. She couldn't miss that shooting star, not for Indie's sake, not for anyone's. When Ethic came back to her, wrong would just have to be right for a little while. She had a feeling there would be no more back and forth, however, and it was what made it hard for her to let him go this time. Alani had taken her place and it hurt greater than any L she had ever taken in her life. It hurt the most.

"The only reason I'm able to love that woman in there is because you showed me that my heart worked after losing Raven. I'm able to love her because I loved you first, YaYa. Thank you."

He leaned in and kissed her forehead. YaYa closed her eyes. She relished those lips against her skin. She locked it into her memory and then reached for his face and pulled him into her. His lips on hers. His lips parting to accept her tongue, as she partook in him. It was their last, stolen kiss and she didn't feel a bit of guilt about it. She felt his hesitation, but he was too caring to spin her completely. YaYa didn't care, however. In this moment, neither Alani or her own husband were a factor. She was taking this kiss. He was lucky she hadn't given him this work, because YaYa had pussy on ice for Ethic whenever he wanted to come get it. Out of respect for the pain he had endured lately, she hadn't taken it that far, but this kiss...there was no leaving without it.

The front door opened and Eazy stepped out with Alani behind him.

"Dad, the food is burning!"

Ethic turned to Alani and his son, as they stood on the porch. Alani placed hands on Eazy's shoulders.

"Let's go back inside, Eazy. Your dad has his hands full right now," she said, before guiding Eazy through the front door. There was injury in her voice. Ethic released YaYa.

"I better go," she said, grimacing.

Ethic nodded, and then rubbed the sides of his lips, pinching them, as YaYa got into her car and drove away.

CHAPTER 17

Ethic walked into the house and headed straight for the backyard. The jovial voices of Bella and Eazy pulled his eyes to the pool. The billowing smoke and orange flames snatched his attention toward the grill. Alani stood, fanning flames, as she tried to pull the food from the chaos.

Ethic came up behind her and took the tongs from her hands. "I've got it," Alani said. Ethic persisted. "I said I got it!" she yelled, a bit louder than she intended. The kids looked up from the pool and Alani closed her eyes. She tossed the tongs on the table and turned for the house.

Ethic was prepared for this. For the blow up, for the rush of emotions that always flooded them whenever they were in each other's vicinity. YaYa's pop-up had added another element to it. He followed her inside.

"Who is she?" Alani asked. Her voice was so small, as if seeing him in the presence of another woman had shrunk her. She didn't want to ask. The inquiry had been on the tip of her tongue since the moment she stepped foot on the patio. She had tried not to ask... struggled to keep her cool because, *who am I to trip?* Yet, here she was... tripping.

"She's a friend," Ethic answered.

"A friend like I'm a friend?" Alani asked.

"I didn't know we were even that anymore," Ethic countered.

Oh, and why the hell did he counter with that? Those words were like gasoline to fire. They ignited her.

She shook her head and scoffed at herself.

"We're not," Alani spat. "We never were, apparently. I'm so fucking stupid," she whispered. "I need my bag. I'm leaving. I should have never come here." Alani's stomach was hollow. Seeing him interlocked in a kiss with another woman obliterated her. The sting of her eyes was embarrassing, and it took all her will not to let him see her cry. She had given him too many tears. The fact that Ethic wasn't moving pissed her off. He was just standing there, arms folded across his chest, staring at her...through her.

"My keys, Ethic! I need my keys," she pleaded. She was seconds away from melting down. She placed her palms down on the marble island in the middle of the kitchen and lowered her chin to her chest. She closed her eyes. *Don't cry. Don't cry.* Her lip quivered.

"Lenika..."

Alani lifted her hand to silence him.

"I'm a fool. I'm sick to my stomach, tossing and turning at night, every night over you. I'm stuck in this shit by myself. Literally trapped in a place where I can't move on from you. I can't stop thinking about you; meanwhile, you're finessing bitches with green eyes and kissing babies like you're the mayor!" Those green eyes really bothered her. "Did I ever even have a chance? Every woman I've seen you with is gorgeous. I mean, perfection," she kissed her fingers, as if she were a chef. "Bad bitches, bodies on point, exotic, with the stuck-up attitudes to match. What were you slumming with me?" *Stop this. You're making a fool of yourself. Just leave. Just scrape up the rest of your dignity and walk out of this man's house. Walk out of his life. Why are you even here?*

"Are we screaming or are we talking? I don't do too good with the yelling and all that. My kids are outside," Ethic reminded.

"And mine are dead." There it was. Her trump card. It was like the big joker in a spades game. When she pulled it out, it just shut shit down. Mic drop.

Ethic leaned against the kitchen counter and took her in. Alani was an unstable creature. Beautiful and dangerous. That anger she carried around armed her like a loaded gun waiting to blow. At least this time she wasn't crying; just mad as hell. Ethic didn't know which was worse.

"YaYa..."

"What type of stupid-ass name is that?" Alani rolled her eyes.

Ethic fought the smirk he felt. He found her jealousy attractive. If she knew exactly how he felt about her, she would never worry about another woman again. "I was with her, briefly, before you," he continued.

"You kissed her. That's not before me. That's during me. I'm sitting in your house, playing with your kids and your tongue... that tongue that you just had between my legs a week ago was down her throat," Alani whispered, as she grimaced in disgust, grasping her stomach, appalled.

"I didn't mean for you to see that. I'm sorry that it made you uncomfortable," Ethic said.

"For me to see it? Or for it to happen? Uncomfortable? It tore my heart out my chest!" She shouted.

"I'm going to offer an explanation because I care about what you think, but one isn't owed, Lenika. You don't want me. She does. She always will, but she can't have me because now I want you, but I fucked that up. You can't turn me away then get upset because the next woman won't. When I'm with you, I'm with you, but I'm not with you. You won't give me you."

"You don't need me. You clearly have options," Alani snapped.

"Fuck options. Fuck the bullshit. Fuck her. She's not a threat. She's a friend that I kept time with, briefly, before you. I want you. Now, what you gon' do with that information? I want to eat your pussy on top of this countertop and move your things in, in the morning. You ready? What's up? Because you can't say no to those things but demand answers when you see me with another woman."

He was distracting her...flustering her with visions of him between her thighs on top of the black, Quartz in front of her. Her body was begging her to oblige.

"How briefly were you with her?" Alani asked. Just like a woman, to only address what she wanted to. She didn't give a damn about the extra shit Ethic was talking. She wanted to know about the other woman. She needed the details. She craved information that would only make it hurt worse. To question what she had witnessed with her own eyes just to give him the opportunity to make it feel better with illogical explanations.

"Very. She's married," Ethic answered. "Don't deflect. What's up? I'll answer every question you got. I won't lie, I won't omit, I am an open book with my woman, Lenika. If you're my woman, put that shit right here in front of me. Let me put my face in it whenever I want. Let me have you whenever I need because I'm in need. Of you. Not her. Ask away! Then, let's quit bullshitting and go upstairs so I can climb inside you, ma, because I'm dying to get inside you. Damn, you don't even know."

"Hmmph," she scoffed. She pointed a finger at him. "You're good. You're something. With your dick print and your dirty mouth and your...all this!" He had her bothered, as she pointed out the brilliance that was Ethic. The undeniable grandeur of his manhood. He was so fine, and he was talking so nasty and it was so uncharacteristic of him. It was hard to stay focused... to stay angry. "You had a bitch sitting in here in front of my face, now you want me to be your woman? You sure? Because as soon as I stepped foot in this house, you should have put her out. As a matter of fact, if you ever wanted to sniff this shit again, she should have never made it pass the threshold. Instead, I show up and she's in your house, sitting on a throne like she picked out the china in this bitch?!"

Ethic's eyebrows lifted. This wasn't Alani. This was Lenika he was talking to. This was Lenika from the Northside of Flint...Susan Street, to be exact...the chick who had mashed out Sabrina Evans for talking shit in high school. He hadn't met this side of her - yet. This might not even be Lenika. This bitch was just Nika. Yep. Nika was the fighter inside her with aggression and words that cut like steel. This version of her wasn't sweet at all. She was bitter and still he wanted to indulge. This version of her was like the Cry Baby candy that tore up the roof of your mouth, but you still couldn't stop sucking on. He knew she had him because this behavior, this tantrum, wouldn't have been tolerated otherwise. He wanted to bust open her wrapper and suck all the sour out until he got to the sweet part. His dick hardened. This back and forth bout of aggression was awakening his authority, challenging his manhood, and he wanted to show her how much of a man he was. He wanted to make her submit and turn those angry screams to ones of passion. His pulse raced. There was an unbearable current pulsing through him and he just wanted to conquer her.

"She's a friend," Ethic reiterated.

"Stop saying that!" Alani yelled. She pointed a finger at him. "I told you that I slap hoes like her. Mop they asses right on up for sitting in my face, trying to be cute. With those fake-ass contacts in her eyes and those gaudy nails."

Ethic dared not tell her YaYa's eyes were real. He just dissected her with his eyes, as she kept going. He wouldn't normally allow the drama, but Alani was so pent up with anger and sadness, he knew she was just letting a little out. YaYa was an easy target. Her real aggression was toward him.

"Lenika." He didn't yell, but his tone pierced her... silenced her.

"I'm not the type to play games. I didn't even know she was coming to town, or that you were coming to this gathering for that matter. She is somebody I used to spend time with. That ended before you. Then, we ended. Then, she showed up."

"Did you fuck her?"

"Does that matter?" he asked.

Alani turned around and closed her eyes, as she balled her fists and placed them on the counter. "I'm going to lose my mind behind you." She said it like she really believed it. She wasn't exaggerating in this moment. She was becoming undone right before his eyes. "How could you sleep with her? How could you touch her, like you touch me?" Her voice cracked, and her stomach hollowed just thinking about it.

Ethic looked around the kitchen before approaching her. One thing that he didn't doubt was that when emotional, Alani didn't bluff. He had made the mistake of underestimating her when he had placed a gun in her hands. He was glad there were no knives in her vicinity and he shook his head because he couldn't believe he was so deep in love with her crazy-ass. He walked up behind her and placed hands on her hips. She felt security in that touch, she felt his need against her ass and she dripped for him. She had to stand up straight because if she didn't, she would allow him to slide her swimsuit to the side and fuck her right there on the countertop. Raw hurt mixed with longing burned in her lenses, as she faced him. He pinched her chin between his fingers. She was a breath away, so close that their noses touched.

"All that slick shit you popping, all this yelling…all this poisonous energy…" she pulled her face away, he manipulated it back to him, as he looked down the bridge of his nose at her. "Stop. It ain't you. It's what I've turned you into. Go back to who you were. I love you in any form, but I'm not particularly fond of this one." Alani calmed in his arms, but she closed her eyes in embarrassment. "Look at me." She did. "She was before you," Ethic stated, honestly. "Nobody since you."

He felt her shoulders slack. This woman who hated him, still felt something, that much was clear. He just couldn't sift through her pain to pinpoint what it was.

"Why didn't you sleep with her?" Alani asked. "When she showed up on your doorstep? She's beautiful."

"Because she ain't you," Ethic said, again, with the honesty.

"You're waiting for me?" she asked. He nodded. "For how long?" she asked.

"As long as it takes," he said, matter-of-factly.

Alani looked off, staring at anything but him. "You're lucky I didn't slap that bitch," she stated, before storming by him. He placed a hand on her stomach, stopping her from exiting.

"Stop," he said. His patience was honorable. She rolled her eyes away from his.

"Order pizza. They'll be hungry soon," she said, as she left him standing in the kitchen alone. Even in the midst of her rage and jealousy, she thought of his children. It was shit like that. It made him ravenous for her. His dick jumped, and he had to adjust himself, as he watched her through the kitchen window. He wanted to fuck her attitude away, put some act right in her.

Chill. She ain't ready.

He watched her glide back into the pool and her smile returned. Alani was back. She was always happy around his children. Golden and loving, like she had birthed them herself. Like she was the baby mama who hated their punk-ass daddy but adored the little human gifts that he gave her. Only she wasn't their mother, yet her connection to them was so nurturing, a stranger would have assumed otherwise. She splashed them, and they gathered around her, laughing as they tag teamed her. When she and Bella ganged up on Eazy, he screamed bloody murder.

"Daaaddy, help! They're trying to kill me!" Ethic stepped onto the patio and laughed, as Alani dunked Eazy under the water.

Ethic slid off his shirt and walked over to the pool. He lowered himself into the water, exposing every muscle on his torso. Alani froze long enough for Eazy to jump onto her from the side of the pool. They both went under and when she came back up, Ethic was hovering over her...in her space.

Why is this man this fine?

"Keep your head in the game, Miss," he whispered, as he licked his lips and maneuvered around her.

He splashed Alani. Then, Bella joined in. Then, Eazy.

"How is this fair?" she shouted, as she closed her eyes. She splashed back, laughing, and it was like a beautiful melody.

They stayed in the water for hours before they decided to

end their fun. They were prunes by the end of the night.

"Can we cut the cake now?" Eazy asked, as they climbed out. Their fingers and toes were wrinkled from the long day. Ethic pulled Eazy under his arm and squeezed him tightly, in an one-armed hold.

"Pizza then cake," Ethic stated.

Ethic ordered the food. "Showers and pajamas. By the time you're done, the food will be here."

Alani grabbed her tote bag from the counter. "I better get going."

"No!" Eazy's gripe turned her on her heels, mouth slightly agape at his passionate protest. "You can't leave before we sing happy birthday."

Bella spun. "Yeah, you have to stay," she added.

Alani paused. "I'm all wet, guys."

"You have clothes. You can shower here. Right, Daddy?" Bella pressed.

Ethic shrugged and motioned to Alani.

She hesitantly nodded. "Okay, sure. I guess I can stay for a little while longer," she said.

Ethic pointed to the staircase. "You know your way around. Make yourself at home."

Alani nodded. She was like a bobble head. Unable to find words and just moving her damn face up and down. She was being jumped by Okafor hospitality and she didn't know how to say no. *Do I even want to say no?* She bypassed Ethic's room and found her way to the guest room she remembered showering in before. She wondered if it was where green eyes had slept. She turned on the shower and realized there was no soap. Wrapping a towel around her body, she turned off the shower and tip-toed to the hall. She knew there was soap in Ethic's bathroom. There was a closet there. She could steal some and creep back without anyone noticing.

She entered his room and walked over to the adjoining bathroom but froze when she saw him. He stood there, head down, eyes closed, hands on the wall in front of him, as he let the water run over the back of his neck.

She gasped. He turned eyes to her, like she was a magnet and his stare was metal. Such a natural attraction. "I... um... there's no soap," she stammered.

Ethic opened the shower door and waited. Alani's chest heaved. There was so much pressure in this decision. To stay or run. *His body...my God. Wait. Why are my feet moving?* She stepped inside the shower. Metal to magnet. Steam rose around them, as Ethic moved to the back, allowing her to get the good spot under the water because he wouldn't be a gentleman otherwise. He reached around her to grab the soap and lathered the towel in his hands. She tensed when she felt the rag touch her back.

"Relax," he whispered. He turned her toward him and Alani looked up into his eyes, as he began to wash her. From top to bottom, even lifting her feet to clean the bottoms and between each toe. Of course, he was meticulous; of course, he didn't miss a spot. Ethic didn't half do anything. With his face at her apex, he paused, and she closed her eyes, anticipating... hoping...she decided right then that if he put his mouth on her, she wouldn't stop him. He didn't, however. He simply divided her lips and let the water gently rinse her there as well. She stood frozen under his touch. He stood and turned her back toward the water and washed the back side of her body. His hand glided over her flesh with so much fucking care.

Ethic put shampoo between his hands and then placed them

in her hair. She held her head back as the pads of his fingers massaged her scalp. It was so intimate, compassionate, like they were an aging couple and she could no longer do it herself. He rinsed her, and she turned to him. He cupped her face in his hands, just staring. There was so much desire in his gaze that Alani could feel it.

"As long as it takes," he whispered.

Alani stepped out, breaking the trance he had put her in.

The doorbell rang.

"There's money in my wallet on the night stand," he said.

She grabbed his housecoat from the door hook and wrapped herself in it. It smelled like him and she relished in his scent, as she placed hurried feet on the carpet. She grabbed the wallet and rushed down the stairs, hesitant to walk through his house in only a robe.

The doorbell rang, again.

Alani rushed downstairs and opened the front door. The pizza guy stood in front of her.

"Three large pepperoni pizzas and wings?" he asked.

Thank God there is still a little bit of hood left in him. All the crispy brussels and green bean casserole talk from Bella had me scared.

She chuckled to herself, as she nodded to the pizza guy.

"It'll be 40 bucks," he stated.

Alani opened the wallet and her hands froze. It fell to the floor.

He has her picture.

She bent to pick it up. Her hands shook, uncontrollably, as her heart lurched in her chest. Her eyes had to be playing tricks on her. She flipped through the photos inside. There was Bella and Eazy in a cute photo from years ago. A picture of

Morgan in a graduation cap and gown. Then, a picture of Love's ultrasound. Her eyes watered. *How did he get this?* She noticed the date was the date he died, and she wondered if the doctor had printed it for him. She flipped, again. The last picture tore her heart from her chest. Kenzie's obituary was folded up in the slot. *My baby.* Alani covered her mouth with her trembling fingers.

"Ma'am? The money?" the man asked.

Alani handed him a 50-dollar bill and took the pizzas, before closing the door. She dropped off the pizza to the kitchen.

Why am I shaking?

She took the stairs two at a time.

She saw Bella first. "Is the pizza here?"

"It's in the kitchen," Alani stammered. "Take your brother to the table. You guys can start."

She was giving orders like this was her house. They were complying like they were her kids and it was normal for her to be waltzing around in their father's robe… like they saw her everyday…as if they woke up to her frying bacon, because wasn't no turkey bacon popping off if this was her house, and sending them off to school while wearing that same robe. She rushed into his room and he stood there. Sweatpants, dick print, and shirtless. Tattoos over skin so dark she almost couldn't see them; frown lines in his forehead, as he wondered about her haste. She crossed the room with urgency, tossing her arms around his neck, causing him to stumble backward. He let the bed catch his fall.

He cared. He cares about the life he took. He honors my baby with his kids. He's sorry. God, he's sorry.

"What's wrong?" He spoke into her neck, as she trembled there.

She was holding onto him like Bella used to do when she awoke from a bad dream. Legs wrapped around his waist, chest to chest, so tightly, like she expected him to slay the boogie man.

"You got to talk to me." He peeled back to look in her eyes. "What's wrong?"

Alani just held him tighter. He put his hand to the back of her head.

"I knew this was too much," he said, scolding himself.

Alani shook her head. "No, it's not. It's just enough," she whispered. "Nothing's wrong. In this moment, nothing's wrong at all."

"Daddy! I ate a slice! Can I cut the cake now?" Eazy yelled and Alani smiled, as she climbed from Ethic's lap.

"You good?" he asked. "You're sure, everything's okay?"

She nodded. "Just give me a minute to dress."

Ethic pulled her hand. "Wear the robe," he insisted. "Come on. We've got cake to cut." She followed him down the staircase, her hand in his.

"Ah, ah!" Alani yelled, as she walked into the kitchen. "No fingers in the cake until we sing. You have to make a birthday wish!"

"Hurry!" Eazy said.

"Happy birthday to you..."

The off-tune song had Eazy smiling from ear to ear, as he stood in front of seven candles atop of a huge, Minecraft-decorated cake.

"Now, make a wish," Bella said.

"I wish..."

"You aren't supposed to say it aloud," Alani said, as she

stood opposing Eazy, leaning down eye to eye over the burning candles.

"I want to," he insisted.

"Okay, go ahead," Alani said.

"I wish that Alani would stay here with us and we could be a family like this every day."

Alani's back stiffened and she stood. She shot eyes to Ethic and Eazy blew out the candles.

"Alright, Big Man," Ethic stated. His eyes were apologetic, as he said it. Alani was speechless. "Take a piece to your room to eat, and then it's time to call it a night. You too, B. It's getting late." It wasn't the latest. They could have stayed up and hung out more, but Ethic wanted time with Alani. He craved it. He would have put his kids to bed at six o' clock if he knew they wouldn't protest. That's how anxious he was to have her alone.

Alani rounded the table and stood off to the side, leaning against the center island, as Ethic and his children cut the cake.

"Good night, Alani!" Bella called before leaving.

Eazy ran back into the kitchen and gave her a huge hug. He was rough, all boy, and she loved it. "Good night!"

His energy was so contagious that she laughed as she rubbed the top of his head. It was wild, knotted, like most new-school boys running around Flint, and it drove Alani crazy. She hated the new trend. "Since you're a big boy now, maybe tomorrow we choose a nice, gentleman's haircut?" She was definitely acting like somebody's mama. Ethic already knew the response. Getting Eazy to cut his hair was impossible. The un-groomed look drove him insane as well, but Ethic knew the battle wasn't worth the war with Eazy. He was very into his uniqueness and didn't allow other people to weigh in on what he wore or how he presented himself. So, when his son piped up and replied,

"Yeah, that's cool," Ethic's eyes widened in shock.

Alani smiled. "Good night, handsome."

Ethic was enamored. She fit so beautifully in his space. That authority, that influence over his kids was miraculous. She wasn't trying to get close to them to impress him. She simply did it because it was natural, and their chemistry proved it. Alani was supposed to be his mate, he just had to figure out how to move past all they had been through, all the hurt that stopped them from wanting to try again.

They waited until their voices carried all the way up the stairs before Ethic spoke.

"I'm sorry about that," he said.

"It's okay," she replied. "They're great kids."

"They're a'ight," he stated, with a chuckle.

"You're a phenomenal father," she whispered. "Probably the best I've ever seen. You have three, beautiful children."

"Four," he corrected, and she didn't protest because she knew why. Love Okafor made four. Their baby mattered to him.

She nodded.

Alani turned to the cabinets and began to scour them.

"You tell me what you're looking for and I can make this easier on you," he offered.

"Liquor," she said.

They're more alike than different, Ethic thought, his mind wandering briefly to YaYa. He didn't like the thought of him driving them to drink, making them sad enough to drown their sorrows in inebriation. Did he do that to women? Did he ruin them? "Strong, hard, liquor. Everything with us is always so dark. So heavy. Tonight, I'm going to get you drunk and we're going to dance," Alani finished.

"Dance?"

"I know I was stepping all on your toes at the debutante ball, but I want to dance, and since the most handsome guy in the house is sent off to bed, you're my only option," she said, with a smile. The way it made his chest feel light, reminded Ethic that he hadn't seen a genuine smile on her face in a long time. This day in his home with his children had lightened her some.

He stood and reached over her.

"Bourbon," he said.

"Bourbon it is," she answered.

The liquor wasn't necessary to change Ethic's demeanor. He was drunk off Alani alone. He counted the hours she had been in his presence, in his home, comfortable. Eight, long, glorious hours and counting. They had finished the bottle that he and YaYa had started. Ethic could handle his liquor. Alani was trying her best to keep up. He could tell she was loose by the way her eyes hooded. She pulled out her phone.

"You owe me a dance," she said.

"You're still on that?" he asked, giving away a half smile.

She nodded, as she bounced from her seat. "One second," she said, as she walked down the hall. Ethic stood and followed her, as she waltzed into his office. He was oddly pleased that she knew her way around.

"Here we go," she said, as she turned on his Beats pill. She connected her phone and turned to him, as the music began to play. The softest melody filled the room, as Alani closed her eyes.

Ethic leaned against the door. She liked this song. He could tell it meant something to her. This was no random selection. Then, he heard the words.

We've crossed the line tonight
An easy hello, but the hardest goodbye

She wrapped her arms around his neck and just stood there, swaying so softly that she never moved her feet. This wasn't about dancing. Alani needed an excuse for him to hold her and he obliged. The lyrics were painful. She was speaking to him.

And if you're falling
I'm falling
I'm falling
After you

At the end of it all I'm coming back to you.

When he heard the last lyric, he cupped her face and took her mouth with his tongue. Fuck the bullshit. He was tired of holding back. He was tired of space. Tired of going without. If she was coming back, eventually, he was ready to press fast forward; and if she wasn't, she would have to tell him that. She would have to tell him goodbye and mean it, sever the cord that connected them because otherwise, Ethic wouldn't stand down. Alani kissed him back, tasting the liquor on his tongue. Hungry for him. He picked her up, pressing her into his need, as she locked her legs around him. Loving her was the most potent thing he had ever felt. To feel that and then have it stripped was damaging to a man. He didn't want Dolce, or YaYa, or Raven. Fuck 'em all. He didn't even yearn for the guidance of his mother anymore. All he wanted was her. He had never kissed a woman so deeply. Alani planted teeth into his bottom lip and bit down, like she was starving, like she was deprived, before pulling back. Lust-filled breaths escaped her. Ethic rested his forehead to hers.

"Take me upstairs," she whispered.

He tossed her over his shoulder like a cave man and she laughed uncontrollably.

"Shh!" he warned, as he gave her a firm smack on the ass. She covered her mouth, unable to stop her glee until they made it upstairs and he tossed her on the bed. Being in his bedroom, in his bed, where their son was probably made, sobered her some. *I want this. Just don't think about it. Just let him love you.*

Ethic stepped out of his sweats and underwear, then pulled the shirt over his head. He pulled at the belt of the robe she wore and exposed the beauty that lie beneath. He placed one knee on the bed, as she looked up at him. There was something holding her back. Fear held her captive, as Ethic placed the other knee down. He leaned forward, his strong body hovering over her and she gasped when she noticed the black ink scribbled on the left side of his chest. Two names had been permanently etched on his skin. LOVE ALANI. They were attached to a pulse made of ink. She hadn't seen it in the shower, but she couldn't miss it now. She touched it, and when her hand connected with his chest, she noticed she was shaking. She tightened her fingers into a fist and snapped her eyes shut. Ethic sat up.

"No, Ethic, I'm sorry. I want this," she said, as she sat up and reached for him. "I'm right here with you."

"But you're terrified."

"I don't want to be," she whispered.

"You know I would never hurt you. You know that, right?" he asked, his tone of voice revealing how injured he was at her trepidation.

"I know that." She sniffed away emotion. "I just can't stop the pit that forms in me when I see you."

Ethic leaned forward, his elbows meeting his knees, as his head hung. Alani was desperate for his touch, as she crawled across the sheets. She reached for him, turning him toward her. "Hey," she whispered. His deep-set brow was wrinkled in apprehension. She placed both hands on the sides of his face and pulled him closer. Ethic was love sick and Alani was medicine. Her lips touched his forehead first and every wrinkle disappeared, as she heard him exhale. For so long they hadn't allowed the sense of touch to occur between them. These stolen kisses were against all the boundaries they had set for themselves, but neither cared. She kissed the bridge of his nose and pressed her forehead against his. "I want you," she sighed. "I don't care how terrified I am. I don't care how guilty it makes me feel. I just can't do this much longer without being touched by you."

He maneuvered his face from her grasp and stood. The revelation that he had slept with her a week before under these same pretenses told him that she hadn't done it for her. She had done it for him. She had served him pity pussy after the pageant, not because she wanted it, but because she felt bad for him. The thought sickened him.

"I care, and you should never give your body to a man that makes you feel like that." Her words had sobered him. "Fear ain't love, Lenika, and I can't lay a finger on your body unless you feel love behind my touch." There was melancholy in him, as he stepped into a pair of basketball shorts. The liquor they had consumed had given off the illusion that they could get back what they had lost.

"Ethic," she said, as she stood, going after him as he began to walk out. He was persistent in leaving and she had to squeeze her body between him and the door to trap him inside. "Who says it has to feel perfect? Huh?" There was desperation in her eyes. "I would rather fear you than love someone else. Please, just come back to bed."

"Nah," he shook his head, before planting a kiss on top of hers. "Not like this." He opened the door and she avoided looking at him. She shrank from the embarrassment of his rejection. It had taken her so much just to open to the idea of him being in her presence, let alone to allow him access to her body, and he had shut her down. *What am I even doing here?* She went to walk by him and he placed a firm hand to her stomach, halting her. "Whoa. Talk to me. I'm trying real hard to be careful with the way I handle you. Why are you upset?"

She shook her head. "Always the fucking gentleman," she scoffed, turning red, as she glared at him. "Where was the gentleman the night you killed my baby? Huh? Where the fuck was he then?"

As soon as the words slipped from her mouth, she regretted them. His stun was visible, and she pushed by him to exit his bedroom. Ethic didn't know what to do. It was her pent-up rage that had caused him to stop in the first place. She hid it well, wanting the world to believe she was healing, but he knew better. A parent didn't heal from the death of a child, especially the murder of one. He recognized the mask of fake strength she hid behind. This slip of the tongue proved that she wasn't ready. She was barely present in his life. After months of not seeing her at all, this past week had felt like a gift. She was finally open to being in his space. He wasn't trying to mishandle her or overwhelm her again by forcing sex back into their complicated situation. It hadn't worked well for them thus far. Her body had a need and he understood because his need for her kept him up at night without release. If she could handle it, he would have never hit the brakes, but her mind and heart were full of resentment. She wanted him sexually, but he couldn't detach his emotions, not with her. Any other man would have manipulated her body without tending to the mess that lived inside her. He refused to do that. Her fragility was important to him. Her mental health was a priority for him. Alani was delicate, and he had the ability to shatter her.

He went after her, as she stormed down the hall, pulling her by one arm and forcing her back against the wall. He trapped her between his arms as he pressed his hands into the wall behind her. He towered over her, his heart thumping in shame and anger. Turmoil churned in his gut. He chose his next words carefully because although her words were callous, they were true. She wasn't obligated to tread lightly or to avoid the subject. She was a black woman and they were the most vicious with their tongues. Their words were weapons that they used to protect themselves when black men failed to do so. They were so deadly because they were dipped in the resentment of abandonment. Fathers who left, boyfriends who cheated, husbands who broke vows, sons who disappointed, it all contributed to the generations worth of black women who shot those deadly words at black men. Black men had failed to protect black women and all they had were slick comments full of disrespect to respond with. Ethic was no

different. He had failed as well, but with Alani, he had done
so drastically. He knew he would be paying her a debt for
the rest of his life and still he would never be able to make
it up to her. Whenever she felt like it, whenever she was
angry or frustrated or mistrusting or afraid, she would lash
out at him. He was prepared for it and he would take it
because he was lucky she was in his life at all. While Ethic
wasn't starving for female attention, Alani left little room
for anyone else to vie for his affection. She had him at her
mercy and he had a feeling she knew it.

"Taking a bullet wasn't enough, so what else I need to do
to show you that I'm sorry?" he asked. "I killed a kid. Not
just any kid either because that alone would not have eaten
away at me as a man...as a father." His voice was full of
anger, contempt, and sarcasm, as he barked the words down
her throat. He wasn't angry at her. He was angry at himself
for moving recklessly, but her comment had caused him
to project his frustrations. If he had put the gun to Lucas'
head instead of shooting from afar, Alani's daughter would
still be alive. If he had been a different type of man, less
gangster, a square, murder wouldn't be the way he solved
his problems. Society had raised him into this, but at some
point, he had to take accountability because he had allowed
it. "I killed the child of the woman I love and because of
that she will never love me back." His eyes squinted, and he
was so passionate that he spat as he whispered the words.
Regret put a tremble in his voice, one that he couldn't
control. When in her presence, she seized control, seized
his heart. She was his queen. "You don't think I think about
your daughter? I see her face every night. I've washed my
hands hundreds of times since, because I still feel her blood,

I still see it sometimes. I see the six freckles that dotted her button nose. I see the blood that came through her missing front teeth, as she tried to breathe in my arms. Her eyes had auburn specks in them and they were so wide that night. She was afraid of me. She looked at me the same way you look at me now. I couldn't save her. I couldn't 'un-pull' the trigger. I'm a father. You don't think I feel that shit? Why do you think Love died inside you? That wasn't your fault, that was all me. That was karma."

Alani's anger dulled, as she saw just how remorseful he was. He had apologized on repeat, but somehow hatred had blocked her from receiving it. The man before her was haunted, and as he described her child in such detail, Alani was overtaken with compassion. She could see her baby in her mind. She had never considered the toll that Kenzie's death had taken on Ethic. She was too busy coping herself, but she saw it, clear as day… repentance. She lifted her hands to his face but lowered her head against his chest.

"How could you, Ezra?" She was weakened by his words, eyes burning, always burning around him. "How could you be like this with me? And be the same person who killed my daughter? I'm so mad at you. I hate you so much. I don't mean to throw low blows, but…"

"Throw them," Ethic interrupted. "I'll take them. All the blows you got, but what I can't take is you storming out of here or you feeling so alone that you check out again," Ethic stated. "Do you know what that did to me? To see you put a gun to your own chin? I just want you back. I want you whole."

"I'm destroyed. You don't want me," she scoffed. "Whatever version of me you're trying to get back is gone. The only way I know to stop this pain is to feel you. Before I knew what you'd done, you touched me, and the pain just stopped. It dulled. You were like Tylenol. I want it to go back to like it was before. God, I just want to feel you."

"Let me back in here," he said, placing a finger on her chest. "And here." He lifted the finger to her temple. "Before I get back in here." Ethic's hand slid up her thigh, as he rubbed her clit.

"Ssss," she sucked in air through her gritted teeth. He was intoxicating.

"She miss me?" he questioned.

Alani's head fell back, as she moaned. "Mmm... she misses you." Ethic pressed his body into her and she gasped as his hardness teased her. She reached for him, rubbing his erection through his shorts. "I can't be with you the way that you want me too. All I can give you is my body, and if that ain't enough..."

Her face melted in yearning, as she felt him grow in her hands. *How is it possible that it gets bigger?*

"It ain't enough. I've had all of you before," his voice was low, throaty, as he moved her panties to the side. "This shit is good, but I want all of you. Every part." He circled her clit with his calloused thumb, while inserting two, thick fingers inside her. "I just got to earn it. I ain't afraid to put in work. You can hate me for everyday of our lives and I'll stay. I'll take all that shit just to have you here," Ethic whispered, as her head fell back. He worked his fingers, curling them as he slid them in and out of her center. She was gushing onto his hand and his dick was brick. Since the first time she wet his dick, he knew that he would crave her forever. Sex with her was just different. It was a spiritual connection that transcended the physical. He felt her soul cum when she reached her peak. Alani was on soak for him and he wanted to drown in her. He needed to muster up some restraint because Alani was begging him to take it.

"Daddy!"

Eazy's voice broke through the air, accompanied by the ringing of a small bell, and Alani groaned. "Saved by the bell," Alani whispered, mischievously, as he withdrew his hand.

Ethic licked her off his fingers and Alani's mouth fell open in shock. She had never noticed his tongue before. She suddenly wanted to sit on his face and ride that tongue until she came. "You can take the master. You're too faded to drive home tonight. I'll take one of the guest rooms," Ethic said. He said it like she didn't have the option to decline. It was a quality she found endearing. He was head of the household; king under this opulent roof and his word was law. She would obey.

"Dad!" Eazy's voice rang and Alani heard the alarm in his tone.

"I see you're raising a little cock blocker," Alani said, with a laugh.

Ethic nodded. "We gone have to have a talk about that," he said. He gave her a wink and adjusted himself, barely able to conceal the erection she gave him. "He doesn't respect guy code yet."

Alani extended a small smile, before heading down the hall. She paused, as she watched Ethic head in the opposite direction toward Eazy's room.

Alani crept to the door and peeked through Eazy's door. It was decorated in a Detroit Lions theme and she smiled as she watched Ethic take a seat in the chair across from Eazy's bed.

"What's going on, Big Man? What you doing up?" Ethic asked.

"What was my mom like?"

Alani immediately felt intrusive and she could see Ethic's silhouette tense.

"She was beautiful," Ethic answered. The gloom in his voice was hard to mask. "She was brave and caring. She saw the good in people, even the bad ones."

"Did you love her?" Eazy asked.

"I love her very much, E," Ethic said. He cleared the frog from his throat.

"Even though you have Alani, you still love my mom?" Eazy quizzed.

Ethic was bemused. He was unsure of how to answer that one. He had never discussed Alani with his children, but it was obvious that his affections for her were transparent. Even Eazy's youthful mind was able to detect the palpable energy between Ethic and the woman he insisted was just a friend.

"Your mother gave me a love that I will never forget. You don't replace people you love. Just because she's in Heaven doesn't mean that I don't still love her. Love lives forever, even when the person you love is no longer around, Big Man. I will love your mom always. No matter who comes in and out of our lives, no one will ever replace her. I've just made a bit of room for Alani. If that's okay? She means a great deal to me. Does that make you uncomfortable?"

Eazy shook his head. "No, I'm okay with that. Mommy says Alani will take care of us now because she is taking care of Love and Kenzie," Eazy said.

Alani froze. There was no way Eazy could have made that up. Eazy knew nothing about Kenzie and Ethic had decided not to tell him about Love.

"Where did you hear those names, Big Man?" Ethic asked. The perplexities of life and death spinning through his mind, as he pondered if it were possible. People always spoke on having angels looking over them and he wondered if Raven was doing that. Was she walking beside them, every day in a parallel Heaven? Would she approve of Alani? Was she looking out for Kenzie and his Love wherever they were? His chest panged at the impossible notion.

"In my dream. I saw my mom and she told me. Alani is going to heal you. Why do you need to be healed, Dad? Are you hurt?"

"Daddy's fine, Eazy. You never have to worry about me," Ethic said.

"But I have to worry, Dad. What if you get hurt, again, like before when you were in the hospital? If something happens to you again, we need Alani here. Who will take care of us if she's not here? We have to make her happy, so she will stay," Eazy said. There was so much passion in his son's voice that Ethic could feel burden building inside his chest. He knew there was a real possibility that Alani would never forgive him fully. As close as she had gotten to his children, he knew that when she pulled away it would hurt them. He had never thought about it before, but hearing how attached Eazy was made him question all the choices he had made up until this point. The last thing he wanted to do was leave his children open to disappointment. Then, there was the sudden Raven talk throwing him off.

"I won't get hurt again. I'm right here. I'll always be right here and when the day comes when I'm not..." his voice cracked. He cleared his throat. "Where will I be then?" he asked.

"In my heart," Eazy answered.

Alani melted, as she watched him rise from the chair to kiss Eazy on the top of his head. Something about witnessing the interaction made her feel better. Ethic had never shared his history with her. She didn't know much about the mothers of his children, but if it was a deal that Eazy's mother wanted to make, Alani would agree. To have Eazy speaking of his mother, taking care of her babies in Heaven was enough to make her emotional. Problem was she didn't know if she could fulfill her end of the bargain. It just wasn't right to move on with Ethic. His transgressions were too great and no matter how hard she tried, she always saw her daughter when she looked at him. She saw death in his eyes, not the possibility of life beyond grief and that was the roadblock she couldn't bypass.

"Who are they, Dad?" Eazy's voice stopped Ethic, just as he got to the door.

Ethic turned. "Who, son?"

"Love and Kenzie?" Eazy asked. "I woke up before I could ask her."

There was a beat where Ethic didn't speak. He lowered his head as he gripped the doorframe with one hand. "They're Alani's...children."

Eazy pushed in a way that children didn't realize they were pushing. "They're dead? Like my mom?"

That one punched Ethic in the gut. Alani too, as she recoiled, leaning her back against the wall to help her stay on her feet. His silence must have been enough to confirm Eazy's questions. "Well, tell her she shouldn't worry. My mom is taking care of them, and if she takes care of us that's fair, right? That will make everything okay?"

Ethic wished that he could make Eazy's dream a reality, but he couldn't foresee that. Ethic was trying to collect moments of time with Alani that he could reminisce about one day when she decided to leave. That's all he knew he could have with her. Moments...never a lifetime, not after the way he had hurt her. Not wanting to get Eazy's hopes up, he responded, "I care for Alani, but she isn't ours to keep, Eazy. She's a friend, but it isn't her job to take care of you, Big Man, it's mine and I'll always do that. We can't ask her to stay, E, but I'll always stay. I'll always be here. Now, close your eyes and go back to sleep."

Eazy turned toward the wall, wrapping his blanket around his body, as Ethic headed for the door.

"Love you, Dad." The Sandman was already lulling him back to sleep. His voice was barely audible. Eazy had no idea what he had put on Ethic's soul.

"I love you too, son," Ethic replied.

He stepped into the hallway and closed the door. He was surprised to find Alani leaned against the wall.

"One day, I'd really like to know about Eazy's mom," Alani whispered.

"One day," Ethic answered. He walked up to Alani and she found her place inside his arms. Like two puzzle pieces, they fit, her arms tucked under his torso, his securely locked around her waist, her head resting on his chest, his chin snug against the top of her head.

"I should go," she resisted, as she broke their embrace.

He had learned not to push her, so instead of objecting, he simply nodded and extended his hand for her to walk by. He remained in the hallway, as she retreated to the guest room to retrieve her clothes. She emerged fully dressed and then he followed her to the front door.

"It was good to see you," Ethic said.

She blushed and chuckled. "Such formalities. Is that what we've come to?" she asked.

Ethic rubbed the back of his neck, as a look of distress bent his brow. "I don't know what you want me to do. When I apply too much pressure you pull back. I'm dropping my kids off to you like we're some divorced couple and shit. I can't step foot inside your house, but they sleep there on the regular. I'm seeing smiles on my babies' faces that were non-existent before you and I'm jealous. Fucked up, right?" Ethic asked, with a laugh, as he rubbed the top of his head.

Alani laughed, genuinely laughed. She hadn't done it in so long that it felt odd. It didn't seem like something a grieving mother was allowed to do. She nodded. "A little fucked up," she agreed, as she pinched her fingers together.

"I wish I could have even a piece of what you're giving to them," he admitted. Her laughter faded, as she looked toward the driveway where her car sat. "I know you got your rules and I know you keep your distance for a reason, but ain't nothing changed with me. I'm in love with you. Just you being under my roof is progress. I'm not trying to overstep here."

"Your fingers were inside me 20 minutes ago, Ethic," she reminded. "I think you're past the point of overstepping."

"That's different," he said. "That's physical. I can get that from anywhere..."

Her eye brows hiked, in offense. "Can you?" She nodded. "I suppose you can. Probably from that *friend* you had here earlier," Alani snapped. "Good to know." Alani confused her damn self. *How am I checking him about anything? He's not my man. He's a grown-ass, fine-ass man. Of course, he can have sex with anyone he wants. Women like green eyes or the foreign heffa he brought to the diner that time. Where do women like that even come from? How are they so...ugh... fuck him and them too.*

Shock wore him, but before he could respond, she relented. "You know what? I'm out of line. I'm going to go." She turned her back on him. Her gut hollowed at the sudden realization that one day Ethic would move on. One day, his efforts wouldn't be so concentrated on her forgiveness. One day, he would make some woman a really good man and that woman would cut Alani out of his life. It's what she would do, so she knew what was coming. His fingertips reaching for hers, stopped her. She held her breath but didn't face him.

"There's no one else," Ethic said. She sighed, in relief, grateful that he had offered the explanation that they both knew he didn't owe.

She nodded and the VISE-GRIP on her heart eased some. She had a little more time to straddle the fence before inevitably walking away. She could feel him over her shoulder. Observing her. Analyzing.

"I'm close to them because it makes me feel close to you without betraying my daughter," she admitted. "I try to guess what Love would have looked like when I look at Bella and Eazy. Thank you for letting them be a part of my life, separately from you."

"Alani..."

She turned to him in stun. He hadn't called her by her first name in such a long time. They had been strangers and strangers called her Lenika. Alani on his tongue, in his brogue tone, filled with such need, did things to her. She didn't want to be undone.

"The day you decide to let me in, I'm here. It doesn't matter who comes, who goes. I'm right here. I'm not leaving," he said.

He drew her into his embrace and she melted. "You promise?"

"On Love," he answered. She knew he meant it. He had put it on their dead son. She leaned her head back, so that she could look at him. He was so regal, so poised, and black and flawed, and fine. He gripped the sides of her face before planting a kiss on her forehead. It was quick, a peck, like he was certain that he would do it again soon...like she was a dutiful wife leaving to play her Lotto numbers and would return in a few minutes. Oh, how she wanted to return. "Text me when you make it home."

She cocked her head to the side. She wasn't ready to fall back into that place of familiarity with him. That was couple shit. This wasn't that, could never be, would never be that.

"You can text me or I can follow you. Your pick, but if you're persistent about walking out of here this late, I need to know you made it," he said.

"I'll text," she replied. She finally descended the stairs and headed to her car. "Oh, and Ethic?" She turned toward him. "Green eyes? She's canceled. Okay?"

He nodded, smirking, as his dick responded to her authority. Alani was unlike any other woman he had ever experienced. "I swear you begging me to fuck you, Lenika. That shit, that sexy, bossy shit you do..." He shook his head and bit his lip. "Good night," Ethic said, as he finessed his beard and shook his head. "Go home while I feel like letting you."

They were back to being strangers, as if the entire day had never even happened.

She opened the door. She gave a half-hearted wave goodbye before climbing in and pulling off into the night.

CHAPTER 18

Alani walked into her home and the stillness of night sank into her bones, reminding her how lonely she was. There had been so much noise at Ethic's house. The laughter, the conversation, even the fighting made it feel like more than just four walls and a roof...he had provided a home for his family...a temporary illusion of one for her. She missed it terribly. She pulled out her phone.

ALANI
Home

She only sent one word. She didn't want to break her promise, but she didn't want to invite him to text more than what was necessary either. Bubbles danced across her screen and she found herself holding her breath, as she waited for the reply. She kicked off her flip flops and tossed her heavy bag aside before heading to her bedroom. She climbed under her covers, as the vibration of her phone announced his response.

ETHIC
I'm here. You're there. That ain't home at all.

Alani's finger lingered over the message as her heart skipped a beat. How could she respond to that? She had no words, so she simply powered off her phone.

Alani climbed into her bed where loneliness kept her up at night. She tossed and turned all night. The clock just ticked by, going from 2 to 3, to 4 in the morning with no respite. Her eyes burned, but her mind was restless. There was no sleep for the weary. This deprivation. This starvation. This eradication of Ethic was self-induced torture.

"Ugh!" she shouted, in exasperation. She kicked off the covers and sat upright in bed, her feet dangling over the sides, as her toes graced the wooden floor. The chill of the wood sent one up her spine. There was no warmth in this house. No family. No life. Sure, Nannie was there, but Alani wanted a man and children. She wanted a family that was growing, not one that was deteriorating. One day Nannie would be gone, and she would be alone. She stood and walked through the halls until she reached Kenzie's room. She paused at the door before pushing it open. Purple walls greeted her.

"You don't want pink?"

"Everyone likes pink, Mommy. I'm going to do purple, so my room will look different."

Alani smiled, as she pressed four fingers to her lips, as the memory flooded her. She had been such a beautiful little girl. Like a little, brown, baby doll, the kind you pay hundreds of dollars for and you can't even open the box. That was her Kenzie...a prized possession.

Alani's feet bravely ventured over the threshold and into Kenzie's room. She sat on her daughter's bed, picking up the unicorn that sat against the pillow, and tucked her knees beneath her before bringing the unicorn to her chest in a hug.

Her doorbell rang, and Alani crawled across the bedspread to peek out of the blinds.

A white BMW sat in front of her house.

She frowned and rose from the bed. Caution carried her to the first floor, as she peered through the peephole. She snatched open the door.

"Morgan?"

Alani peered over Morgan's shoulder and saw Messiah sitting in the driver's side of the BMW. It was the middle of the night. What was Morgan doing at her door at this hour? What was she doing here at all?

"He loves you," Morgan said, stubbornly. "I don't see how or why, after what you did. After what your brother did..." Morgan's words caught in her throat, as she shuffled on her feet and blinked away tears. "You're nothing like my sister, you know?" Morgan's tears were falling now, but she rubbed them away with her palms, sniffling. "He was so in love with her and we lost her that day...at the park...there were so many gun shots...my sister bled out in his arms..."

Morgan's shoulders hunched over, as her face crumpled from emotion.

"I don't want him to love you like he loved her. If he loves you like that, he'll forget her. He'll forget that I'm family and I was here first. He's all I have...he's my dad," Morgan's voice quivered. "What is a father supposed to do when...your brother...he..." Morgan choked, again, as she looked down. Her hands fumbled as they went inside her Gucci cross body. "I know he killed your daughter, but he was only protecting his...I have something you need to see."

Morgan handed Alani her phone.

Alani took it and pressed play. The gruesomeness before her eyes caused her to cry but she couldn't tear her eyes away. Her blood brother and his friend had brutalized Morgan. She covered her mouth and looked at Morgan in horror, as she shook her head.

"Ethic would never hurt an innocent child. Your brother deserved everything he got. Your daughter was an accident," Morgan whispered. "I just thought you should know."

Morgan took her phone and turned to leave.

"Morgan?" Alani called, distraught. She could see the effects of what Lucas had done hanging onto Morgan. It was a part of her scars. Every woman had them, maybe not the same type, but women collected events in their lives that tarnished who they were. This rape was one of Morgan's, although Alani suspected she had many more. Alani empathized with her more than Morgan could ever imagine.

Morgan turned.

"I'm sorry for what my brother did to you," Alani whispered. Morgan stared at Alani for a long time.

"I'm sorry for what your brother did to *you*," Morgan answered. "This is all because of him." Then, she was gone.

Alani closed her door and was deafened by the sounds of the video, as it played in her mind. She was flooded with a different type of pain. One where the reality of someone you loved crashed into the fantasy you had always imagined them to be in your head. Her brother had been her baby. She had practically raised him, but the streets had grabbed ahold of him and Alani wasn't strong enough to beat them. She grabbed her notebook and a pen and then began to write. She couldn't keep these emotions inside. They would spoil her. Her entire insides would go rotten if she didn't let this go. Disappointment-filled, her pen flowed. Her fingers cramped, and the inside of her middle finger was bruised, she wrote so much, but she couldn't stop. How could she stop after all that she had been through? This was her testimony. These tears blotting her ink were evidence that she was going through a test. There was war being waged over her soul and she had been letting the devil win. She had to get it out. She had to purge. She had to find the light. The light was in this book…in her story…because… all of this tragedy had to lead to something. Hers. Kenzie's. Ethic's. Morgan's. Nannie's. What did it mean? How could she get it to end? Tears had never felt so good. These ones felt cleansing, like the ones that came to you when you were in the throes of laughter or witnessing a miracle. She had to get this out of her system because the pain had been festering. She was infected with it, and if she didn't do something about it, it would kill her. These words were her antibiotics. Morgan's visit was the painful needle that had administered them. It was agonizing, but it had to come out in order to let it go, and she wouldn't stop until it was gone.

CHAPTER 19

I don't want to go back to school tonight," Morgan whispered, as she watched the city pass by outside her window.

"You've got class tomorrow, shorty," Messiah reminded, as he steered the car with one hand and interlocked the other within her fingertips. Their conjoined fists felt powerful and he lifted her hand to his lips.

"I don't care," Morgan answered. "I'm tired of being away from you at night. I'm tired of sneaking around." She turned to him in her seat. "I want to move in with you."

"Mo, I thought you weren't ready..."

His eyes shot to the small splint on her finger and he wondered if he was ready for this. That finger was a reminder that he was capable of hurting her. Could he handle this without mishandling her?

"If he can love her, I can love you. I just want you to love me too, Messiah, because right now, it feels like my family is moving in a new direction. I'm grown now and I'm not his real kid and he wants to love her. I have no one. Who's going to love me?"

"I am, shorty. I'm going to love the shit out of you, until I can't no more," Messiah said. She lifted shocked eyes over to him. She knew how uncomfortable voicing the words made him. "I love you, Mo. I don't care who knows. Who approves...

who don't. Fuck 'em. I just want to keep you, shorty. Me and you. That's all I need."

He drove her across town to his home in the suburbs, and when the car ticked into idle, they both sat in silence. Lost in their own thoughts, they each had burdens they didn't feel like sharing. Messiah climbed out first and walked around to Morgan's door, opened it, and then took her hand. She followed him into the house, knowing that they were about to take whatever this was between them up a notch. It didn't matter. She would have followed him to hell and back if he asked her to. There was a weight on her chest, an emptiness in his gut, a fear in the air because they were both afraid of what it meant to only have each other and no one else.

Messiah was afraid of disappointing her because he knew he would - inevitably. He knew he should stay away from her. His soul was black, and she was so godly. They didn't match, but she needed him. She was telling him that she was lonely and afraid, and he couldn't let her feel that...he couldn't let her think that. Messiah would die for her and go to hell early, because he for damn sure wasn't welcomed into Heaven. There were so many secrets he was keeping. They were from two, different walks of life; two, different sides of a familial war and she didn't even know it. Nobody knew it, but he did, and he was a snake for even working his way into her heart. There were things about him that she would never understand. He would lose her one day because of that, but he wanted to enjoy her in the moment. He wanted to be loved by her because a woman had never done so before. The thought of the day he had to let her go haunted him daily; and right now, it was eating through his consciousness, causing something physical to manifest inside him...something painful. He felt like killing somebody. He sat on the couch. She stood near the door, her back against it. Silence.

"When I hurt you..."

"You won't," she whispered.

"When I hurt you," he continued, like it was a certainty. "Remember I loved you first. Remember I tried. I'm trying so hard to keep shit separate that it's killing me, shorty." He hung his head so disgracefully that Morgan gasped.

Morgan took docile steps toward him and stood between his legs. He buried his nose in the V of her tiny shorts. Those, along with the Burberry bikini top she wore, barely covered any skin. He kissed her through the fabric.

"I want to fuck you, Morgan," Messiah said.

Morgan's eyes widened in the slightest, as his crass words jolted her. He pulled at her shorts, roughly snatching them down and she stepped out of them. His finger traced the outskirts of the checkered-print bikini bottoms and he kissed her stomach, dipping his tongue into her belly button, playing with the M belly ring she had there. Morgan grabbed a handful of his locs, as she sucked in a breath. "I've been gentle with you, but my head is all fucked up and I got so much shit in me that's so fucked up and you just keep loving it like it's okay. I need to let it out. I need to beast on something, but I go hard, so I'm going to need your permission, shorty, because it's different than what I been doing with you and I need to hear you say yes. I need to know that you want that part of me too."

The way he said it, Morgan knew that it was the part that no one had ever chosen to love before. It was the part that embarrassed mothers, frustrated teachers, and enraged fathers. It was rebellious, treacherous, and dangerous, and she didn't give one single fuck because she loved that part too. She would be the first person in his life to show him there was value in that part too.

"Yes," she whispered.

The truth needed no time to manufacture. Her daddy had taught her that, and when Ethic had repeated it growing up, she knew he had taught him too. She said it, instantly, without hesitating, so Messiah would trust and believe her. Then, the nigga became Houdini because her bikini bottom disappeared.

Messiah turned her around and Morgan let out a yelp of surprise, as he planted teeth into her right ass cheek.

She heard his belt buckle and then felt him stand behind her. He needed her. She felt it, against her skin. Aggression in the form of an erection. A slap to that same side of her ass, clearly his favorite. Before Morgan could fully feel the sting, he picked her up by the waist and lowered her onto his dick. The anticipation of being the recipient of this had her soaked for him.

"Damn, Mo," he grunted, as he turned and lowered her body to the couch. She planted her elbows there and he wrapped his fist around her hair, pulling, to get her to back up on him further. He started slowly, grinding in and out of her with care, as he watched himself disappear and reappear inside her.

She could tell he was treading lightly. He was afraid to hurt her. Afraid to show her this side of him.

"Fuck me, Ssiah," she whispered.

Her neck snapped backward, and he pounded her. The sweetest pain she had ever felt filled her pussy, as he beat it up. The way he hit the target in the back of her made her think he had never gone all the way inside before, like he had been using restraint every time before now. She couldn't remember him being this big, always satisfying, but never this long.

"Agh!" she cried.

He split her sea, sloshing her wetness around, grunting with every stroke. His grind was so feral that Morgan was slipping off the couch and he followed her, tailgating her pussy so tightly that there was no escape.

"Fuck!" she screamed. "Messiah!"

"Take it, baby," Messiah said, between clenched teeth, as he rode her to the floor. He released her hair and her head hung forward. Sting. Another slap to her ass. That arch in her back deepened. "Good, baby, keep that ass just like that. Take this dick. Damn," he moaned, as he grabbed her hips and drove his pelvis, down then up, so deep that she called out his name.

"Messiahhhh!" His fucking name.

The visceral attraction to him made her cream and he felt her dew on his manhood as he lifted a foot to the couch for leverage. His balls slapped against her ass, making it clap, as she threw that freshman 15 in a circle on his dick.

"I told you I was no...fucking...good," he gritted. She was so wet, and he was so far inside her that strings of her juices . stretched onto him. A grunt of appreciation came from the back of his throat and he hit that shit harder. Morgan clawed at the carpet in front of her as, she stretched her arms over her head.

"Messiah!"

Messiah felt the tip of him swell, as a prickle traveled up the vein on the underside of his length.

"Shorty, shittt," he moaned, as he wrapped a strong arm underneath her stomach and pulled her into him. There was no space between them, as Messiah changed strokes, going in circles.

"Babyyyyy," Morgan's legs were tucked under her thighs and spread wide to make room for him. Her chest was to the floor and her ass was in the air, as Messiah knocked down her walls. "Aghhh lovveeee youuuu!" Morgan came first, Messiah came last, pulling out onto her back. Morgan was still in position, heaving, as she rested her head on balled fists, her messy hair falling around her face.

"Did I hurt you?"

Morgan came back on her legs, sitting upright. She turned to him, placing manicured fingertips on the sides of his face. She shook her head and kissed him. She had never cherished someone so much. Messiah's full lips enveloped hers and he pulled her to her feet, devouring her tongue. Scooping her up in his arms, he made his way to the stairs, with effortless strides up to his bedroom. The love they shared was so young and passionate. It was all-consuming.

"Are you sore?" he asked.

She pulled back and pinched two fingers together. He knew a little meant a lot. He had gone too hard and he made a mental note to dial it back to love making. He carried her into the bathroom and placed her on her feet before leaning over the tub to stop the drain. Flashes of the first time she had sat in that tub caused her to step backwards, knocking over toiletries that were sitting on the sink. He turned to her and her face, stricken with dismay, vibrated through him like a lightning strike. He stood and took her face into his hands.

"Hey," he said, his deep voice, so close that she felt his breath on her lips. "You're never unsafe with me. Fucking ever. You hear me?" He knew where her mind went. He just knew her. She was his. Why wouldn't he know?

She nodded. He turned and let the water out the tub then turned on the shower.

"I got to take a call. You shower," he instructed.

Morgan washed quickly, feeling vulnerable without him at her side. She wondered how long it would take for her to rid herself of the images of that dreaded night. She was raw but satisfied between her thighs and she exited the shower, surprised that there was still a pulse of need in her clit. She left puddles on the tiled floor, as she made her way to the bedroom, but she paused when she heard Messiah's voice on the other side of the door.

"I told you. I'm over that shit. I'm not doing shit. Let that beef die with him, it ain't mine to iron out."

She held her breath, feeling like she was out of place. She didn't know if she should walk in to interrupt or stay put. Messiah had ceased talking, but she was sure it was only to listen.

"Fuck family," his voice hissed. "I'm done with all that. Only family I need is sitting under my roof right now. I'm out. You want it done so bad, do it yourself."

Morgan knew she shouldn't be listening at that point and she hurried back into the shower and turned it on. His business was his business. She didn't need to be involved in that. As long as he came home unharmed, that's all she cared about. She placed the towel on the sink and stepped back into the shower.

"Ssiah! Can you hand me a towel?!" She called out loud. She knew he would end the call and crawl back into their bubble. It was where he belonged anyway.

When he entered, she stepped out the shower and the scowl on his face softened. He walked up to her with a new passion, as he took her lips, tasting them like he was liberated to do so whenever he pleased.

"I can always come home?" he asked.

Recognition resonated in her eyes and she nodded. "Always, baby." She frowned. "Are you okay?" she asked, as he wrapped her in a towel.

He nodded and scooped her. Her legs straddled him in midair. His cocky-ass was still naked, as he carried her to his room. He laid her on the bed and spread her legs, east to west.

"It's more than a little sore," she whispered.

"Let me make it feel better," he hummed, already kissing her clit.

Messiah couldn't stop sucking on her pussy if he wanted to. The way her other hole clenched when he trapped her clit between his full lips made him go harder. He licked up, then sucked, long and hard, as he pulled his head back, slightly tugging on her engorged pearl.

"MESSIAH, NO! WAIT, BABY. SIAH, WAIT!" Morgan's legs trembled, as Messiah got comfortable, laying between her legs like it was where he rested his head all night. He pushed her legs back farther, holding them open wider, as he worked his tongue.

"I've got to pee, baby. Wait. You're going to make me..."

"Hmm hmm," Messiah moaned. He was damn near kneading her clit with his tongue, waiting for her body to release the sap that only came from intense pleasure. That feeling that Morgan was feeling wasn't urine...it was an orgasm and Messiah was determined to make her squirt. Her back arched. *Damn, this pussy so fat.* He had suspected that Morgan was sitting on gold. In fact, he had forced his mind to an appropriate place every time he interacted with her because the fly shit she used to wear left little to the imagination. She was too pretty to have whack pussy, so he had known it would be good, but Morgan was playing on a different field than other women. Messiah's eyes closed, as he savored the taste of her. She was an addiction.

LICKKKK, flick, flick, flick
LICKKKK, flick, flick, flick, SLURPPPP

He was in a zone, changing his speed, eating her to a rhythm that had her bucking like she was possessed. Morgan's moans bounced off the walls, as he lapped at her sweet, pink flesh. There was no need for fingers, his tongue was doing all the work, parting her labia, massaging her budding clit, and never forgetting to lick her depths on the way up and down. Messiah had never enjoyed delivering this type of orgasm, before Morgan, but with her he had found a new obsession. Her scent, her flavor, it melted onto his tongue like butter on a hot skillet and slid down his throat like the finest champagne. He caught a buzz off her pleasure. They moaned like crazy. Morgan's falling off her pretty lips, one after another, as she called his name, begged him, prayed to him, praised him. It didn't take much from her to get him worked up but his name...the name she had admitted to wanting to say for years...the name that she had claimed before he even knew she was interested, the name that she had drawn inside hearts next to her own. His name on her tongue, in the tone of her voice, where the 'S's sounded like 'Z's and came out a little raspy, was his ultimate weakness. He couldn't remember how he had survived before her. How had he run around the world without having her to retreat to? It was like he couldn't even recall a time before her. He had tunnel vision. Morgan vision. She was breathtakingly blinding. His inept heart had found a reason to pump warm blood instead of the ice it had been surviving on.

"Ooh... don't stop," she whimpered. Messiah grabbed beneath her ass and pulled her further down onto the edge of the bed. He pulled on her clit like it was a piece of stubborn taffy, before moving it in circles, pressing his tongue against it, adding pressure, before sopping it back into his mouth again. Morgan was so wet that she felt it dripping between her ass. "You making a mess. Clean up your mess, baby," she whined. *Her bossy-ass,* Messiah thought, but loving it because only she could tell him what to do and how she liked it. Only Morgan could command his actions and thoughts without much effort at all. He obliged, obediently. Her eyes were closed, her teeth clenched, and her fists gripped the sheets beneath her, as Messiah went lower. His thumb replaced his tongue and he stroked her clit like he was playing guitar, pinching it a little as he inserted two fingers. All it took was one lick of her most sensitive hole for Morgan to explode. She dripped like a leaky faucet.

"What are you doing to me??!!"

Messiah stood, and his body was at attention. She laid on his burgundy sheets, heaving, exhausted, but in pure euphoria. Tears filled her ears as they slid without effort from her eyes.

"Why are you crying, baby?" Messiah asked.

"I want to have your baby, Messiah," Morgan whispered. "Can we? Please?"

He steeled, as the weight of her words pressed down on him. He looked Morgan in the eyes. She was high from bliss, fresh off an orgasm, sweaty, her hair sticking to her neck as her breasts heaved up and down.

She don't mean that shit.

His mind told him she was speaking out of emotion, but damn if she wasn't stirring feelings of possibility within him. He would never even consider a child in this cold world with anyone else. He had never wanted a kid before her. They were needy, snotty nose, little mu'fuckas, but he could see his needy, snotty nose, little mu'fucka so clearly in his mind. The idea of an unbreakable bond, of forever with Morgan... the thought was almost like taking a pull of the highest narcotic. It lifted him. It heightened him. His pulse raced, and his throat went dry. "I want you forever and ever..." she whispered. Messiah eased into her. "And ever," she moaned, as he pumped into her.

"You gon' have my baby, Mo?" He whispered.

"Yes, boy, yes," she groaned.

Messiah tucked his arms beneath her underarms and balled his fists at her temple as he grinded. His strokes were slow, but deep and long, as he studied her. Her eyes were closed, her mouth was open and her nails scratched his back, probably drawing blood, but he liked that shit.

"Agh!" Morgan cried.

Every muscle in his body tensed, as he pulled out slowly and dove in again. Slow. Deep. Long.

"You gone give me a family, baby? Give me a shorty, Mo?" he asked, his voice cracked. The only person he had ever considered family was in a grave. He had relatives, never family, that's why it was so easy for him to say fuck anybody. Fuck everybody. Except her.

"Yesss, Messiah," she whispered. His heart quickened because he knew she meant it. He could see a mini version of them, hopefully a boy because a girl would bring him karma like a mu'fucka. He wouldn't mind a little homie that he would name Nazim. He was already wishing.

He was buried in the groove of her neck, as he whispered in her ear and fucked her with so much passion it felt like they would leave a dent in the bed.

"I just want to have your baby, Siah. God. I don't want you to ever leave me," she cried. He pulled back to look in her eyes, but never stopped his stroke. The contortions of her expression symbolized satisfaction. He was making a woman out of her; and despite her age, she was making a man out of him. Could he really be that? A man? A real one? Be a husband and a father? Could they have that regular dream? He wasn't a regular nigga but for her he could try.

"God, this dick is so good. My man is so good. Your heart is so good. God, your tongue is soooo good," Morgan was speaking in delirium. Seeing her in this state, Messiah felt his heart swell. Morgan was the only one who would speak goodness over his name. Everybody else would tell a different story, a much more callous edition, but to her, he was good. A prickling burned his eyes. The connection he felt to Morgan made him vulnerable in a way he had never been before, and he had to squeeze his eyes closed to control himself. He had always perceived emotion as weakness, and Morgan brought the bitch out of him every time, despite his intention of fighting it.

Morgan grabbed his face and wouldn't release his gaze. "I want to be in your life forever, Messiah. Don't pull out. Just be with me. Let's create forever."

He wanted to shoot up the whole club right then and there, but he knew it would be selfish. *What about school? She's young. She deserves better than me.* She kissed his lips.

"I'll have every single one of your black ass babies, Messiah. They're mine. This dick. Your seeds. Your heart. It's all mine." Messiah picked up speed, going deeper, hitting it harder, as he cleared her hair from her face, so he could get a view of perfection. Morgan was the sun and he was so close to her that it blinded him. "Messiah!" she screamed. Fuck if his name on her lips didn't get him every time. He felt a tear, mixing with sweat and glided down his cheek. His mouth fell open, as guttural sounds of his soul leaving him came out in grunts. Morgan pulled his face to hers and their tongues danced. She kissed him, deeply, passionately, stealing his oxygen as he transferred all his energy to her. Messiah emptied himself into Morgan and when every drop of his seeds was planted, she wrapped her arms around his back and pulled him into her body, holding him, consoling him. She felt his tears. The convulsions of his chest revealed that he was crying too. Whatever they had just done, it was beautiful. She didn't speak but her stomach contracted, as her tears grew stronger. She had done it. She had cracked through every part of him and he was allowing her to see every vulnerability. She knew they wouldn't address it after the fact, but he didn't rush to move. She had earned this victory. His tears were the trophy. He just laid there, in the groove of her neck, as her soft hands consoled him.

"I love you, Shorty Doo-Wop," he whispered. Her heart melted. He said it first and without being asked to. He wasn't reciprocating, he was supplying, and for the first time since losing her family, she felt like she belonged to someone.

"I love you, too."

CHAPTER 20

ONE MONTH LATER

Alani looked at the word count on the bottom of her computer screen, in awe. 120,472. Words. Written. From her heart to the page. Alani felt empty. She had unloaded it all - the passion, the hurt, the pain, the confusion, the betrayal, the animosity, it was all there in front of her in the form of a manuscript that she entitled, *The Ethic of Love.*

She looked at her cell phone. It had been silent for four weeks. Ethic hadn't sent one message or called one time since Eazy's party. There had been no pop ups or visits from Eazy and Bella. He had given her space. He was waiting. *As long as it takes.*

She pressed print and lifted from the table, as her heart beat uncontrollably in her chest. She felt lighter, calmer, than she had since losing her daughter. She could see above the pain, today, and for the first time in a long time she felt the notion of forgiveness. It wasn't about Ethic. It was about herself. She forgave herself for failing as a mother, for not protecting her babies, for allowing their lives to slip through her fingers. Alani had put all those things into her book and let them go. She dressed simply, in jeans, a slim-fit, long-sleeved, black t-shirt and sandals, and then grabbed her tote and carefully loaded the pages inside. She walked over to her laptop and pressed send, hoping that her old professor would see growth and value in her writing enough to allow her to return to class. Alani was ready to climb from under her rock and resume living, resume dreaming, this book was the first step.

She grabbed her Polo hat off the coat rack and covered her awkward head. Her hair was growing back and neck-length, so her options were limited. She hadn't been to the salon and it was too short for a decent ponytail, so a hat was her only option today. It didn't matter. He had seen her at her worse and still wanted her. The hat was an upgrade compared to where she had been. She tucked her hair behind her ears and pulled it down low, before stepping out into the sun. For the first time in a while, she actually felt it. It warmed her skin and Alani lifted her face to the sun. She could feel her skin reacting, it was like she was a seed and after months of struggling through the dirt, she was reaching the surface to soak up those rays...she was growing.

She didn't call first, because the sound of his voice would rattle her. When she found herself at his doorstep, she took a deep breath and centered herself before ringing the bell.

The Hispanic woman that answered the door smiled.

"Can I help you?" she asked.

"Hi. I'm Alani. Is Ezra home?"

The woman smiled. "Aghh, yes, Ms. Alani," Lily answered. "Please, come in. I'll get him for you."

Alani waited in the foyer, heart racing, as she paced. She felt him before she saw him, and when she turned, he was standing at the top of his staircase. His eyes were on her, shocked and curious, all at the same time.

He took a seat on the top step, as Alani craned her neck to look at him.

She frowned. "You're going to stay there?"

"My words can reach you from here. My hands can't," he said. "Just respecting your limits."

"I think it's called self-control," she reminded.

"Goes out the window when it comes to you," he admitted. He put elbows to his knees, as he leaned over and peered down at her. She stood at the bottom of the staircase, the height difference made her feel small. She felt like the common girl coming to address the king.

"I need you to come with me somewhere," she said.

"You want to let me know where?" he asked.

"Not really. I just need you to trust me," she answered.

He stood to his feet and swaggered down the steps, closing the space between them. He released a heavy sigh, taking her face into the palm of one hand. She leaned into him, as her breath caught and her eyes closed. Alani's hand shook, as she went to remove his fingers from her skin, but instead, she placed her hand on the outside of his to keep him there. She frowned, absorbing the energy that was Ethic Okafor. It had been so long since she had allowed herself to enjoy this touch, to appreciate it, instead of resenting it. Her tears were unstoppable. They fell, running into his hand, as she pulled in oxygen to calm the storm. Her eyes fluttered open and she saw gratefulness in him. His wrinkled forehead and a stitched brow accompanied his disbelief. She didn't cringe, she didn't pull back. He was touching her, and it felt like before...like before she knew. There was something different in her stare, something that screamed for him, and when she reached up, putting her hands around Ethic's neck, he caved into her. He couldn't help the sob that escaped him, only one, before he was able to restore his countenance and maintain his composure. He held her, flesh to his body, one hand on the back of her head, the other, under her shirt to feel the silk of her skin against his rough hands. She felt so good in his embrace, like he had found a piece of himself that had been missing for months. He didn't know what it meant, he didn't know if she would pull back, but he needed this hug as much as she did. It was replenishing, reviving, and as she quaked in his arms, he rocked her from side to side.

"I miss you," he whispered. "Fuck, I need you."

They stayed there, for minutes on end, absorbing the magnitude of this moment. A hug, so simple, but extremely intimate was monumental for them. It felt like a win. It felt like the first day of spring after a long, harsh winter. It was like Alani was opening her windows, letting out the dust and the gloom that the long season had brought into her home. She was airing it out, airing out her soul, and he was the wind sweeping through the curtains, blowing them beautifully, reminding her that ice, no matter how hard, always dissolved. Her frozen heart was melting.

She pulled back. "I really need you to come with me. Can Lily get the kids from school?"

Ethic was a man who noticed things. He observed actions and reactions, noting human behavior because the way people moved told him what people didn't speak. She had said the kids...not your kids...not Bella and Eazy...but the kids, as if half of the responsibility was hers. He had many worries about Alani but her love for his children would never be one.

Alani wiped her eyes and blew out a breath, in an attempt to keep her nerve as she led him to the car.

They were silent, as she drove through the streets. She gripped the steering wheel at ten and two, her fingers wrapped around it so tightly that they were red. When they pulled into her church's parking lot and she put the car in park, the silence was loud.

"I need you to know God, Ethic," she whispered.

He didn't look at her. His stare was transfixed on the brick building in front of him. There was fear in his gaze, intimidation. She had never seen him look like that. She had never seen anyone look like that.

"I've tried to live without you. I've tried to hate you. I took my time hating you and this past month something changed. I saw the video of Morgan's rape."

Ethic went rigid, but his eyes didn't move.

"If we have any chance at all. I need you to learn about your faith and receive God, Ethic. I want to forgive you, but I need help. Sometimes, my faith in us will grow weak and I need your faith to be strong. I need you to believe in God so that I can believe in you," she said.

"You can't force God on a man, Lenika," he whispered. He placed both palms flat on the dash board. "I want you more than anything I've ever wanted, but this God shit ain't for me. I just can't." He shook his head. She was asking him to do the one thing on Earth for her that he was afraid to do. Trust in a God that he felt had failed him repeatedly.

"You called our bond devilish," she whispered. "It came out your mouth. We're bonded by demons and secrets and sin. That's not a gift, it's a curse and I can't break it. I've tried, and I can't," Alani whispered. "I hate you. Do you hear me? I hate you! Why are you still here? Why do you still want someone who hates you?" Her face was scrunched in utter confusion.

She couldn't wrap her mind around it. How could he give her access to him after almost killing him? After doing something as hurtful as hiding a child from him? He still sought her. He even allowed her to be alone with his children without worry of revenge. "You can't let go either, can you?"

Ethic didn't respond, he only blew out a sharp breath, as he massaged the back of his neck. Everything between them was so hard, so resistant. It was like trying to make two puzzle pieces that didn't match fit. They were forcing themselves together when they had every sign that the universe had designed them separately. Their destiny was to be apart...their bond unnatural. "I hate you and I want to kill you. I want to slit your throat in your sleep for what you did to my daughter, but I can't because it would hurt to watch the world lose you. It would hurt me to hurt you. When I shot you, after the shock, after I realized what I had done, I kept your blood on my body for hours. I refused to let them wash it off because I didn't know if you were going to live or die, and in case you died, I wanted to feel you, I needed to feel your blood on my skin to remind me that you were real. That's sick. That's not sane. That's not even healthy, but I can't let go. You make me crazy with irrationality, with need, with pain. So, I need you to meet God. I need you to come with me to seek God because I think you're the devil. You have some demons in you and they have attached their hooks in me because I can't let you go. You're everything I ever wanted, but you're not godly. You're such a beautiful man but it feels like a mirage because you don't believe in anything. I need you to be a man of God...to believe in God. Not in the creator, not in karma, not in a higher power. I've heard all the nicknames you use when explaining your spirituality. I need you to open your mind and your heart to God. You have to believe in Him because he's the only chance we've got. God is the only love powerful enough to heal what you've broken. Please, Ethic!"

Alani was desperate, grasping at straws to find a way, any way to get past everything that stood in their path. They needed a miracle. She needed a miracle and she knew that only God was in the miracle granting business.

"I don't believe in a God that takes women and babies. What kind of God adds that type of pain to the world," Ethic said. There was animosity in his tone. He sounded like a little boy who had sat on the stoop all day, waiting for his father to arrive, only to be let down. Maybe he was, maybe he was that child who had prayed to the ultimate father and he had never shown up. Maybe God had failed Ethic in his history. Alani didn't know, but the tension in his shoulders, the lines in his forehead, the skepticism in his eyes, the anger in his shallow breaths...the devil lived in him and she had allowed herself to fall for him.

"Then believe in me," she shot back. "Trust me enough to know I won't lead you toward anything that would hurt you. Love me enough to find God through me. We've connected physically, and we failed. Mentally, we failed. Emotionally, we failed. None of those connections are strong enough to keep me here and I want to be here. I want to be a mother to those kids and to look at you and not see what you took from me. I want to love you, but I am destroyed, Ezra, and I know you'll never admit it, but you are too. You were broken way before I came along, and you won't talk about it to me. You won't even talk to me about Raven!"

Ethic was on her in half of a second, gripping her chin. "Don't mention her name! You don't know anything about her," he said, between clenched teeth. Alani teared, not from pain because his grip was firm but not harmful, but because he had enough skeletons to start a graveyard. He was full of hardship and devastation and meeting her had caused it all to overflow. His agony was showing, despite his most valiant efforts to hide it. Alani maneuvered her face from his hold and looked him square in the eye. "Connect with my spirit. You have to believe in God for Him to make this impossible love between us seem possible again." She reached for the collar of his jacket and gripped it tightly, as she bowed her head to his chest. The burning of her eyes brought on her tears. She didn't even want to cry. She was tired of weeping, tired of weakness. It had never been a part of her DNA to be so fucking helpless, but life had a way of beating a woman up. What else was there left to do but to let her sorrow rain down her cheeks?

Ethic blew out a breath of frustration. He had never been angry with her before, but today, in this church's parking lot, he was livid. Alani was forcing his hand, asking him to believe in something, someone, some entity that had failed him time and time again. He had seen preachers leave the pulpit and come cop dope from his workers. Others he had seen take money from their congregation and use it for self-gain. He was supposed to follow these men? He didn't play sheep. He was the shepherd of his own church, his own belief system...the streets had saved him. Where was God when he needed Him? Where was God when his mother was burning holes into his back? The block had fed him, sheltered him, and he became a leader with a gang of killers and hustlers behind him to make up his flock. She was asking him to change and abandon the tangible for the intangible or she would leave him. His chest was split open. The ultimatum was worse than the bullet she had put in him. Ethic had always been a freethinker, he developed his own code, lived by his own man-made law. Church, religion, God, required submission. How could she submit to Ethic if he was on his knees submitting to some shady-ass pastor? How was a flawed man supposed to be the bridge between him and a God he didn't even trust? Ethic wanted to decline. His pride wanted to walk away, but his innate reaction to even the thought of losing Alani was unbearable. Ethic had gone a lifetime without someone to consistently love him. He had given out a lot of love, but he had never been the recipient, not long enough to feel worthy of it. This was his chance…with her…a second chance that he didn't deserve. Where had she come from? A woman so pure-hearted that she would allow her child's killer a chance to know her. It hit him all in an instant. Alani had come from God. That was why she was so magnificent. *Maybe she's what He gave me after all that praying. Maybe all the suffering prepared me to love her.* It was all so hard for Ethic to fathom. *Maybe.* He lifted her chin with one finger. "Stop crying," he whispered.

"Stop hurting me!"

His chest caved at the potency of emotion in her voice. When had he become that nigga? The one that hurt women so drastically? The one who fucked up so immensely that he changed who they were on the inside? "You refusing this… saying no. It ends us, Ethic. Just do this for me," she pleaded.

"Do you know what I've done in my lifetime? You know what I did to your child's father? I'd be a hypocrite to go to God and ask for forgiveness, knowing that if I had to do it again, I would. God don't want me."

"God made you!" Alani screamed the words, she was so desperate. She couldn't understand how he didn't know this. It was like she was sitting at a table trying to teach a kid that one plus one equaled two. It was so easy...too easy of a concept to evade such a brilliant man. Spirituality was tricky that way, however. It required faith and Ethic had none. She took a deep breath to calm herself and lowered her voice. "He will never not want you and He'll show you that you don't need to do anything. You didn't have to punish Cream or anyone else. It's not your job, Ethic. It's His, but you don't know that because you don't know Him. You won't fully know me unless you know God."

"And I want to know every part of you," Ethic replied, as he gripped her face in his hands, using his thumbs to stroke her cheeks gently.

"Then come with me. Do this with me. I swear I will never leave you, if you just do this. You asked me. That night. Not to run when I discovered the worst parts of you. I've seen them, and I ran, but I'm not running anymore. If you do this, I'll never run. Just please, please..."

Ethic could feel her conviction, he could hear it. This was important to her and she was important to him. He nodded.

Alani's eyes rose in disbelief. "Okay?"

He felt the stress building in his chest. He wanted to say no. If she were anyone else, he would have, but she was his world and he would do anything to keep her. "Okay."

His feet felt like they were stuck in cement blocks, as he stepped out of the car. Alani hustled quick feet across the pavement as she tucked herself under his arm, intertwining her fingers with his.

"Don't leave me," he whispered. His words halted her steps. She had heard these pleas before. The morning she had found out he had murdered her daughter. He sounded so childlike in this moment. This wasn't Ethic the man standing before her.

This was Ethic the boy. This was the baby who had begged his mother not to go. She had left anyway. She had abandoned him anyway. Alani had tried, but her heart wouldn't allow it. She couldn't detach herself if she wanted to.

Alani shook her head. "I won't leave. I'll love the darkest parts of you," she said. She reached up to pull his face to hers, kissing the tip of his nose, and then his lips.

One peck. Then two. Then, the lids of his eyes. She wrapped him in her arms, again, securing him, securing them. "The darkest parts," she whispered.

It was the parts of his mother he had loved despite her actions. Alani was offering him the same and it weakened him. Hand in hand, side by side, they walked into the church. Together...

TO BE CONTINUED IN THE FINAL BOOK...
ETHIC 4
COMING 2019

Whew!!! Three books in six months, just because y'all love Ethic so much! My brain is numb!! Now, I need some time to craft the ending to this story. It requires patience. Ethic's conclusion can't be rushed past this point. I've lived with him in my mind for a decade, so I want to make sure that I do him justice. Once he's out of my head, he's gone for good, so I have to get this ending right. I have to prepare a goodbye for the character we have all come to love. I have to decide if I want it to be happy or sad, good or bad; whether it entails life or death. Ethic was only supposed to be one book. The depth of this character, the beauty in which he thinks, and the pain he endures has transformed this into an entire series. I've never felt passion for writing like this before. I've always loved it, but this is something else. The inspiration behind this love story is different and I thank you all for taking the journey with me. It's a beautiful story. Little girls have Prince Charming, grown women with melanin skin now have Ethic Okafor and he is a king. I feel lucky to be the one telling his story. Ethic and the love he has for Alani. The love she fights for him. M&M's crazy passion. Bella's journey from little girl to a young lady. It's all just the perfect recipe for my pen. Ethic IV will only be available to purchase in one place. It will NOT be on amazon or in book stores. It will ONLY BE AVAILABLE at my personal store. To reserve your copy, pre-order at...

https://ashley-antoinette-books.myshopify.com

-xoxo-

Ashley Antoinette

CPSIA information can be obtained
at www.ICGtesting.com
Printed in the USA
LVHW091721150319
610803LV00002B/380/P